Love on the Run
Series

MICHEL PRINCE

ALWAYS A GROOMSMAN
Copyright © 2023 by Michel Prince

ISBN: 979-8-88653-135-0

Published by Satin Romance
An Imprint of Melange Books, LLC
White Bear Lake, MN 55110
www.satinromance.com

Published in the United States of America.

Cover Design by Ashley Redbird Designs

PROLOGUE

MINE

Could rage burn through your veins like acid? A mix of flames and stinging blades cutting their way through the pipelines of your body. My palm heated up from a sharp stab answering my question. The pendent on her necklace imbedded into my flesh. No permanent branding to seal me forever with the trinket around her neck. Her gaze cried out to me as if she'd done nothing to bring this upon herself. Against my hand her heartbeat thudded, the artery along the column of her neck thick as fear forced the thick liquid throughout her body.

From behind me, hands clutched my shoulders, yanked me backward, and tossed me to the floor. Three men, if that is what they considered themselves, acted as if they'd done something to stop me. No one will stop me from punishing the woman responsible. The one who tortured me for hours only to deny me access. As if I was not the reason they were all here. She cowered, being consoled by the succubus beside her. The women acted as if they were the victims when we both know who was wronged in this moment.

Lies permeated the air thicker than the humidity on this island choking me. The men formed an arch, trying their best to

1

manhandle me down the stairs. Sending me away as if I were the interloper and not them.

The pressure lingered like a ghost in the center of my palm where I pressed tightly to her throat until I no longer had to hear her excuses and lies. Cracking my knuckles, I wondered if they were stiff from how long I held them, locked, fingers digging into her flesh. My heart seized in my chest, reminding me that the acidic rage still coursed through my body.

The world around brought my senses to a fevered pitch. The buzzing of the light in the sconce irritated the last of my nerves. The last flutters of a trapped insect, suffocating, dying, for what? An unnatural yellow light, luring them in, teasing it with promises only to be cut off from all reality. A position all too familiar to me in this moment. The light distorted the true color of the wall as anger dropped a haze of red over my eyes.

Their words lost on me, the echoed mumbles disappeared into the crashing waves, nullifying unnecessary excuses. As if I hadn't seen with my own eyes. My touch, not alone on her body, the smell of him lingering on her skin. She was mine and mine alone. Her hair wasn't right, the shampoo not the one I had used when I massaged her locks, taking the care needed for them to shine. Only I knew how to properly care for her and yet when I arrived to get my room key she was not there. Not where she belonged, waiting for me to arrive.

Instead, she thought she could go out, half-dressed in front of those that were less than me. Flaunt what was mine without me there to claim and protect. Glancing up the stairs, the smug look on his face as his friends did the dirty work. Tossing me around. Slamming me into the wall with their cheap shots. Keeping me from making it up to the top of the stairs. All because of her. Eyes narrowed, lips pursed. Glaring at me. Keeping me from what I had claimed as my own.

"Go to your room," one of them said.

"Not without her," I snarled, reaching for my bag only to find my luggage was gone. Glancing down the cobblestone path, I could see the glint of silver as it disappeared around a corner.

Taking off, my pace caught up to the little shit stealing my luggage, his dark eyes glanced over his shoulder before breaking out into a run.

"Get back here you little shit," I called. "Security, security."

Surely this resort had to have someone watching it. By the time I caught him by the back of his shirt, he stumbled a bit, then twisted and got away. His hands clutched my bag and tossed it over a wall. It landed with a thud as he faced me. His gaze darted around, trying to find an escape as if in this moment I'd let the little shit go. Catching his rumpled polo with two hands, I tossed him against the wall with what I hoped was enough force to knock it down. His body arched and crumpled like a discarded candy wrapper.

The kid scrambled, his legs flailing as I caught him again and he swung at me. Turning to avoid the contact had him spinning fully. The force used sent him in a whirlwind as his fist grazed the concrete wall and had him in an almost full turn. Fear had his eyes wide and mouth agape. The power escaping him flowed into me. Egging me on to teach the kid a lesson he would soon not forget. Lunging, I dove toward him, only to smash face-first into the wall as he darted away, disappearing faster than I could turn around.

As if my week hadn't been shit, month really, with her testing her boundaries as if I hadn't put them fully in place. She agreed and now was reneging. All of it sent my blood boiling. I didn't know which room they were staying in and when I turned to the pathway realization slammed into me that my room key, phone, and wallet had all been tucked away safely in my luggage when I was at the party. Only a shitty-coated paper wristband acknowledged I was where I was supposed to be. I needed to regroup. Attack this in the morning, with fresh eyes.

Right now, even the air hurt me as I cut through the pathways and made it to the cabanas on the man-made part of the beach.

The resort was quiet, staff wasn't lingering which explained why my damn luggage was stolen. Crashing on the plastic mattress of the cabana, my mind swirled. My heart pounded, fury bubbled up and tipped the scales. Minutes, hours, days might have passed for all I could focus on. Tugging down my baseball cap, I tried to block out the light bursting forth from the cloudless sky. The moon mixed with security lights, melding into me needing help, as I lay out undisturbed, not even a random security guard patrolling to toss out the man lying in a cabana.

I didn't need my phone to see the images sent to me over the last twelve hours. The ones of her and him had been branded into my brain. Fueling my need to track him down, to beat him for touching what everyone knows is mine. His hand brushed along the velvety skin of her neck. Brushing back the satin locks and—

A sound echoed in my ears, the light movement of sneakered feet on stone. Rolling to the side, I stayed low in the cabana. Peering over the edge to see the kid from the night before. Probably going to get my property from where he'd hidden it. Mine, the word slamming into me from a dozen directions. Why were people trying to take what clearly belonged to me?

Arms and legs moved of their own power, my ability to calm myself left behind at customs as I tackled the kid. Wrestling him to the sand before he tossed a handful into my eyes. Stabbing bits of grain irritated and blinded me temporarily. Through blurred vision I chased him, scrambling down the steps to the real beach. Stumbling, my feet tripped on the last few steps, twisting my ankle and sending a shock of pain along the outside of my leg.

My eyes watered as I tried to find him in the early morning sun, grains of sand mixing with my tears that tried to clear away the foreign bodies lingering there. Wiping at my eyes, trying to clear the sand as figures moved and voices called to me in the distance. I turned only to have pain shear its way through my skull. Sending me flying backward, pounding sent another fission of pain, knocking out whatever I had left of light around me. My heart thudded and crashed into the center of my chest as thick wetness poured down my face. Gasping, I breathed in coppery liquid, the saltiness not from the sea air, but my blood as I swallowed back. Choking me as it caught in my throat, cutting off my ability to breathe as I began to drown. Exploding bones in my face made it impossible to see who was behind the voice I heard rising up between the waves crashing into the beach. My hands unable to move as the last sensations I could acknowledge were sea slime, sand coated leaves beneath my fingers. No longer could I feel her flesh or smell the other man on her. All of my senses were calculating and acknowledging the fact I had lost everything, including my life in a matter of hours.

ONE
BEST RUN, LEAP AND GO STRAIGHT DOWN

A few days before

"Now the best way to cool off when you're in Jamaica is to head into the Caribbean Sea for a dip."

With expressive hands splayed wide, Serena Love kept her eyes on the DSL camera her husband Conner held steady in front of her. The camera sported a mic where most would have a flash, but it allowed her to get a clear audio most times without needing to wear an earpiece.

Behind the camera, his face was a firm line of disappointment she had become all too familiar with. Long ago he gave up trying to tell her no. It only tended to egg her on, but as they worked their way to the front of the line, she could see the worry tightening on his brow. A few uneasy wrinkles, with each additional line she had to worry the man would stroke out from stress. She missed the days when he shook his head and smiled. Damn him for wanting a long life with her by his side.

Making sure to keep her place in line at the top of the cliff, she continued in her reporter voice, *"Rick's Café in Negril has become a necessary stop for all visiting Jamaica. Whether you come by sea or land, thrill seeker or like the love of my life, watcher of the insane like me, this is one stop you want to make."*

Conner's camera swept the area from the open patio-style bar with the signs showcasing Rick's Café in pure black, green and yellow Jamaican style. A flag flew on part of the cliff where divers weren't allowed. Beckoning ships from the sea with a promise of a good time. A makeshift wooden diving platform was high in the sky where only locals who had dived from this area were jumping to earn tips from tourists for the fantastical acrobatics. Playing up the crowds with options on how they would dive into the clear turquoise waters below with a strange ability to avoid the jagged gray cliffs and boulders around the edges of the pool.

The atmosphere was a mix of the overly confident and the slightly fearful. Each step closer to the spot where aluminum bars guided the way to the best place to jump had her belly tightening a bit, though she'd never admit her skin raising or her unease to Conner. Instead, she focused on her research, bringing the watcher along and making them feel as if they were right next to her in the Caribbean sun.

"Centuries worth of cliff diving have made this inlet a spot well known to those in Jamaica. Between two and four each afternoon, the tide waters are at their peak, making this the best stop before the evening parties begin at the adjacent café. While you may not qualify to jump from the diving platform, the steps coming out of the cove have a few stops to give you a place to jump in and cool off. Personally, I'm choosing the top spot from the land." Serena's head turned and Conner followed with the camera up to where a diver stood on the wooden platform probably fifteen feet higher than the edge of the cliff. *"I'll leave the big dives to my friend up there."*

The man, skin dark with a shine reflecting the sun from his last dive into the waters below was hyping up those standing with their phones at the ready to capture his death-defying leap. A few younger kids, no more than ten or twelve were running around collecting cash from those willing to reward the man for the brief moment of entertainment. Circus barkers could learn from these kids and the man high in the air. Goading the crowd to begin clapping, the beat slower than the collective heartbeats in the area.

With a shake of his head, the diver brought his hands to his side and bent his knees. Everything seemed to move in slow motion as Serena's heart clenched and her fingers absently wrapped around the heart-shaped pendant as she nervously ran along the chain of her necklace through the latch. Her head lightened a bit from lack of oxygen as she held her breath. His arms rose as if they were pulling him from the platform. His dive flipped twice in a tuck before straightening out like a seagull after its prey in the waters below as people gasped and clapped as he disappeared with a splash Olympic divers strived for in the pool of liquid blue.

Tourists leaned over the edge of the unfenced cliff, while others buried their faces into their significant other's chests, waiting for news of the diver's return to the surface. In the pool, the "lifeguards" unpaid and unlicensed, really a part of the show and locals that would split a pot at the end of the day, waded at the edges as a white ring of bubbles from the impact widened, then vanished, becoming part of the seawater once again. Hands sliced through the surface of the water seconds before his head, and the crowd rewarded the man with a burst of applause.

Serena uncurled her fingers from the pendent and placed her hand in the center of her chest, relief washing over her as she released the air from her lungs. Trying to hide the fear and slow her heartbeat in defiance of the adrenaline flooding her bloodstream.

"Baby," Conner said, the camera clutched in his hand, but dormant at his side. "You good?"

"Of course, that was amazing wasn't it," she replied, trying to keep her unease from her husband.

"Not the word I'd use," he replied, a fourth wrinkle cutting its way across his forehead.

Nerves bubbled up in her belly when once-in-a-lifetime shots were being done normally. Perfect moments, not always ones where she had to perform, but you couldn't coax a whale to breach on demand. When a chef is performing a trick when cooking, there was only so many times they were willing to be inconvenienced for a blog. And sunsets, with an undisturbed lake surface, glass-like and reflecting everything could be destroyed in a millisecond when geese decide they want to hit the water.

While Serena could muster the strength to jump off a cliff, there was no way, if the cameras had a glitch, she was doing it again. Once accomplished thrills rarely have had her making second leaps in the past. Only right now she was fighting back a dozen tragic scenarios because, while petrifying, she knew this was more than video content. This was a chance to experience flying without a net. Adrenaline tripped off every nerve in her body, causing her skin to gooseflesh even though she wasn't cold. Not in heat like this, with the Caribbean sun high in the sky, sending rays to the island like coals on a grill.

Very few times in her life had Serena questioned her ability to complete a task. Growing up with her father, who had immigrated to the United States from Nigeria as a child only to become an ambassador for the United States, never wanted to be without his family when assigned to a country. Which meant Serena had a forcefield-like bubble around her all the time. She would walk down a street others would avoid, zip line across a jungle, or swim under a waterfall with little to no trepidation because her mother didn't even protest. Having grown up on a farm in a rural Minnesota community she relished the fact her daughter was seeing more than wide acreage, a handful of lakes, and the local truck stop. That had been how she was raised and once she went out on her own the feeling was still there. Taking chances, trying the food, or in this case, taking the leap as if her security detail was in place to keep the dangers of the world at bay.

"Serena," Conner's grown man tone made her warm and smile. The protective nature of him was a mixture of adorable and annoying. Both had her brushing back the flop of blond hair he usually had hidden under a ballcap. "Do you know how high we are?"

"Not really."

Being the planner, worrier and geeky savant that he was, Conner had told her a half dozen times but knew she would block minor details if they could possibly make her come to her senses. *What fun would that be?* She waved her hand up to get him to restart the camera then approached a man near the platform for tourists. The young Jamaican gathering tips for lifeguarding those jumping in the cove below smiled brightly as she approached.

"Hi, sir, how high is this cliff?" she asked while pointing him toward the camera.

"'Tis thirty-five feet ma'am. You think you're up to the challenge?" The man's accent was thick to the point Serena wondered if it was all for show or natural.

"Always." Serena beamed brighter than the sun beginning to set.

"Going over is the easy part. May I suggest a tip so we can save your life should that become necessary?"

"As in a bit of advice? Or…"

The man's fingers began to rub together and Serena crossed her arms.

"So, you'd let me drown down there?" she challenged, even though there were a half dozen signs warning jumpers they did it at their own risk.

Jamaicans knew the importance of tourism, in her research she found close to ninety percent of the country's income was driven by tourists. Those employed, or in this case, making their own way to hustle money from those looking for adventure.

"I'm sure your man would jump down and save you, wouldn't you, sir?" the faux lifeguard said.

Now it was Conner's turn to glare.

"But," their little lifeguard salesman said as he took in the two tourist faces with a bit of care. "We already have five of us swimming down there and we can get to her quicker if there's a problem. But there shouldn't be a problem, should there my lady?"

Serena motioned Conner who pulled seven thousand Jamaican dollars out of his pocket, way more than the going rate of three, but what was fifty dollars when it came to his wife's well-being?

"I want her safe," he warned, slapping the bills hard into the hand of the man before centering the camera on Serena again.

"Wait? Are you the lovely runners?" the man asked, his accent smoothing out, or maybe Serena was becoming more accustomed to the inflections after a week on the island.

"Love on the Run," Serena corrected. "Are you a fan?"

"Ya, you made me want to go to Norway—in the summer, though." The man clapped his hands together and smiled broadly. "I can't believe I'm going to be on the channel."

"You will," Conner said, sure to add the passive-aggressive warning, showing his nerves were only slightly higher than her own. "If she doesn't get hurt."

"She'll be fine," he assured.

"I don't suppose you have someone that can jump and we say she was Serena, do you?" Conner questioned.

The man looked from Conner to Serena and back to Conner. "This woman? This specimen of beauty. We have beautiful women on the island, but Ms. Love—" his hands moving in the shape of Serena's curves.

"Missus," Conner corrected. "And come on, there must be someone. Serena, please."

"We have watched over twenty people jump so far," she pointed out, wishing he would stop adding pressure on her.

Below, the horseshoe-shaped cove could only handle one pontoon boat's worth of passengers at a time. They'd considered the party boat with stops to snorkel and see the coastline, but she needed the freedom to adjust their timeline and capture all they needed. So instead, they took a taxi ten minutes from their hotel.

Capturing images of the rocky ridges with the hand-carved steps jackknifing up to the top where they stood. Railings and stopping places for those who wanted to jump, but were avoiding the big drop from the top. All of that would have been limited if they were stuck on a party boat schedule.

"Fine, let me double-check the clauses on your life insurance. You know it's ninety minutes to the nearest hospital." Conner mocked as he pulled out his phone and she shoved on his chest. "I'm not sorry. I love you and I'd prefer it if you were alive."

"That is really selfish of you," she replied with a wink as she moved her hips from side to side and stretched. Making sure the tankini she was wearing didn't ride up as she removed her flip-flops and passed them to Conner.

He shook his head and stuck them in the side pocket of his cargo shorts.

"Will you be here with a big kiss when I come back up?" She beamed.

"Aren't I always." Conner's bright golden smile shone back, bathing her in warmth, before he knelt and pulled out the waiver from his backpack. At some point, he would be sure to get signed by the lifeguard happily holding the tip.

"No worries my man, your wife is gonna be a'right."

"Ready, Conner?" Serena asked and he tucked away the release, refocusing his attention and the camera on her.

"Not even slightly, my love."

Shaking out her fingers Serena stretched her neck from side to side and got camera ready. Conner brought the camera up and she gave him a nod.

"Guess it's my turn. Rick's Café, in Negril, will be my reward with food, both traditional and Americanized the best way Jamaica knows how." Serena twisted her long braided locks up into a bun while smiling at the camera. "Love on the Run is all about capturing the moment, and as I look down into the crystal clear water below we have lifeguards that got the okay that they've been paid from my new friend."

Serena tugged on the guy's arm who'd taken the cash and she grinned, tourist style for the camera. "Um, hi, I'm Trenton and don't you worry about your pretty little wife here, she's gonna be just fine."

"Any tips for our viewers around the world?" Serena asked and Trenton held one of the bills between his index and middle fingers and winked before tucking it into a bright red lock box that said Tips for Lifeguards.

"Tips are good, but first question my beautiful lady, can you swim?"

Serena instantly liked Trenton. He knew the game, and all that was involved in pulling in a crowd. A showman for sure who would refocus on those behind her once the magic of her moment was gone, because she was one of many he would need to charm today.

"Yes," she beamed.

"Are you drunk?"

"No, but I think I should be." She laughed.

"I've had a few shots of rum that's why I'm taking the money and my best friends will save you," Trenton said. "Now, you see the spot in the middle?"

Serena peered over the cliff to the turquoise pool below. Other cliffs, one barely five feet, another probably fifteen or twenty had people taking leaps and creating a white foam when they hit. Circular patterns from their entry disappeared as the sea washed into the inlet.

"I do." Serena motioned for Conner to angle the camera down to catch the shot. Down on the steps leading up to the café, Josh, her tech wizard of a personal assistant was below ready to get video from another angle.

"Yeah, that didn't make me feel better about this," Conner grumbled.

"A'right. Best run, leap, and go straight down, do not try to dive, I don't care what color medal you got at the Olympics, this is Jamaica and the cliff does not bounce like a board." Trenton then tapped his nose. "And if you don't want to smell the salty sea for the next three years, my lady, hold your nose."

Serena let out a cleansing breath. Gave Josh a thumbs up, and then one to Conner who she hoped would not close his eyes.

"Kiss for luck?" she asked, knowing the man could never say no to her. With a deep kiss, he pulled away and she prepared to give one of her signature lines.

"This is Serena Love about to put my words into action. I say it's hot in Jamaica and Love on the Run is going to show you the best way to cool off. Jump in the sea and let the waters cool you."

Run, leap, hold your nose. The moment her bare feet left land Serena floated through the air like some Bugs Bunny cartoon. Her feet still moving, but unlike the cartoon, there was no running back on vacant space. Nope, the humid air around her whooshed in her ears as she plummeted thirty-five feet until she was enveloped by the warm waters of the cove. The land had been less than two seconds away and yet it seemed like a lifetime. Water rushed in her ears; breathing wasn't even a thought at this point for her when she opened her eyes. Under the salty water, they stung, but still she couldn't look away from the sight of brightly colored fish and dark-skinned legs treading water illuminated by the sun breaking through the veil of blue. The legs were a good distance away, but not in a rush to save her.

Only she didn't need saving. Reaching her arms above her head she pulled them down and made her way to the surface in less than a handful of kicks. Breaking the translucent, superficial ceiling as she took a giant gulp of air and arched her back. Soon she was surrounded by the pay-as-you-go lifeguards who were trying to move her away. Maybe she should have chosen one of the more remote spots. Normally she did, but Rick's was tossing her a few bucks and a free meal to jump there. All Serena wanted to do was float on her back for a few quiet moments and enjoy the sensations, but this was a tourist spot and there was a line of people who wanted the few seconds of free fall she had just experienced for herself and the tide was moving out.

Instead of quiet, she could hear Josh calling from the rock steps. "Serena, say the name."

Flipping in the water, Serena swam over to the edge of the cove where the steps went into the water. Tepid in her first few steps to make sure her footing was solid and more importantly hadn't been damaged when she hit the water at close to thirty-two miles per hour, if Conner's calculations were correct. There was no doubt they were correct, they were always correct and beyond that, she had shoved them from her mind while jumping because what kind of an idiot would knowingly create a situation where they were going thirty-two miles per hour without a safety harness. She knew who—

"I'm Serena Love," she said as her hand wiped water from her face and she stepped on tipped toes up the stairs. *"And this has been Love on the Run, Jamaica. Make sure to click subscribe and check out all my adventures. Message me with where you want to go so I can find the best places to take you for a visit, but right now I'm going to take my lifeguard's advice and have a few shots of rum in my other favorite Caribbean way to cool off. A frozen rum runner with some beef patties. Remember runners, miles expire, so take the trip."*

———

"Please say your angle was good?" Serena asked Josh as she fully emerged from the water and began toweling off.

The kid, just out of director's school, took the PA job until he could find backing for his script. Barely twenty-five he'd been with the Loves for a few years now, upping her camera game and helping expand her vlog.

"I'm going to mix it with whatever Conner might have gotten. Add a little music…some mid-air stops if your face is right." Josh was going down the rabbit hole he usually did when plotting out scenes for video mixing.

No matter what, it would be amazing, and way better than Serena's early ones done on her phone in quick Insta-approved bursts. When they took on the curly-haired graduate, her page blew up and is now receiving sponsorship and has been shared by millions. Josh was only five years younger than her, but in comparison to the way she and Conner grew up the poor guy was barely an infant.

In a way, he was a good addition to their team because of his awe when they traveled, especially to places she'd been to as a kid. No longer seeing places with virgin eyes it was a good thing to have him along to remind her how beautiful, quirky and exciting the world could be. Bright colors weren't the only thing that caught people's eyes when on vacation. It was the tiny passages, the wonder, and the Earth under their toes. All of it needed to be explained in detail to take the watcher along for the ride. The way the flower smelled, how sweet and juicy the mango was, and the energy naturally flowing in the market with goods both manufactured and handmade. The tiniest detail catching the ear and imagination of their followers.

Glancing up to the top of the stairs, she saw the love of her life who sweetly scowled down at her. Conner's tanned skin, a mix of the week they'd spent in Jamaica and their regular travels, was a far cry from when she first met him. A gym rat by nature, the former international basketball player spent all his free time doing one of two things indoors. Working on his outside jumper or attempting to create a puzzle game to confound and entertain the masses.

At six-seven, lean yet muscular build and stunningly blue eyes, he was built to play the sport, but international pay wasn't on the same scale as in the states. This meant her husband had to find a side hustle and his mad genius computing talent meant most days he could get caught up and lost trying to solve any puzzle put before him. That is why his last three game designs were more than likely downloaded and earning him ad revenues by three-fourths of the people waiting in line to eat today.

"Did you age?" Serena teased her frazzled husband.

"Only about fifty years since I married you, my love," Conner said as he brought his forehead to hers while holding her shoulders. "Must you?"

"Well, you're not gonna do it." she challenged, but not really, as she tightened the floral print sarong to her still damp hips. When she wanted him to do something, she would shrug her shoulders and say, 'If you're not up to it.' But this wasn't one of those times. Now they were going to dine, review video and decide when and where to go next.

Their plane tickets said Minneapolis as it should since at some point they did need to make their way home. But after that, there needed to be another video and another spot. Even when her father had been stationed to a place for years, she had visited nearby countries. It was impossible in Europe to not take a train and cut across three borders for a fun weekend. The spirit to move, go, learn was so deeply ingrained in her if Conner hadn't needed a home base for his company, they may have never purchased the condo.

Other reasons, beyond the inability to sit still, had Serena wanting another adventure. The *World Traveler Channel* was one of her closest followers, she'd watched them like, comment and even share her posts to their pages. Only when she woke that morning their interest in her appeared in her inbox. An email with an offer to sit down and talk. Though she wasn't sure she wanted planned out trips with a crew of ten with her, shot and reshot scenes to capture the right moods, what had been a joke and dream now sat, like a treasure waiting to be opened with a single click of her mouse. The get-a-ways with Conner had been the way they spent their year-long honeymoon. What had been sharing her adventures with friends on her private page soon turned into a chance for a business. One where she was actually having fun when she worked, for nearly seven years that had been their life. The idea of leveling up was natural, even if she'd already thought she was at the top of the mountain only to see another peak, hidden just beyond her view.

Josh was now their errand boy in a way, but knew to give

them the space they needed. WTC wouldn't let her do things on her own timeline and she knew that, which meant any butterflies of excitement she was feeling about a potential contract would have to be tamed.

Freedom was a luxury she had and cherished. What had been a vacation, turned into a life, a third turn could create a job. And a job meant toil, work, and worse yet, growing up.

After sitting and being given their first round of drinks, Serena retrieved her phone from her bag as the sun continued its descent into the sea. The pinks and purples melted into the darkening sea, and yet there was calm all around her as the party atmosphere picked up.

"Oh," she said, sitting up straighter. "Remember Bethany?"

"Your German tutor Bethany or favorite cousin Bethany?" Conner asked while giving the waiter a thank you nod as their appetizers were being placed on the table.

"Cousin, she's getting married."

Conner choked on the jerk spiced shrimp. "I'm sorry, what?"

"I know you thought she was a bit—"

"Self-involved."

"I was going to say...you know that might be it, but she is fun," Serena acquiesced. "Yes, she wants to live in every moment perfectly, and if you're lucky you can go along for the ride."

"Gee, I wonder why she's your favorite cousin," he replied with a wink. "When's the wedding?"

"Friday," Serena said, furrowing her brows. "It says this is my last call for RSVPs and she wasn't sure why I hadn't responded because the invites went out over two months ago."

"I wonder if she sent the invite to the condo." Conner spun his fork a few times before offering her the shrimp on the end.

"Has it been that long?" Serena asked, covering her mouth as she ate the heavily flavored crustacean with the type of heat bringing out flavor instead of overwhelming a person at the beginning. "Wow, okay." Reaching for her cocktail, she tamped down the tiny bit of fire burning on her tongue as flavor gave way.

"Yes, it has. I'm pretty sure the patio furniture on our balcony has to be ruined under a pile of snow."

"What month is it?" Serena asked. Days, months, years, hell time in general shifted once she wasn't on a school schedule land-marking her life with important dates. Now her life had become a bit of a blur, with little more than a handful of birthdays and a very important anniversary to keep her focused.

"February, hence, the influx of pale people in the Caribbean," Josh said, still flipping through the uploaded video on his laptop. "You know we could overlay you screaming, we didn't quite capture it fully. Maybe we'll need to get waterproof sound equipment to keep everything one hundred."

"I could help with getting you to scream." Conner's hand slipped to her thigh with a light squeeze.

"Wrong inflection," she replied, but didn't remove the hand that had located the slit in her sarong. She loved when his pinky would stroke along her inner thigh. "Back to the invite. Auntie Louise hasn't been filling my inbox, texting or anything. That's odd."

"Not really," Conner said. "You remember what she said at your grandfather's birthday a few years ago."

Serena dug through the memories of the few family gather-ings over the years and realized her father's line had been written off long ago. When he was made ambassador, both sides of the family distanced themselves in a way. No longer would they have family gatherings like they once had from the pictures kept in the library at their homes. Visits had a high chance of being cancelled due to a crisis occurring and although her mother was comfort-able with her father's side of the family hers was less receptive to their little girl marrying a man from another country. Especially since that country was in Africa. It didn't matter that he'd spent his formative years in Wisconsin. From what her mother explained a full-on Nigerian wedding had her Lutheran parents dumbstruck between the bright colors and long traditions. Not wearing a white dress had her great-grandmother ready to collapse from the idea of it all and once her parents were stationed around the globe it never was the same.

"I would feel horrible if I missed Bethany's wedding. Especially since it's just an island hop or two away in the Dominican Republic."

"Or, you'd feel horrible missing out on another island on your quest for world domination," Conner countered.

"I've been there before, once, but I've never heard of Puerto Plata."

"That's the spot with the Rio thing," Josh said, leaning back in the chair.

"Carnival?" Serena asked with a bit too much hope in her heart.

"No, the Jesus thing."

"Christ the Redeemer?" Conner questioned. "They have a Christ the Redeemer statue and no one knows about it?"

"Hi, I'm a human and I know about it." Josh swallowed a bit too much of his drink and coughed a bit. "Look it's not as big, but it is a replica on a hill, mountain, whatever. Puerto Plata doesn't get all the pub Punta Cana gets, or Santo Domingo, but it's a big city on the island. Kinda like Montego Bay. Metro, yet, beachy."

"It would just be you and me," she offered, placing her hand on his. "You know how weddings make me all—gushy."

"Ours did that's for sure." Conner turned to Josh, whose dark eyes were as mournful as the sigh he released.

Tucking away the camera equipment and laptop, Josh pushed back from the table before snagging his drink. "This can wait. I'm going to make sure I properly experience Jamaican rum brands so I can write you a report when my eyes open. Until then, I'm going to dance before I'm banished to the snow globe."

Drink in hand, Josh found a few young women who were dancing, even though it wasn't really that type of spot at the moment.

"You and me?" Conner countered, brushing back the few braids that had loosened from her bun. The heat from his fingertips seared her cheek and set off more than butterflies in her belly. "We could get a flight for tomorrow and find our way there. Rent out a bungalow by the beach."

"She's got places for guests at a resort," Serena said, then finally had time catch up with her. "Did you say it's February?"

"No, Josh did. Why?"

"A Valentine wedding, it all makes sense now," Serena smiled, then leaned on Conner's shoulder. "A trip would be better than a box of chocolates and flowers."

"You're already splitting the trip in your mind between a regular Love on the Run episode and an all about love compilations on where to go for a romantic getaway." The quirk on the corner of Conner's lip made her warm in all the right places. Mind, heart, and a bit further south.

He'd always been her rock. Her biggest cheerleader and the man willing to take on the world with her.

"You think you can handle all the camera duties?" she asked.

"You think you can choose to not jump off a cliff when offered?"

"I could, but then I wouldn't be the woman you married."

I MARRIED A ROMANTIC GENIUS

Musical advice should be listened to repeatedly until your foolish heart accepts the words. For Conner Love, he should have listened to Jimmy Soul and married an ugly woman. Not that Serena didn't make him happy, and he saw no reason that would change, but never having to worry would be nice. Her lack of fear of the unknown had nearly crippled him early on in their relationship. Sure Jimmy Soul was singing about the woman being loyal, still there was the dream Serena would find a place and plant her feet.

Then again, if she did, would the beauty he found in her deep brown eyes disappear like the sun had over the horizon as the stars salted the sky above? Her heart was full of wanderlust, but not in a bad way. The few times he couldn't go with her on a trip she came back a bit disappointed. Not because the place wasn't magnificent, but because he found half of her joy came from his reaction. Showing him a new place or strange fruit.

That is why he was scanning the internet for flights to switch and as always, cashing in the flight home. Did he want insurance on this flight? Yes, yes a thousand times yes because he'd never know if they were going to leave in a week to go home or follow the next suggestion that hit Serena's Vlog.

He marveled at the way the woman slept contently before a trip. Like a kid who got the toy they wanted on Christmas Eve, so they didn't care about waking early or any other present coming in the morning. Curled on her side, just her foot poked from the covers as the curve of her ankle teased him a bit.

A light knock on the door caused her to stir as he went to get their room service order. Tipping well, because that seemed to be the unseen cost with vacations on the islands, he took the tray and set it on the table knowing the smell of freshly brewed coffee would wake his bride. Not that she drank the stuff, but the smell reminded her of mornings and soon she was rolling over in the bed as her eyes batted away sleep like a tennis player balls from a serving machine.

"Please say pancakes are on that plate," she mumbled, dragging herself from the bed as if it were the sea and the wave was receding back to pull her under.

"Banana pancakes, with strawberries cut up on top," he replied, flashing the lid from the plate all burlesque style. Just a peek, but did you really see what you thought you saw?

"Tease."

"No, the tease is the coco bread I had them make for us for the plane."

"I married a romantic genius," she said, slipping from the bed in just a pair of silver colored boy shorts and matching lace bra.

For all her in your face out and loud Vlog behavior, she was demure in so many ways. Wearing a tankini yesterday instead of a bikini. Her body was for him. In the morning light, he could see her skin had darkened a bit from the normal tawny coloring to a rich amber from the moments when she let her brain settle and rested in the sun.

His parents didn't understand their lifestyle. Not that they ever really got him once college was over and the only teams calling him required a country code to call back. They understood him being a jock. Playing ball. Working toward a career, with the understanding he would pair it with a college degree. One he might actually be able to find a job with. Computer sciences fit his love of gaming, the way he tended to unearth cheat codes others couldn't find and the fact he could take apart, and thankfully to avoid his father's wrath, put together a computer on a rainy Saturday when he was in second grade.

This, his father saw as a reason to put him in sports. Idol hands and all. Now, no matter how many games downloaded or contracts signed the fact he married a wild hippy with braids and a love of flowing skirts didn't help his father's belief that his son was lost to the world. Maybe they should go home after the wedding. Show they weren't as lost as they appeared.

"What time is our flight?" she asked, taking a sip of orange juice before cutting into her pancake.

"The shuttle will get us at noon, so we'll be at the airport in plenty of time." He chose the fresh fruit plate, since he knew all of it had been grown on the island and couldn't get any fresher. "I was going to go for a run before we left."

"Aw, you're so healthy, I'm going to say goodbye to the island, take a few more shots and see if there are any appropriate dresses for sale at that little market we went to on Tuesday."

A chill ran down Conner's spine. Josh was set to fly out a few hours before them, so he knew the kid was practically out the door by now. No way would he let his wife wander in a flea market alone. Safety and practical reasons would have to delay his workout.

"That sounds good. Maybe you'll find a gift or two there."

"You don't trust me," she challenged, setting down her fork.

"Serena, you are five foot nothing—"

"Four," she bit back, then waved her hands all ninja style. "I'm quick and slippery."

"And I've enjoyed that on more occasions than I'd like to admit."

Playfully, she tossed a piece of strawberry at him and he caught it in his mouth.

"Brat." Leaning back in her chair she smiled. "You know I can take care of myself."

"And yet, who's the one coming to save you? The last thing I need is some guy snagging a purse and you chase after him only to find a dead body."

"Once, that happened once, and if I hadn't tripped over the dead guy, I would have caught him."

"Instead, we extended our stay until you found out who the real murderer was."

"I got a commendation from the Police Chief," she boasted, her shoulders straightening a bit. "And three marriage proposals."

"Of which you accepted two."

"Are you worried my second fiancé little Bennie is nearing double digits and soon will come to sweep me from your arms?" Serena's arms swirled a bit before she placed the back of her wrist to her forehead and lolled it back in pure love-struck fashion.

"Please I've already pre-booked the tickets for that kid's eighteenth birthday. I'm dropping you on his doorstep annulment papers in hand."

"Annulment?" she gasped in under overly dramatic fashion. "As if our—" he watched as she calculated the years to Bennie's birthday from their wedding. "Fifteen years together meant nothing."

"He's Catholic," he replied, and she sat forward and took another bite of pancake. "I'm assuming he'd want to get married in the church, not a drive-through chapel."

"Oh, that makes sense. Very practical of you, but tell me are you regretting your claiming ways, Conner Love?"

He scoffed. "Don't try to change the subject and I was going to ask you to marry me before you found a body lying dead in an alley."

Serena's dark hazel eyes narrowed a bit. "Wait? Did you order the hit in some elaborate solve the murder mystery and earn the brownie party way?"

"There were brownies?" he joked, then refocused his conversation wandering wife. "Can you admit, when you are left to your own devices things go sideways?"

"On occasion—" she began.

"Every day is an occasion with you, my love."

"It is not my fault." She absently cut another bite of pancake. "We've been here for a whole week and—"

His hand instantly shot across the table to cover her mouth as he knocked on the wood of her chair. "Don't do it. Don't you temp the Gods, Serena Anaborhi Love. We have a good six hours before we are in the air, and I would like to get there without the distraction of a newly rotting corpse."

The inside of his hand became wet, and he pulled away from palm licking wife.

"So you're taking me shopping, then?"

"Why not a nice jog?"

"Haven't you noticed joggers always interrupt or fall over a murder scene?"

THREE
WHAT'S BETTER THAN A VACATION WRITE-OFF?

There was something in the water of Jamaica. No matter how many times she'd had coco bread stateside it wasn't the same. Even at the Carifest in Minneapolis, the flavor was not the same as it was on the island. Flipping through social media, Serena ate her bread and waited for their plane to be called. For a woman who made her living off of social media, she had been absent as an enjoyer of what it had to offer.

Refollows happened, but rarely did she scan the pages and take in the life others were having. If she would have Bethany's announcement and subsequent barrage of wedding planning breakdowns should have caught her eye. She would have called her cousin, but she knew the woman was in full on last chance wedding planning mode. That drama she wasn't in the mood for.

A quick apology text, making sure to let the woman know she was the most important thing and that all plans were scrapped to attend her wedding.

I wish you would have gotten back sooner, you should have been in my wedding party.

While Serena wanted to point out the phone can ring and she does pay attention to most text messages, it would fall on deaf fingers. All the love she had for the queen that was Bethany she knew better.

It would be bad to replace an issue couple wouldn't it?

Serena smirked. *Depends, what's the issue?* With a wink emoji.

One of those drama couples. Bethany replied. *Donald never would let me.*

Then I guess you're stuck. Serena replied as relief released her tensed muscles, glad she was out of the duties involved with a wedding. *I'm so excited I can be there for you either way.*

A simple K was returned and Serena began researching the Puerto Plata area.

"Isn't this supposed to be our Valentine getaway?" Conner asked.

"What's better than a vacation tax write-off?" she countered. "Besides, there's a whole different vibe in the DR than there is in Jamaica. Each of the Caribbean Islands are more than just beach and fresh fruit you know."

A loud bang made Conner jump, and Serena furrowed her brow at him.

"Wait, I've solved it," she said, and he gave her a questioning look. "Construction."

She pointed to where they were moving bags of cement on a part of the airport being upgraded.

"You're acting like you've lived in a warzone and have PTSD," she said, then used her thumb to scroll on her phone. "Trust me, that's far from a warzone noise."

Kazakhstan hadn't been her favorite place to live, but the meal culture believing in multiple appetizers may have created an unrealistic expectation for life. One needed more than a bread basket or a cheese tray.

"I'm assuming you've booked us into the resort," Serena said, putting aside her phone and reaching for her laptop.

Editing needed to be done. A quick shout-out to her followers she did all the time in the airport. Never saying where she was going, especially on this trip. If she was going to tie it into Valentine's Day, this could be a year from production.

"Stop," Conner said, closing down her laptop and setting it to the side. "I'm asking for ten minutes of—"

The sound of power tools filled the smaller airport, and he shook his head.

"Let me see if I remember Bethany right," he said, lifting his hand to let her continue her notes about Jamaica.

"Oh, you remember her. My father's younger sister had her quite a few months shy of the first anniversary of her marriage."

"And by shy you mean?" he said, leading her words.

"It was closer to her wedding date."

"The scandal."

"At the time, yes. It threw the whole Isola clan back in Nigeria into a tailspin of not so silent condemnation about what happens when you come to America."

"The horror," the deadpan look her husband sported knowing full well the Nigerian half of Serena's family would pull traditions out of their ass when necessary even though they were more than fully Americanized since she had been born there.

"Right, so Auntie Louise was beside herself, claiming her sweet child from God had been born early. Fragile and in need of extra care." Serena shook her head. "I was the only one dumb enough to think an eight-pound baby had been born four months early. But I was only five and she was smaller than me."

"What you're saying is basically Bethany has been spoiled her whole life?"

"Yep." Serena beamed. "I got the best of both worlds with her. When I was with her, I got the best of everything and went to any place she wanted. And when I was at home my father praised me for not being a spoiled brat like my cousin. Such a win-win for me."

A text came across Conner's phone and he let out a sigh. "I've got to handle this before I get on the plane."

She waved him off, then decided it was time for her usual live update.

"*Hey there, Runners,*" she began as she held the phone out just enough in selfie mode so they couldn't tell exactly where she was. Airports had a general quality to them that allowed her to keep people engaged. "*About to take off from a beautiful location to go to another. I think I got a little sun this time around.*"

The viewers ticked up on the upper corner with hearts and thumbs floating on the screen. Euphoria filled her veins from the instant gratification of it all.

"*Now, no guesses as to where I've been or where I'm going, but we all know I'm going to have stories to tell.*" She flipped the camera to a booth where Conner sat dutifully on his laptop with his earbuds in, having a conversation. "*Look at him. Being dragged around the world and working like a dog. Isn't he the most adorable man in the universe?*"

He got sun too, say it was an amazing beach, *Travelslut234* texted in the comments. While others were just posting jelly, take me with, don't care where I'll come.

Flipping the camera back to her, Serena replied, "*Yeah, Travelslut, he did get some. Poor man, I had to coat him with sunblock to keep him from turning into a lobster. Something tells me I need to take him somewhere raining for a few weeks.*"

This started the barrage of what women would do with him in the rain, mixed with others from men, offering an even better option for her. This is usually when she blocked the comments and finished up with what she was planning on saying.

"*I'm heading to a wedding, destination of course, and it makes me think back to the wedding of Old Man Love and myself. You ever get that way? Wanting to revisit a place just for the memory you created there? I usually don't, but I'm getting all gushy and gooey. What can I say, I like the guy I married.*"

More hearts flooded her screen in approval as she tried to capture a good tag to get the watchers over two thousand for the live stream. Letting out a sigh, she gave the camera a wink.

"*That's it, runners, all you get. Right now I see you're giving me suggestions of where to go, and haters I've already been there, got the T-shirt and made sure to put in an offer on a nice condo next to the Lake of Fire."*

Why trolls existed in the world confounded Serena. What did one get from trying to make another's day bad? Negativity had her turning into a Costanza and wanting to yell 'Serenity now.' In a way, the fact her feed garnered her over a few thousand watchers was good. She wasn't everyone's cup of tea, but damn scroll away.

"Remember, miles expire, so take the trip."

Clicking off her phone, she tucked it away and waited to see what disaster Conner had been pulled into. Family or work. There was little in between even if Serena had made the suggestion to the Secretary of State that Conner could negotiate a better Mideast peace accord than most. The way his fingers were typing she assumed it was work. While he did piece work out to a hand full of coders, that didn't mean tragic fails weren't a hundred percent on him.

When he closed his laptop and pinched the bridge of his nose, she steadied herself. Prepared for whatever would come her way. That was how they were together. Each helped the other unburden themselves. At least it wasn't a family thing. She would have enough of that with her Auntie Louise.

FOUR

THIS IS ONE OF THOSE ALGORITHM THINGS THAT WILL MAKE MY EYE TWITCH

Heat of the island hit on the jet bridge, customs in the DR, the local nickname for the Dominican Republic, was smoother than in Jamaica even with most of the pages filled with stamps in their passports. The fact the two of them shared a medium-sized bag, and each had a backpack confounded Conner. When he was younger, his parents would fill the trunk with suitcases packed to the gills.

Serena was a master at finding a place to wash their clothes. Usually while they went out for a tour of the city, but still, he admired his wife for her ingenuity to travel light.

Something he wished his contract labor could figure out on their own. Their firewall had been breached, but they acted as if data was being compromised. It wasn't this time, instead the hacker just gave all the users a ton of game currency and he had to get it back. Most users wouldn't even notice as they didn't log on in the half-hour when the money had been dropped. But he currently had to determine how much money he'd just lost over what he hoped would be a one-time prank.

To avoid being called out for stealing, he left those who'd logged on during the dump with their new funds. The last thing he needed was to be gamed himself. His first few apps had been sold to bigger companies, which had been perfect. Conner got money, with only time as an investment, and could focus on basketball. His agent even helped with the contracts for less than his normal fee. But once he was done playing ball it only made sense to control all the rights. At first, the venture was simple. Now he understood how much those other companies were having to deal with on a daily basis.

Flipping through his phone the whole ride to the resort, he was watching for any blogging news that could hurt Gaming Love. With a new game set to launch in a few months, he had to make sure this hadn't been a test run for something bigger.

"Everything okay?" Serena asked as they sat in the back row of the shuttle van. "You were quiet the whole flight."

"Hackers," he said, no reason to worry his wife over business. "I'm in a catch twenty-two with them. On one hand, I want to beat them into a pulp from messing with my tech."

"And on the other you respect the skill," she concluded. "Anything really bad?"

"I'm having Amy review the numbers." There was a difference between worrying his wife and lying to her. He wasn't going to take the chance of being caught up in a lie if this turned into something more.

Conner may help Serena with her Vlog, but it was hers. He held the camera, took the shots she wanted, and did his best to make sure she didn't wander off and get lost. Much like he wouldn't advise her, she wouldn't him.

"Numbers? As in they broke in and took your money?"

"It's a weird thing. They gave coins to players which means they won't need to buy or try to earn more through watching ads."

"This is one of those algorithm things that will make my eye twitch, isn't it?"

"Even on a good day," he said, trying to shove the early estimates of half a million dollars from his mind. He stupidly asked for the worst-case scenario and now had that lead weight resting in the center of his gut. Wrapping his arm around Serena, he pulled her tight to his chest.

The hit, no matter how big, would be hard, ego-wise, more than money. The Love's portfolio was diverse, each of them with their own money and one joint account. Serena was the one with eight digits. The trust from family money set her up before she even graduated high school. Once she went to college, the education was paid for by her grades and not her parents. The wandering woman had room to discover what she wanted to do in life. Getting caught in the air around her had been intoxicating at first.

His salary wasn't on the scale of the 'one and dones' who'd left him behind in college. The games were where he found a fortune. Something his family expected him to focus on more.

'How much more could you make if you actually sat still and focused on the job at hand,' his father admonished right after Conner had paid off the man's mortgage twelve years ahead of schedule.

'George,' his mother tried to intercede. 'Say thank you. Conner, we can't —'

'This is from your wife isn't it?' his father barked. 'No way you made this from some game about bubbles.'

'Serena doesn't even know I'm doing this,' he replied. 'And after what you just said she never will.'

There was no way he could explain losing a half million to his parents when their home had taken barely a hundred grand to pay off. He needed to backtrace the hacker. Using his free hand he quickly texted Huey, that guy could track down anyone. Conner refused to let this weigh too heavily on his mind. For the first time, their trip was their own. Josh wouldn't be knocking on the door to try to catch the right light when Serena's hands were wandering on his body.

"Think this is our stop, my love," he said and Serena uncurled from him.

Gated, with guards brandishing weapons, he wasn't exactly sure how comfortable he felt about staying at the noted five-star resort. Were those stars real? Did they have celebrities and that's why they need the AR-15s or had he missed something as they drove through the city? Lord knew the white-washed building was modern, with tiled floors and crystal clear pools visible from the check-in desk. Paradise was only a few steps away from a man needing a semi-automatic weapon.

Their bag was stickered with the resort logo, adding to the ones Serena decorated the hard plastic luggage with. Serena spoke four languages, Spanish being one, and easily conversed with the front desk clerk. Soon they were being driven in a golf cart to the building where their room was. Open and airy, Conner did love that places near salt water had tiled and not carpeted floors. A quick tip and soon they were settled into their room.

"It's quieter than I expected here," Serena said as she stood on the balcony. Only the sound of the ocean crashing beyond the walls of the resort could be heard.

Conner was reviewing the passport map and guide to the place. An all-inclusive resort, he was already working his excuses to avoid the timeshare pitch session.

"The desk clerk said they would take us around tomorrow to show us the property. I guess they have a dozen beaches and over thirty pools."

"It's a timeshare. Do you want to move into the villas? Stay on the beach forever."

"That would be boring," Serena said as she came back into the room and closed the door. "So, I'll set the screen and you'll post up behind me to help get away from any sales reps?"

"It's cute when you try to use basketball jargon."

"I'm great at my basketball jargon, you're just jealous."

"Am I?" he said, snagging her around the waist and pulling her to the bed. "I will say one thing I'm jealous of."

"What's that?" she asked when he leaned down to kiss her lips.

"The shower in this place is at least twice the size of ours at home."

"I can't even remember ours at home," Serena said, bringing her hand to her face. "Okay, it's official. We're going home after this wedding."

"But can we use the shower first?"

Her delicate hand slipped from her face as a knowing smile crossed her lips. "Yes, but I'm hiding all the soaps, so they'll refill tomorrow."

"I would be disappointed if your cheap ass didn't steal all the hotel soap."

FIVE
YOU'RE BEING A NERD

"B *reakfast buffet, breakfast buffet, breakfast buffet,*" Serena sang as she danced awkwardly with as little rhythm and as much ass wiggling as possible. "*There is a breakfast buffet.*"

"You know it's probably going to be bad as two-star chain hotels. Make your own waffles that never beep right when you flip them."

"Be still my heart, admonishing what was your lifeblood in your youth."

"What can I say? European style breakfasts ruined me for all others," Conner grumbled and rolled over in the bed. She wasn't sure exactly how long he'd stayed up working on his issue last night, but Serena knew one thing, she didn't get the ass he loved by skipping breakfast. "You're going to let me wander around all sexy without you?"

"That is a danger, seeing as that's how I found you. Wandering around all sexy." His voice was deep with gravel, a true indication of how late he was up. "You know I love you, right?"

"But…" she said, waiting on the inevitable.

"Never mind, they won't let you make me a plate. Not here."

"Nope," she replied, holding her flowy skirt between her thumbs and middle fingers as her toes pushed up in her strappy sandals like a two-year-old with a big skirt. "Isn't it wonderful?"

"Breakfast in bed would have been wonderful." Conner rolled onto his side, the cut of his bicep tempting her as it curved to his shoulder. She had a thing for broad shoulders.

"You had enough food in bed last night," she quipped and turned on her big toe to get the room key and place it in the hip wrap purse she wore when exploring.

"We're not coming back to the room anytime soon are we?"

"There is a whole city to explore and experience. You know Bethany will demand we lay on the beach and drink all day when she gets here."

"The hell you say?" he mocked. "What type of person goes to a tropical paradise and—"

Thank goodness for throw pillows. The one from the couch hit Conner squarely in his face and he conceded. Packing the camera and equipment in a bag. They went to breakfast and soon were sitting at the table with the concierge setting up a tour of the city for tomorrow, but today they would check out the mini Christ the Redeemer. The packages were enough to block the roaming time-share salesmen for a few days.

"At least I'm not making you hike up Mount Isabel de Torres," Serena reasoned as they joined with the other tourists in a shuttle that would take them to the cable car that would carry them over the trees and to the top point of Puerto Plata.

"Making me?" he questioned. "Because I'm pretty sure you were the one who rolled over in Jamaica when I kissed your forehead and asked if you wanted to go for a jog."

"I only have so many steps in my life and you want me to waste them moving faster than necessary to get where I need to go?" she teased. "Then turn around and go back over those steps so I can go home and you know maybe tomorrow I'll run with you before we explore."

"The shower?" he questioned as his hand moved over her thigh.

"It should be illegal and I need to take specs to find us a plumber to install it at home."

"Would that make you stay home?" he asked.

"There is a high possibility I may stay more than three days," she reasoned. "Or we could let the timeshare guy sell us on the resort."

He chuckled and soon they were getting instructions as Serena took still shots with her camera. A mix of signs, flora, and street life. Having been in so many countries around the world she shouldn't be surprised when she saw a man on a moped with a woman on the back and a toddler in the middle. But when they zoomed down the street she had to stop and shake her head. Necessity she could understand, but it didn't help her unease.

Stepping on the tram, she had to steady herself. Hadn't she leapt from a cliff less than twenty-four hours ago? That wasn't the same as riding a tram, with the random rocking back and forth. Trees occasionally scraped along the bottom as they rose high in the sky.

"You okay, my love?" Conner asked as his fingers intertwined with hers. "This view is amazing."

"I believe you," she replied as she examined the polish on her toenails.

The younger riders in the tram were on their knees on the seats, turned backward with their faces plastered to the glass enjoying the rise. The grinding of the cable above Serena had her heart clenching as she let out a long breath of air.

"You have to explain this to me?" he prodded. "Yesterday—"

"I could step back and say, nope. Right now, I have zero control of the world around me. I'm in a tiny little metal box creaking its way up a mountain at an excruciatingly slow pace." She lifted her gaze to his. "A mountain."

"As opposed to the cliff you jumped off of yesterday?"

"Pish posh," she said, waving her hand to distract him. "Oh

no, Mr. Love, I'm not giving you my cheat code. If my insanity made sense, you would have conquered the game and be bored with me like a round of solitaire."

Conner spent the next ten minutes distracting her until the loud click of the door allowed her to jet out onto the grass and solid ground. Height wasn't the issue. When she spun around and saw the view, her heart stopped. A sea of green from the tops of the trees melted into the white, red and gray roofs of the city finally flowing into the blue of the Atlantic Ocean. The near cloudless sky shone bright on the world below.

Swapping out the lens on her camera to her seventy-two-hundred, Serena captured the layered landscape before her. A familiar hand rested on the small of her back and she tried to stay focused.

"And this doesn't bother you?" Conner whispered in her ear, sending a charge down the column of her neck.

"You need to stop," she replied a bit breathlessly as she turned her head to the side and encountered the lips of the man leaning down to her height.

In bed, they could be somewhat even in scale, but on land, she remembered exactly how much of a height difference there was between them. The fact that in a minute, when he stood tall and slipped behind her, she could completely disappear. Becoming engulfed in the man who she barely made it to mid-chest on.

"You know, telling a gamer there are cheat codes sends their minds reeling with all sorts of ideas."

"Save it," she replied. "We have plenty of time this week. Even with me grabbing a few shots here and there." Her voice lowered and she mumbled something.

"What was that?" he questioned.

"Huh? Did I say something?"

"Yes, you did," he pointed out, knowing whatever she said she was trying to hide.

"So, I noticed in the brochure passport thingy they have scuba certification here."

Conner crossed his arms. She'd tried this in a dozen countries, and he wasn't comfortable with her getting certified outside of the United States. Call it prejudice, but licensing and laws allowed for additional safeguards.

"No." His tone so harsh her head pulled back as if he'd slapped her.

"What?"

"I said no, it's a two letter word, spelled n-o," he repeated.

"It's not registering? Are you sure it's not slang? Is this one of those things you type to get an angry wife emoji to appear on your texts?"

"One usually does pop up right after I say it," he said, unable to tamp down his sarcasm. "Doesn't change the fact I don't want you to have an embolism from a poor oxygen mix."

"Ugh, I swear you're the only person who actually reads disclaimers. Why did your parents teach you to read?" she replied. "Did they know you'd go beyond comic books?"

"No." he shook his head and she snapped a picture of him. "Alright boss lady, let's do that research thing you love so much."

"Exploring, with the direct result of retaining knowledge."

"You don't want me to say you're being a nerd," Conner joked, and she stepped away to swap the lens back to her twenty-four-seventy.

"We only have room for one nerd in the family and you are it, my love."

Flipping the camera on her phone, Serena checked to make sure the headband style wrap holding her braided locks back from her face was in order, then added a little lip gloss. Nothing major, just enough to make her lips glisten as Conner shook his head. The two of them wandered through the domed building, reading plaques on top of what she had researched when she woke before Conner that morning. Once they stepped outside, she became the documentarian again.

"*Unlike the original Christ the Redeemer in Rio, Puerto Plata's version on top of Mount Isabel de Torres was on top of a domed fortress.*

Window lookouts proved to be useless when clouds or fog rolled in on the mountain high above the city," she explained, and Conner walked alongside her as if she were talking to a friend and not a camera lens. "Puerto Plata has another seaside fort we'll be visiting tomorrow, but right now, Runners, the sky is clear and we're going to make sure the area is secure."

Conner followed her lead and scanned the area below, making sure to sweep the whole view in a metered pace to avoid the Josh fallout. Once he'd done that, he turned the camera toward her and she continued.

"Guess we're safe, Runners, which means we can go on to the botanical gardens." She smiled. "You didn't think we took a tram here for a statue, nope like everything in Puerto Plata, there are layers to uncover."

———

"Serena," Conner warned, knowing the young man about to approach would garner attention he shouldn't.

His wife had been lost in a moment of clicking images of the plants and flowers, but all it took was a 'Hey missus,' to get her to stop. The kid couldn't be more than fourteen wearing a dirty, navy blue, polo shirt and khaki, cargo shorts a few sizes too big. If they were pressed and clean, Conner would say it was a school uniform of some sort. The only thing he knew was the kid was on a hustle, and Serena had a soft spot for kids.

"Hey missus, dollar?" His hands were stretched out in front of her.

"Do I have a dollar?" Serena asked as she scanned the kid. "Aren't you supposed to be in school?"

The kid smiled broadly, used to begging, and with hopeful eyes that the woman would pass him money and move on.

"Hey," a man called and the boy jetted away into lush foliage off the path, leaving only the sound of rustling leaves behind.

Conner continued, with Serena in tow, curving along the path of fresh plants. Higher altitude and pure oxygen from the leaves clearing his mind a bit from the messages he prayed would be on his phone once they were back in a cell service area. Here he was acting as if they needed to stay down at the resort to chill and actually relax when really he was waiting on Amy's figures and Huey's report.

Once Conner had learned to code, even the simplest ones, his brain never silenced. Only a basketball court could he stop the matrix-style numbers from falling in front of his eyes. Serena turned around and the digits disappear as if the braids in her hair had whipped them from the space before his eyes. This is how she'd captured him back in Latvia. Who backpacked through Latvia? Especially a young black woman fresh from college. Taking, as she termed it, a gap year before deciding if graduate school could teach her more than immersing herself in the world.

'A dissertation can make me an expert on one thing,' the young woman bundled up in a pea coat with a thick scarf around her neck said. Her hair was under a knit cap, a tangle of curls attempting to be tamed. 'My father, of course, expects me to get a doctorate in something, but the fact is he doesn't care what I get it in means he wants the title and not the education.'

'Or,' Conner countered as he sipped the black tea from the disposable cup as they walked the streets in Valmeria, Latvia. 'He wants you to choose courses you enjoy and not demand you become what he wants.'

'Personal experience?' she questioned, either oblivious to the stares they were receiving from the locals or unwilling to give the gawkers the satisfaction of acknowledging their rudeness. Either one made him envy the woman and want to know more about her.

'Tall kid, must mean I was meant to play basketball,' Conner replied.

'You don't like it?'

'No, I do, but I'll never find a home with it,' he replied. 'I'm not at that level and I can accept it.'

'Then quit,' she stated plainly, as if that option was one he hadn't considered.

'To do what?' he asked.

'*What do you like to do beyond honing in on the only American girl for thousands of kilometers?*'

'*Kilometers,*' he replied with a light laugh.

'*I try to adapt to my surroundings, blend in and all.*' Now she was the one drinking the warm beverage as they found a park and sat at a table with a chessboard etched into the surface.

'*In college, I studied computer science. Learned coding.*' His fingers absently traced the perfectly symmetric board in front of him. '*I recently sold two games.*'

Serena's hand hovered over the second row of her board, then she moved an imaginary pawn out two places. '*Your move.*'

"Hey? Where did you go?" Serena asked, jarring him from the day he met and fell in love with his wife.

"Happy places," he replied.

"You sure?" she questioned.

"You were there, how could it not be."

"Flirt," she said, then pushed up on her tiptoes and he leaned down to lightly kiss her lips.

"Dollar?" the teen was back, his tanned skin sporting a few scrapes Conner hadn't noticed before.

"School," Serena countered since it was a weekday Conner understood her urging. They'd been in enough impoverished areas to know the only chance these kids had, no matter how street-smart, would come from education. "You speak any more English?"

"Sometimes," the teen admitted before shooing away a grade school aged kid whose face scrunched in frustration before running off toward other tourists.

"What's your name?" Serena asked and Conner wondered if the woman knew how to put up a wall between herself and danger.

"Derian, who you?"

"Serena, and this is Conner." She arched her eyebrow and Conner did his best to tamp down the smirk pulling at the corners of his lips. "So, you gonna tell me why you're not in chemistry right now?"

"Field trip," he replied, his smile wide.

"And your teacher lets you beg on poor tourists?" she challenged.

"Extra credit, the more I get, the higher my grade. Wanna help me get an A?"

"Serena, come on," Conner said, knowing his wife a bit too much and seeing one of the employees of the place heading their way.

"You know this city well?" she asked.

"Yes, ma'am."

"Fine, tomorrow we are going on a guided tour I'm sure I'm not going to like," she said. "If you help us really see the city I will reward you."

"Where are you staying?"

"No," Conner interjected, his wife could have some leniency when it came to safety, but he had limits. "Tell us where to meet you or a good place to ditch our tour guide."

The kid narrowed his eyes in thought. "Those guided tours tend to take you downtown at some point. There's a central park area. I'll find you there."

"Get," the worker for the botanical garden came up. "Scat. Leave these people alone."

"Why? So you can sell them overpriced larimar?" Derian asked as he back peddled toward the entrance. "Don't buy any jewelry from these guys. I have the hook-up."

Derian scurried out of the area and back down toward the statue outside.

"I'm sorry about that. Don't listen, we have a stunning collection of handcraft…"

The man's voice droned on about the precious stone exclusive to the island. Conner and Serena listened and at one point she tapped him to begin filming for content. That was her world. He just held the camera and prayed to get away.

SIX

YOU DO REALIZE BACON IS INVOLVED?

"Got a text update from Bethany," Serena said as they sat to eat breakfast after the jog she agreed to take that morning. "Or more I was tagged with a picture of a half dozen people I don't know showing them all on the plane."

"They're coming in today?" Conner asked, a bit too much excitement lacing his voice for her liking.

"Guess so, we'll be on our tour."

"Fifty bucks says Derian either doesn't show or takes us somewhere we shouldn't be."

"Why shouldn't we be someplace?" she asked, stabbing a fresh piece of melon with her fork. "This island—"

"Has spots we shouldn't be."

"And so does New York, Western Kentucky and Botswana. Doesn't mean I don't want to visit and take my chances."

"Western Kentucky?" he questioned.

"Churchill Downs," she said, and he shook his head to let her know she'd guessed wrong. "No?"

"North central Kentucky, and since when do you want to go to a horse race?"

"Have you seen the hats?" she asked, falling into a poor

attempt at southern drawl. "I could get all fancy, have a mint julip, and cheer for a filly."

"You got too much sun lately. I'm thinking you need to check out Antarctica."

"Joke all you want, Conner," she teased, but not really. "We could slide down to Chile and hit it around this time next year."

He shook his head and closed his eyes a bit.

"What? You code all over the world instead of sitting in a dark room with too many energy drinks and nuked meals." Every part of her wanted to know what was going on with Gaming Love. Conner wasn't one to hold on to secrets but until he had a resolution he would never think of sharing. Unfinished issues were like unfinished programming. Not to be seen unless her help was needed to sus out a problem.

"Have you heard from the ambassador?" he asked.

"The usual. He is grateful I'll be here to represent the family properly." Even in her mind she could hear the blah, blah, canned response she could have received from any of her father's staff members, but actually received directly from him.

"He has met you, right?" Conner joked.

"I know," she balked, knowing she was far from the standard-bearer when it came to traditional family values. "I was thinking we do need to get Bethany a gift when we're out, since we found nothing in Jamaica for her."

Conner nodded in agreement. "I'm sure any tour guide here will happily take us to a giftshop and take their cut from the sale."

The game was the same in most tourist traps. Unpriced items, all subject to negotiation, and Serena had learned how to play early on. Watching for marks from cheap imports that may have been worn or rubbed off versus the real hand-crafted items.

"Speaking of which, what time is it?" she asked, wanting to get the sweat from their beach run off her.

"We have about an hour," Conner said, and she quickly drank

her orange juice and finished the custom made omelet. "Didn't it feel good to run?"

She cut her gaze at him. "Jog, I jogged."

"Will you jog with me tomorrow?"

"You know you're pushing it on the for better or worse part of our verbal contract," she said as they left a few bills in a tip for the waitress and headed back to their room.

"Promise me tomorrow you will go for another run?" he said. "For me, I need the processing time."

"But do you need me to process?" she questioned, hoping the man might actually divulge what was really going on. "If so, I'll jog with you."

"What I'm hearing is a yes." He smiled, and she shook her head.

Today's package had them jammed into a minibus with nearly two dozen people. Slipping away from the group would be easy if Derian showed up as they traveled around. They drove past the Atlantic Coastline and every part of Serena wanted to pull a cord and jump off. But the shuttle bus didn't accommodate that feature. Why would the tour guide tease them? Telling them about the great statue of Neptune protecting that side of the island from hurricanes and not let her out. More importantly, she swore there was a sign for fish tacos on a shack with a make shift bar.

"Breathe my love," Conner said as he leaned back in his seat allowing her to be glued to the window. "You have any idea how twitchy you get when you can't go rogue?"

"It's not right. I'm a wild animal. I need to roam free," she whined and brought her knees up to her chest. Curling into a ball on the seat before leaning against the window as if she were five, and they'd spent the whole day touring.

"So not fair," Conner said, rubbing his knees that were pressed against the seat in front of them, out of basic lack of space.

The tall man's burden she called it, but they were the perfect match for each other. She could get stuff from the lower shelves, he the higher. Massaging the muscle connecting his thigh to his knee with the palm of her hand, he let out a satisfying sigh. The rhythm and unconscious actions they both had together hadn't been a struggle or learning process. Serena understood any ride, bound up and longer than twenty minutes could cause him pain. Why he put up with her constant need to travel, she'd never understand, but appreciated all the same. From the moment they met, it was as if their bodies were lockstep and hearts unwittingly came along on the adventure.

'Oh, I hate you right now,' the words were louder than Serena had expected. Thank God she said it in English.

Honestly, she thought the words had stayed in her brain, but damn somethings were sacred and the last bacon bun in the coffee shop should have been hers. She'd been eyeing that bad boy from the moment she got in line. Watching as people were served a slice of honey cake or a muffin instead. Each step she took closer to the glass hope had bloomed brightly in her chest for the doughy, croissant-shaped, pastry that had a bacon concoction in the center. A mix of crispy, salty, sweet and doughy. The fact they weren't served world-wide had her considering Latvia as a permanent residence so she could have them on demand. And now this mutant in front of her had taken the last one.

'Is there any particular reason?' a man with a midwestern accent asked, making her step back a bit, or was it the cool, crystal eyes and the crooked grin he sported? Sure, she had to crane her neck to see the man standing, in her mind, two feet over her, but it was worth a trip to a masseuse to work out the strain.

'Bacon bun,' she said, pointing to the breaded goodness being slipped into a white paper bag. 'Now I'll have to hunt down another place to get them and I'm at least a minute from passing out from starvation.'

His lips quirked into a half smile as he took the bag and a covered to-go cup from the clerk. 'You know what makes it even worse?'

'What?' she wondered, playing along with old Too-Tall-Jones and his devastatingly handsome good looks.

'I've been here for two months now and I can honestly say, this place has the best version.'

'Dagger to my heart,' she said, holding her hand to her chest. 'And here on the holiest of days.'

'Let me guess, it's your birthday.' His lips pursed as if she were some scam artist set on stealing his bun.

'Oh, god no, not the day my father said the Earth stilled and Satan's minion was let loose on the planet.'

'Then what day is it?' he asked.

'The day I met you. Can't think of a more important day in history. At least not in my lifetime.'

'Wow,' he said, shaking his head. 'And here I thought men were supposed to be the ones with cheesy lines.'

'You do realize bacon is involved?' she prodded. 'Bacon, the gateway meat. The temptation that makes millions reconsider their religions.'

'That does the up the ante, but not sure it warrants the level of best day in history,' he challenged. 'Besides, you'd need to give me your name if we were to have officially met.'

'Serena Isola.' She extended her hand right as the clerk barked something in Latvian because they were holding up the line. 'What should I get?'

'Coffee, tea, the honey cake looks good today,' he suggested. 'I'd hate for you to pass out from starvation especially when I'd be to blame.'

'The worst part of this whole thing, mutant man, is there is no way that's enough to satisfy you.' She shook her head. 'You're going to tease yourself and then be stuck in a really bad spot. Still hungry, moving into anger as you wonder why you didn't get a full meal instead of a simple pastry.'

'Now you're an expert on my needs?'

'Someone needs to be since it's obvious you need assistance.' Serena straightened her shoulders.

'Says the woman who will be pointing and praying as she orders from the menu,' he replied, then leaned against the counter and lifted his white bag to his nose. 'They sell out fast here, this one is still warm.'

'You know what could fix this?" she suggested, facing off with her *sexy nemesis. 'Give me the bacon bun and I'll buy you a piece of honey cake.'*

Lowering the bag, he gave her a wink. 'Tempting, but you'd need to give me more than honey cake to get me to give up this bun.'

'That could be negotiated,' she said as she struggled to make her tea order, but her now gentleman hero stepped in and helped. With a small paper bag dangling from her wrist, she walked out of the shop with the man who finally introduced himself.

'Love, Conner Love and yes, Love is my last name.'

'Dang, I couldn't even call you out for being cheesy,' she said when he flashed his passport for her to examine. He split the bun in half, giving her the bigger piece. As they walked, she wondered how it took less than four steps outside of the bakery for their steps to match. Even with the height difference, she wandered down the street without a care in the world as she sipped her tea and eating her bun with a man she knew instantly she would share more than a pastry with.

The bus jerked to a stop, and she gathered herself. Prepared for the rehearsed tales of the where they were at. To her surprise, it was a school, not the usual tourist stops one would assume. Here they would explore the kids in navy polos and khaki shorts, pants, or skirts.

"Now, this school is sponsored by your resort. Fully funded and open to the children whose parents work there as well as neighborhood children."

The sales pitch was in full swing and Serena's stomach clenched. Children being used as props for the daily tour stop disrupting their day.

"Chill, baby," Conner whispered in her ear, his arms wrapped tight around her belly, enveloping her by his tall frame.

"This school goes all the way through to high school."

"I know."

"Derian wore this uniform."

"Maybe," he said, moving his hands to her bare upper arms and rubbing them up and down to help calm her. "There isn't a crest, so who knows how many schools around here wear the same thing."

"It makes me uncomfortable," she said as her belly clenched as she peered into the room with kids sitting at long tables all facing a chalkboard.

The teacher stopped her lesson so the kids could interact with the tourists like this was some strange zoo. Stepping to the side as the students answered questions from the tour group in either English or Spanish. She couldn't take it anymore and moved to the hallway with Conner behind her where they ran into the teacher.

"Do you even really teach them?" Serena snapped at the older woman, whose face tightened from the insult. "They are innocent—"

"They are far from innocent," the woman countered, her eyes dark as they responded to Serena's outrage with as much vitriol as she could. "If twenty minutes of foreign guilt allows me to purchase textbooks from this century or offer them free milk with lunch, it's worth it."

"It feels wrong."

"Go to a public option," she said as she crossed her arms. "I swear every few months I get one of you through here. The self-righteous, so sure they know how to teach these children better with limited resources."

"Not every day?" Serena asked, the acidic bile inching its way up her throat.

"If it was everyday, they might stop the tours," the teacher explained. "We have successes here. Many of our students are able to find ways into a secondary education of some sort. Some tradesmen, starting in their final years. This is a necessary evil."

"Doesn't it teach them to beg to foreigners?"

"Life does that," she stated. "And yes, we know, use the cutest ones, but is it really any different anywhere in the world?"

Serena glanced into the room where a young girl was showing

off some of her work. The hesitant responses mixed with a beautiful smile reminded her more and more of the day before.

"Do you know a boy named Derian? I know it's a long shot, but we ran into him up at the botanical gardens yesterday."

"I've had a few over the years, but there is a young man in our secondary school who tends to wander."

"No wonder he was drawn to you," Conner teased his wife. "Like minds."

"If it is the same young man he's a good boy. His mother works at the resort and that is how he can come here, but she's a kitchen worker and doesn't make much."

Their tour guide reappeared, and the teacher moved away from them. Soon they were moved on to a school store where people could donate as well as purchase locally sourced items. Hand-drawn pictures, carved statues, and confections made by the students in the upper-level classes. Serena was still uneasy, but she took a card so they could donate once they were back in the room. Kid and parent themed items wouldn't do for her cousin's wedding gift and so she purchased a bit of chocolate before they moved on to the next stop.

"I may have had one too many samples," Conner admitted as he tucked away the three bottles of rum in the camera bag. Rum factory tours were always dangerous. Lord knows Jamaica's had been. Though he wasn't sure if his wife's lack of enthusiasm came from the sharper flavor in comparison to Jamaica's sweet rum or if she was still upset from the school.

"One of those will be part of our gift, right?" she asked. "Because you know Bethany isn't going to tour anything beyond the walls of the resort."

"Sure," he replied, trying to recall the flavors he'd chosen for his least favorite. "But does she drink?"

"Officially?" Serena replied, and Conner gave a knowing nod.

The tour tended to be a balance between photo-ops and buy now stops. A museum about amber, followed by a jewelry store where both amber and larimar being shaped into exclusive pieces. He saw the light in his wife's eye at an amulet. The rich blue so similar to the sea, with strains of white cutting through and silver wrapped around in a web-like pattern ready to be strung on a chain at the length she found acceptable.

"Remember Derian said to wait on the jewelry?" Conner pointed out, though the piece would be stunning with a chain long enough for it to lay between her breasts.

"Yes, but," Serena said as she placed the amulet in the exact place he'd been picturing. Her spaghetti-strap linen top with a plunging V-neck had been tormenting him all day. How was it they'd been together nearly seven years and instead of getting the itch to leave he was more attracted and in love with her each day? "All of this is custom, so even if he takes us to a better spot I won't be able to get this same piece."

"You're right," he said, not really one to say no to her anyway, and he wasn't exactly sure how he was going to broach the subject of not going on to the real Puerto Plata tour with Derian.

Nothing against the boy. It was the fact it seemed every doorway in this downtown area had a man, some old, some young, sitting with a shotgun or bigger weapon on their lap. Were they guarding the upper apartments? The store? It didn't matter. He was a Midwest kid, used to hunting weapons and had no issue with guns per se, but this seemed a bit excessive. Even if the town was the second largest in the country. And he knew if they did meet up with Derian he could take them where the men sitting watch were there for a reason.

Loaded back into the bus, they only had to go a few streets over and the bus parked again. The rotation to photo-ops had the tour director explaining more of the history as they entered the area. Pigeons flew in and landed around the wrought iron benches in search of crumbs or treats. Their gray bodies already pudgy from the good life in what was being touted as the downtown historical district.

The people from their group wandered around. Snapping pictures of the double-decker gazebo in the squared-off central park with the only green coming from the palm trees. Large white stone bricks reflected the heat from the unfettered sun bearing down on their group. Statues of founders and generals greeted them on the edge, and a church built centuries ago by missionaries was open for visitors.

Their guide let them wander, his gaze mindful of those who would disrupt the supposed safety of the area. Part guide, part security, even though those around knew the tourists were going to be out. Two-story buildings had open air porches wrapping around the upper levels, a mix of apartments and professional tenets. Wooden signs versus signs of family life, the clearest indicator. Despite differences in economics, climate and politics, humans tended to be the same around the world. If nothing else, his travels with Serena showed him more than McDonald's was universal.

Southern United States, or the eastern coast, could mimic the buildings probably put up around the same time. Historical buildings with a feel not unfamiliar to him. Serena took pictures, then switched the camera to video, panning around the square he could see a sadness in her eyes. Stopping her focus as she searched out for their escape from the tour guide.

"Hello Mister," a voice from behind made Conner turn to see Derian sporting the same outfit from the day before only a bit cleaner today. "You get the Missus."

"Does your mom work at the resort?" he asked only to receive a broad smile.

Their tour guide rushed over speaking, his words fast and tone unmistakable even if Conner couldn't understand Spanish. Derian responded in kind and Serena made her way toward them. Her smile fading with each step as hands were added to the admonishment between the older man to the teen. The silver wrapped around blue larimar pendent reflected the sun's rays bouncing with her steps, sending flashes of blinding light toward him as if it were a lighthouse flashing Morse code.

"Hey, he's not bothering me," Conner said, trying to calm down the angry guide. "We're friends."

"You're friends with this—this—"

"Yes, I am," Conner said, right as Serena stepped into the space.

"Hey, Derian, you're late," she said.

"He's early," Derian replied, cutting his eyes to their guide. "Or your group hasn't been impressed by my city yet and wanted to move on quickly. Which was it?"

"Look here, boy," the tour guide said. "You need to leave these nice people alone."

"Actually," Serena said. "He's offered to take us to a few places we wanted to check out."

The tour guide's face reddened, then calmed. "You must stay with the group."

"Like you haven't lost people before," Derian said. "Besides, you know I'll get them back safely. Can you promise the same?"

"Go," the guide said as he placed his hands on Conner and Serena's shoulders, pushing them toward the church and away from the teen.

Although Conner had been wanting to take a pass on the "real" tour from the kid, the obstinance of the man pushing them away had him standing firm. There were taxis as well as other services that could be called.

"You know how to get to the beach bars with the fish tacos?" Conner asked, and Serena's face lit up.

"Oh man, Carlos' is the best. We can be there in—"

"I'm going to tell your mother," the tour guide dropped the ultimate kid panic threat known in modern civilization.

"She was right when she said you were the slow one," Derian said. "Next stop, fish tacos."

"He knows your schedule, right?" Conner said only to get a hard glare.

"You up for public transport? Either that or gang members, cartel probably," the tour guide warned. "That boy there has only one destination."

"What's that?" Conner asked, insulted for Derian.

"Cárcel de Rafey."

"And that would be?" Serena questioned.

"Prison," Derian said. "Can we go?"

"We are not responsible—"

Conner waved off the man as they moved through the city, walking a few streets over until Derian saw a cab and waved them over.

"You got cash, right?"

"Maybe," Conner said.

"You're American you all have cash." Derian spoke a few words to the driver as Conner and Serena slid into the backseat.

His wife unphased as if they weren't taking their life into their own hands.

"No," Derian said when the driver tried to make a left hand turn. He then followed with some fast paced Spanish again, making Conner grip Serena's hand tighter.

Serena, true to form, was completely transfixed on a mural along the edifice of a street long building. He knew growing up she'd seen things. Been numbed to a great many things, but how basic survival fight or flight didn't take over when it came to her he would never understand. Then again, if it had, she may have never walked aimlessly around Valmeria with him.

"There an issue?" Conner asked the words enough to have Serena turn to him a bit confused.

"No Mister, no problem," Derian assured and the taxi driver cut his eyes at Derian, who countered with a look three times harder than a kid his age should be able to make.

Two quick turns and they were back on the parkway with the ocean clearly visible from the road. Derian relaxed in the front seat and the acid bubbling in Conner's stomach was settling down. Usually the heat of islands made hunger dissipate, but maybe the air-conditioned bus they kept getting on and off tripped it off. Strange, the whole hunger thing, but it did explain the heft of people in cooler climates. Nothing better than comfort food on a cool evening. Now the thought of fish or shrimp tacos, fresh, cool and with the perfect amount of veggies mixed in had him ready to get out of the car. Or maybe it was the tight backseat causing the ache in his knees.

When the car slowed, he quickly dug out bills and Derian held up his hand. Negotiating with the driver about something. Conner had little doubt the driver spoke perfect English. All islanders tended to because of either former British rule or current tourists being a large part of the economy.

"Six hundred peso, that includes tip," Derian replied and the man once again tightened his jaw to the kid. "Number, I'll call when we're free."

"If I'm free."

"You want one fare or four?" Derian negotiated. "Middle of the week, you know people aren't waving too much."

Conner fished out six hundred pesos and passed them to the driver.

"I'll be around," the man said, his eyes warning Conner, but the more warnings about Derian he received the less he was believing them.

"We good?" Serena said, her legs halfway out the passenger door as she turned her head, the soft, velvety, hazel brown eyes and full lips questioning his hesitation. Common place for the two of them. They were opposites in so many ways, like magnets in one way repelling and running it in two different directions, but if flipped it was practically impossible to pull them apart. "My love?"

"We are. Can't you smell the grilled food out there?"

"I can and it's physically paining me that you're preferring a backseat to whatever is five steps from here."

There was an elegance when Serena moved, the way she would slip out of the car. Training perhaps, or just who she was as a person. Though she said she only was in ballet for a year, she could be mistaken for a dancer any day of the week. Gliding in a way until her feet sunk in the sand at the far edge of the beach. He followed, always followed, when it came to Serena. Dumbstruck with a beauty unmatched and that was saying something for a man who now had traveled around the world at least one full time.

Carlos' stand did not disappoint. Clapboard structure with bright colors and a bar that could withstand the elements because if the bar top fell off or was destroyed another two-by-eight board could be put right back on to replace it. Unvarnished, but well-worn from years, if not decades, had smoothed out the wood's ability to have splinters.

Conner scooped a bit of ceviche on a tortilla chip. Bright colors from fresh tomato, corn, red onions, cilantro and shrimp were the perfect mix of sweet and salty to stave off his appetite as he sat on a stool. His forearm rested on the bar top as an ice-cold beer cooled his fingers. The Atlantic, so different from the Caribbean where they had just been. Hard crashes of waves bringing in gusts of salt air instead of light breezes. The sound mingled and mixed with the sizzle of the grill in a symphony lulling a traveler's senses.

They weren't the only ones at the bar. Locals came up, ordering meals and infusing the musical nature of the world around. Maintained with bright colors and matching waitstaff, places were serving others along the beach and maybe it was the smaller structure of Carlos' grill that made it appear to be more popular, but Serena had taught Conner to always go with where the locals eat. Not the tourists. They may go hand in hand, but places like this stay around because of those who live here, not those who travel.

For him, it was the safety of a place that appeared to have been sanitized in the current decade that was a draw, but only once has it gastronomically failed them when they went outside of the tourist spot. Serena told him he needed a better gut, one that could take the challenge.

'Didn't the players call you a goat?' she asked as he lay on the bathroom floor, his belly on fire with cramps he believed had to rival birthing pains.

For Serena, a quick dose of Imodium and the pain and diarrhea had stopped. He on the other hand couldn't keep the pill down long enough for any possible healing properties. Although he was sure he was near death, she assured him once it was out of his system he'd be right as rain. A little hungry, but good. He believed he would never eat again. Unlike previous girlfriends, Serena sat on the tiled bathroom floor. His head in her lap, he'd pass out and come to find her setting down a book as she helped him in whatever way she could.

'Goat is different in sports,' he groaned. 'And I was far from earning that title, it's an acronym.'

'For?' she questioned, uncapping a bottle of water and passing it to him. 'Sip, don't chug. And don't do that weird let me see if I can get this all in one big gulp.'

'I'm not sure my throat can perform that function anymore,' Conner groaned, the words stung as they made their way along his raw larynx. Even sipping water set off a fire as it crested the back of his throat and he silently prayed it could make it to his stomach. 'In sports, it's greatest of all time. Which, clearly I am not.'

'But you can hit those three things,' she said with her non-sports knowing jargon trying to be supportive.

'Yeah, my love, I can hit a three.'

The ting of a metal spatula dicing up the white fish on the flat top the cook had on the side of the grill jarred Conner from the memory.

"You know why this bar stands up?" their cook, who did say to call him Carlos, asked.

"Why's that?" Serena asked, camera recording the whole interaction.

Pointing the spatula to a set of rocks about twenty yards out to sea with a statue in middle, Carlos went into detail. "Neptune, he protects us from hurricanes. Haiti gets decimated, and we have a sprinkling. Neptune man, he controls the seas."

Carlos gave a spatula salute to the bronze statue, greened now from years of service to the island standing guard. Trident in hand, keeping his eyes on the water, Conner had to give it to the man. Haiti, on the other half of the island, was a hot spot for destruction, though he doubted they only got sprinkles when swirling clouds were overhead. Today was bright, clear blue as far as the eye could see, and the ocean met the sky in an almost seamless fashion.

"You told the taxi driver four fares," Serena said finally putting down the camera that had to have three dozen pictures taken in the last twenty minutes. "What will they be?"

"Food, stop one," Derian said. "Next place is tourist, but not for shopping. And you're not dressed for hiking so, I was going to take you through some neighborhoods. Let you meet people. See the prison I'm destined for."

"Derian," Serena admonished.

"There's a good spot up high and the prison is below it," Derian said, his eyes cutting to the ceviche bowl in front of Conner.

"Did you order?" Conner asked the kid who might hit ninety pounds after a swim in the ocean.

"No, Mister."

"Conner," he corrected. "And she's Serena."

"Wait," Carlos said, stopping mid-plating of their tacos. "Serena, Conner, I knew I knew you. Runners use the miles."

Carlos' eyes lit up like Christmas, New Year's and exploding fireworks on the Fourth all combined.

"No way," he said slapping at one of his regulars. "My stand! My stand is going to be love running?"

"Love on the Run and yes," Conner said, then shifted his backpack around to get the release needed. "And you wouldn't mind signing a release form would you?"

"Release form?" he asked.

"Yeah, we can't pay our spots where we stop outside of paying for our food or admission you understand."

"Are you kidding," Carlos said as he continued to plate the tacos. "You can have these for free letting me on there. I'll need a second cook."

"We'll pay for ours," Conner said. "But how about a batch for Derian who brought us here?"

"This kid, I love him. He's a good boy," Carlos said, ruffling Derian's hair. "And not because he brought you guys here. I've been watching him running up and down this beach for years."

Serena and her love of education having heart let out a sigh. "You're the first person to not warn us about him."

"Ah, no one likes to be out hustled in the Dominican, and Derian is a hustler and survivor," Carlos said. "But I've always been of the mind of we get more done together than apart."

"And yet your most loyal customer can't get an empanada," the customer grumbled from the side.

"But I used you to fix my steps," Carlos rebutted. "Didn't even ask for a discount."

"Ah," the man scoffed, his hand admonishing Carlos who raised a frying basket out of the oil then dropped it back down.

Belly full, soul infused from a good conversation the Loves hit a shopping center with high-end items, allowing Serena to get Bethany a perfect gift. The sculpted image of two lovers, smoothed and shining crafted from larimar was breathtaking and he could see his wife slightly coveting the item for herself. She then found a necklace, silver chain links with the local stone shaped into a dozen ovals creating a chain of blue dots. The necklace could wrap around the wrist and even linked in a way to drop it low into a V.

"Versatile and perfect if she's going for the something blue aspect of a wedding. I'm totally giving her this before the wedding. It's not a Nigerian tradition, but we both know Bethany is probably going to use the best of all the wedding customs that she can try to claim."

"What if she doesn't like larimar?" Conner questioned.

"Then she shouldn't have been married in the Dominican Republic because it is breathtaking." Serena's hand absently went to the pendent around her neck as she watched the clerk wrap up their purchases in shiny white paper, with offsetting bells in a shade of slight gray that could only be seen when the paper was angled perfectly.

Derian was hanging outside the shop on a bench. The teen earned his money by telling histories Conner hoped were true about the island. Serena taped them all, making Conner wonder if she would be doing two episodes out of this trip. Valentine's Day one next year for sure. But would there be one just about the place in general?

A group of kids, still adolescents but older than Derian, showed up and hassled him a bit. At first, Conner was going to step out and intercede, but the body language changed. Derian was pressured by them, but led the kids away from the store. Much like when he was in the taxi, Conner couldn't help the feeling Derian was doing what was best for the Loves. All he hoped was it wasn't at the expense of his own safety.

SEVEN
I'LL GET MARRIED NAKED

The high-pitched squeal coming from Bethany pierced Serena's ears when they entered the bar. She should have expected the entourage after the tagged post with nearly a dozen people, but it still surprised her that so many had come to the destination wedding. With a bejeweled crown befitting the Queen of England nestled into the thick curls atop her head, Bethany had every indicator possible to man when it came to bride-to-be status. Including the white satin sash with the golden letters spelling B-R-I-D-E cutting across her body.

Bethany's skin, flawless as usual, was a deep brown, with eyes only a slight shade darker. Full lips and high cheekbones, she could be the poster child for what a Nigerian woman should look like. Though if the scowl on Auntie Louise's face meant anything, she was not enjoying the non-traditional wedding about to take place on a tropical island.

"Everyone, this is my oldest and dearest friend," Bethany explained to the group of people who appeared to know each other. "My cousin Serena."

"Hey." Serena slipped back into her role as second fiddle, taking pressure off herself to be the entertainment and hostess with the mostest situations.

This wasn't a she's the bride type step back and let her shine. Nope, Bethany always took center stage in all things. Might be why when Serena and Conner married it was a whim, the joy numbed for a moment by her father insisting on a retroactive prenup. Nothing worse than an 8:00 a.m. knock on a honeymoon suite door.

"Oh my goodness, you're Conner, right?" Bethany said, wrapping her arms tight around him. "We've met, right? I've met you, I know I have."

"Yes, in Minneapolis, you came to our house," Conner said and her cousin let out a trill of laugher.

"Oh my God, you're right, great view that place has. Then you've met my fiancé," Bethany surmised. "Of course you haven't. Donald, Donnie," she called out, then lowered her voice for only them to hear. "Isn't his name horrible? I don't ever think I'll be able to get used to it." With a nasally whine as if the name had been stuck in the back of her throat, she repeated in a myriad of pronunciations. "Donald, Donald, Don, ugh I give up. Maybe I'll call him Dearest."

"Like dearest departed?" Conner asked and Bethany's eyes widened then blinked three times. As if the information was being reviewed by a computer and the spinning wheel was about to time out.

"Oh my God, that's funny. You're funny. Is that why you love him, Serena?" Bethany gushed with her right hand now clutching Conner's upper arm and her left resting on the middle of his chest. Conner gave Serena a save me from the molestation occurring right now look. "You two must just laugh your way around the world. I couldn't of course, with my job. Have you gotten a job yet, Serena?"

"My Vlog is my job," Serena countered, though she doubted Bethany heard her.

"Did Uncle tell you they accepted me at Burns and Stein?"

"No," Serena said as her cousin continued to run her over at the mouth.

"Partner track from the start, of course. With my grades, it was a no-brainer right? I mean, really, why do people think law school is so hard?"

"Because they go to an accredited one." The little bite wasn't normally Serena's style, but old Don hadn't made it from the bar and Bethany was still petting Conner like he was the stripper for her bachelorette party. Undergrad wasn't the issue. Law school made one's head tilt a bit when they examined the degree on the wall.

"Oh, Miss Ivy League," she snipped as Donald arrived, thankfully, and Bethany cuddled into her man.

Bethany was taller than Serena, most were after age ten, but her fiancé barely had an inch on her. Although she insisted it was a love match, Auntie Louise would have not only approved, but more than likely picked the man. Older, closer to Serena's age than Bethany's with a rounded face and skin a rich dark mahogany.

"'Ello," he said, extending his hand to Conner, his accent almost as thick as Serena's grandparents had been. "I'm Donald Usman."

"Conner, welcome to the family, this is—"

"No need for introductions. I am a big fan of Love on the Run."

"You are?" Bethany asked, her face twisting a bit in confusion, or possibly jealousy.

"Serena has shown me so many wonderful places to visit. You make me want to give up my law practice and use my miles." He laughed. "But I suppose I'd have to earn a few first."

"Right, honey, you would." Bethany snuggled closer. "And you're too busy working so hard."

"All for you."

"Are you still living in New Jersey?" Serena asked.

"Practically New York. It's a taxes thing, and the commute is worth it, though I wonder when we start having kids—"

"Tell me," Donald asked, and Bethany's face instantly

pinched. "Are you going to stay on here and do an episode? Will our wedding be part of it?"

"We have been shooting a bit since we got here."

"Oh, you did not come in just now?" he questioned.

"No, we were getting ready to fly home when I got the text from Bethany," Serena explained. "I'm not sure how we missed the invite."

Auntie Louise spun toward the bar, and things were beginning to make a bit more sense.

"It doesn't matter. You're here now and I'm sure our spa day tomorrow can accommodate one more." Bethany took Serena's hands in hers, lifting the unpolished nails and examining them. "You've been on the road so much you'll need a rest. Don't worry, it's a treat I'm giving to all my bridesmaids and you should have been one, but I had to make a cut somewhere."

"Spa day?" Serena's belly twisted a bit as the gaggle of girls were dragging her away from Conner.

"Yes, now it's time to meet everyone and get this woman a daiquiri," Bethany called out to the bartender. "Strawberry right?"

"Yeah, prefect."

The men were moving over to a table on an outer patio where cigars were permitted and a brown whiskey bottle was filling glasses. Conner and Serena weren't the type of couple that needed to be with each other twenty-four seven, but in situations like this she was uneasy with the divide and inebriation.

"Serena," Auntie Louise greeted her with a kiss to each cheek.

She was the only one in traditional dress with a bright blue buba and matching iro and gele head tie. Intricate gold thread had been woven in a geometrical pattern. Switching between triangles and squares, Serena did believe the love of patterns had to come from her Nigerian heritage. Lord knew her mother was the queen of solids.

"Have you proper attire for this occasion?"

"This one right now? Getting wasted with your daughter?"

Auntie waved her off, the insolence of the American child could only be seen on her, never the perfect Bethany.

"You know what I'm saying. Everyone will be in traditional dress. Donald may live in the US, but he is from a good family," Auntie Louise said, her back straight and proud, as if she was ignoring the behavior going on right behind her.

"You talked Bethany into wearing an iro, buba and gele? Like full-on Yoruba style?" Serena was a bit impressed because the whole idea of the day-long wedding where Bethany was the center of attention made sense, but a whole day? And Bethany not wearing white, both seemed a bit extreme to her. The pinched lips of her aunt told the true story.

"The gele only for now, but I have a few days to convince her."

"Why are we not having this wedding in Nigeria then? It is beautiful, especially in the countryside. Dominican is nice, but—"

"Donald did relief work in Haiti with his church years ago. Obviously, that side of the island would not be acceptable, but here, some of his friends could make the journey. It was a compromise. Especially when we found out his family has a villa on this property."

"They bought the timeshare spiel?" Serena had to hold in a laugh as her aunt's gaze bore into her. "That's awesome. Someone has to do it."

"Since Bethany and Donald will be vacationing here regularly, bringing children and the like she wanted—"

"Wait, is she pregnant?" Serena asked, more to irritate the woman who herself had a rushed wedding following a positive test.

"She would never, Bethany has remained chaste." Arms crossed and nose in the air Auntie Louise could block out a hurricane coming full speed through the bar at this moment. The hurricane had moved to distract the current matriarch so her chaste daughter could do a few body shots off of her betrothed. Not really the traditional way she was raised. But it did look fun.

The whole group of friends had sucked Conner into their orbit, which was a feat in and of itself because she'd noticed he'd gone back to his phone and all the trouble there.

"I have had a long day of travel. Late nights are for the young to prepare them for sleepless nights later. But you would not know of that blessing yet would you?"

Let's just throw a Serena is selfish, wild and unable to conceive log on the fire. Serena and Conner hadn't made a conscious decision to wait, or not have any at all, when it came to that subject. Nope, not even a thought. Auntie slipped from the stool where she'd been sitting and pushed her tall glass toward the bartender. Condensation covered the slick surface and obscured the half-melted ice cubes floating in pale pink liquid. Probably pink lemonade, if she knew her aunt at all.

"Good evening, Serena. Tell Bethany I took my leave and not to worry."

"Yes Auntie Louise." Serena stood to make sure the woman was steady. She was older and there may have been a shot of something in the drink. "Goodnight."

The more she watched her cousin the more she wondered if there had actually been an original invite. Nothing about tonight screamed traditional and even if her father was swamped with work, if a traditional wedding was called for he would come. More importantly, Uncle David would be here somewhere. There were family meetings, gifts, meals all of it to assure the match was good and strong. No rush to the altar in the way Serena had done it.

As Conner lifted his glass with the group, Serena couldn't help the smile coming from deep inside her. They can say it was her western upbringing or her father's wild ways when it came to her mother, but Serena couldn't have imagined a better partner in life than Conner. They were on the same plane of existence. Getting each other from the start.

No matter the circumstances, she hoped her cousin was truly happy. This was far from the dream wedding Serena and Bethany would play at in the few shops that offered traditional dress in Milwaukee where Bethany grew up. Running up and down the aisles of brightly colored clothing adorned in threads of gold, silver, or bronze shimmering in the overhead lights.

Tucking the mess of curls Serena sported under the gele and making her feel so grown. The fabric folded in such a way it was a mix of a crown and a turban. Loose in comparison to the tightly wrapped headdress of the Sikhs, puffy and still she never felt as if it could fall off. Even with two giggling girls trying them on after they had been custom woven and made.

'You'll wear blue and I'll wear purple,' Bethany mused as they stood facing the mirror. 'I'll probably marry before you, sadly.'

'Why would you say that?' Serena asked a bit rebuffed by the comment.

'Mama says you're too skinny and no man wants a skinny girl.' Bethany's nine-year-old musing had her holding a buba to her already budding breasts. At fourteen, Serena was barely forming any definition to say she was a girl. 'Besides, you're too light.'

'Light?' Serena questioned.

'Yes, a Yoruba man wants his woman dark like me.' Bethany ran her hand over her rounded cheek as if to inspect and make sure her perfect skin was exactly as it should be. 'There is not enough sun in the world to make you attractive enough.'

'You really need to stop listening to your mama, Bethany,' Serena rebutted.

'No, I shouldn't. My momma knows what she's doing. See? My papa is a good papa that is always buying me things,' Bethany said, pointing her toes to show off the latest sneakers even though the girl hadn't played a day in her life. 'I will catch the eye of a good man and papa will buy out this whole shop so everyone can be at my wedding.'

Moneywise, Serena's family was no better or worse than her cousins. Yes, her uncle had generational wealth which gave them a better foundation, but still the little spoiled brat Bethany could get under her skin even if she was younger. Cousin or no cousin, she was going to lay out some basic facts to the kid.

'And why would you limit yourself to Yoruba men? I have seen handsome boys all around the world. But you are right about one thing.'

'What's that?' Bethany asked, her eyes rounded with wonderment.

'You'll probably marry before me because your mama is gonna pick out some nobody just so you can be traditional. I'll never be traditional.' Serena pulled the gele from her head and her long curls tumbled down her back, freeing her in more ways than one. 'My husband will be my friend, lover and equal. I will choose him, not the other way around. And if I want I'll get married naked.'

Serena stormed from the bridal shop and sat on the curb outside. It didn't take long for her mother to show up with three dum-dum suckers as she sat next to her on the curb. Eyeing them warily, she snagged the root beer one and removed the wax paper wrapping. Her mother did the same with a lemon-flavored one then tucked the bubble gum one over her ear like a pencil. Her mother's ash blonde hair had been pulled into a misshapen bun that hadn't been there when they entered the shop. Maybe from her trying on a gele, or just to make changing clothes easier.

It was then the bright canary yellow of her tight outfit shined as much as her hair. The buba similar to the one she wore when she married Serena's father. Then her traditional costume had been a rich emerald green. Serena would sneak into her mother's closet when her parents were at some official dinner and run her hands over the satin fabric.

'Naked huh?' her mother said as the crinkle of the wax paper wrapping being removed from the sucker was somehow louder than the street noise. 'Guess we'll only be able to send close-ups to your grandparents and say the rest of the wedding pictures were burned in a tragic fire.'

'Bethany is easily shocked,' Serena replied while letting the root beer flavor melt on her tongue then shifted the candy to the side. 'But why not? Some ceremonies the bride wears little more than a strap of fabric. At least my color scheme would be simple.'

'Would we have to dress to match?' her mother asked then placed her hand on her belly. 'If so, please allow me at least six months to tighten or better yet see a surgeon and heal.'

'Whatever, she was being a brat.'

'Would you have expected anything less?' her mother asked. 'You *know your Auntie Louise has been trying to live down a shame most have forgiven or forgotten a decade ago. It's all in her mind at this point.'*

'She and daddy are so different.'

'She was raised as a girl. Boys get a little leeway in this world,' her mom said then stuck the sucker in her mouth for a quick taste before removing it once again to speak. 'The first girl at that. Lord knows Auntie Olivia is nothing like Louise.'

'What are you raising me as?' Serena asked.

'A kid for as long as I can. What's this getting married nonsense all about anyway? Your daddy and I are trying to make sure you see the world and are never in one place long enough to fall in love. We're mad geniuses he and I.' Her mother gave her a slight nudge.

'What about college?' she asked. 'Aren't I getting four years free of your meddling where men roam wild and free.'

'Vassar?' her mother said with a nod. 'Or some other women's college like Spellman.'

'Spellman and Morehouse go hand in hand in many ways,' Serena said pointing her dum-dum toward the street before popping it back in her mouth.

'Vassar it is.'

'What if I'm a lesbian?' Serena countered. 'More and more states are making it legal to marry.'

'That's it, we're going with an online college with you locked away in a panic room at the embassy of our choosing.'

'You sure? You might forget me if you have to bug out quick.' Serena cut her gaze to her mother.

'For the last time we didn't forget you, we were told you had been retrieved from the school.'

'It was a Saturday, I was held hostage for three days,' Serena bemoaned, though the experience hadn't been what the movies portrayed thanks to a woman in the group who refused to let anyone touch her.

'And your father nearly carpet-bombed the whole country to get you back,' her mother said. 'Who knew those self-defense classes actually

took? That's it, you can go to a co-ed college, but you're not allowed to fall in love until you are at least thirty-seven.'

Serena let out a light laugh. 'Why thirty-seven? Aren't you thirty-seven?'

'Yep, and right this minute I realized if your father came up and told me he loved me I'd actually believe it.'

'So the past fifteen years were what?' Serena asked. 'A test run?'

'Youthful exuberance? I don't know. I just want you to see and experience everything before settling down, which would be hard unless you marry a man like your father,' her mother said with the stick of the sucker bouncing. 'Maybe I'm in the mood for a forever home this week. I'm sure it will pass.'

'It better,' Serena said. 'Because daddy is due for a new post once the presidency switches.'

'Right now we need to get you an appropriate outfit for your Auntie Olivia's wedding,' her mother said pushing up from the curb and wiping off the dust from her skirt. 'And remember Auntie Louise is trying to curry favor with your grandmother. Bethany is receiving the backlash of that. Something tells me she's going to be less like Auntie Louise and more like you.'

'Why?' Serena asked as she took her mother's extended hand and was pulled up from her crouch.

'Because she came running in the back with us and said the gele is all I need, I shall be naked and free like Serena. We're going to dress to match like American flower girls.'

Serena pulled up her phone and flipped through old pictures posted to social media. Though she'd run away and eloped with Conner, she had channeled her ancestors and wore a full wedding dress. Complete with a gele, iro and buba in bright emerald, just like her mother and standing next to her in a tux Conner smiled brightly. The poor man not really understanding what he'd just signed on for.

Looking across the bar, the sexes had separated again and she found where the men were gathered he gave her a look that shot straight through her heart. Warming all parts before she was quickly dragged away to be with Bethany and the gaggle of female wedding party members.

———

"Okay, so quick rundown," Conner said once the whole group came together because the food was being served and everyone was enjoying a late-night snack. The usual fare of fried, bite-size treats, nachos, fruit, and some pastries he remembered from the morning buffet. Either way, it allowed them all to keep eating, drinking and enjoying the night, and that was the point of a good wedding. "Who are all of you?"

A redhead stood, her hands moving with every word. "I'm Katelyn, Bethany and I were college roommates at Northwestern, keep 'em flying," the sorority style in which she said the words told Conner it meant something, but he'd never been a Wildcat fan, so he had no clue. "Which means she won't let me get drunk enough tonight to tell all the best stories about her, but I still have my maid of honor speech, so watch out."

"Yeah, can someone get this woman some water please," Bethany said as she mocked like she was waving over a waiter. "Honestly, she's a cheap drunk who would leave with five bucks and come back wasted two hours later."

"I'm not cheap, I just get people to pay for me," the young women beamed with pride and turned right to Conner. Serena instantly slid her hand around his shoulder and rested her head as if it had been such a long day. "Who are you?"

"Me?" Conner countered. "Just the husband of this beautiful woman. Serena, Bethany's cousin."

"The Serena," Katelyn balked. "Oh my God, we're practically dealing with royalty the way Bethany describes you. I'm so glad you could make it."

"Well, thanks," Serena said as she sat up and reached for a cocktail plate to fill up with a variety of appetizers.

"Joey," the man next to Katelyn said with considerably less fan fair. "Groomsman, I work with Don in New York."

The table continued introducing themselves. Four groomsmen and five bridesmaids for some reason. A second Kaitlynn who they were told spelled her name differently, Chelsea, Yvette, and Emma. All friends and Conner wondered if the younger female cousins were going to show up as junior bridesmaids from Auntie Olivia's side or if Bethany was going with only her true blues. For Donald, it was a blend of friends, family, and coworkers. One Abaeze claimed to be a mix of all three. In addition, Eric and Evan rounded out the four-man crew.

"So what's the deal? Four Groomsmen of the apocalypse?" Conner asked.

"Hey, what can I say?" Don said. "Some people found their way, while others missed the flight."

Emma gave a half-interested harrumph to the comment, then helped Joey refill his plate.

As the evening progressed, stories got louder with laughter, catching the attention from those around them.

"You know I saw the wedding pictures of you, Serena," Bethany said, her words slurring a bit. "Mother says I'm bringing shame not having a traditional one like you."

"Traditional?" Serena coughed a bit on her drink before setting it down. "Me?"

"You ran away, yes I get that with a white man—"

"The horror," Conner admonished as he decided to use the alcohol to numb the numbers tumbling through his brain like boulders off the mountains taking out trees, road, and making wildlife run for shelter. Serena squeezed his hand and he nuzzled along the column of her neck, a trace of the floral smell of her soap still on her skin. He was tipsy, but was it enough to take their leave graciously and find their way back to their room?

"But still, I knew you weren't going to get married naked."

"Wait, that was an option?" Conner asked, coming out of the stupor of alcohol and lust. "I was not consulted on all the options.

Don, how much were you asked about when it came to this wedding?"

"Not enough if the Isola clan has no issue with nudity. No wonder I was told Yoruba brides were the way to go," the bride-groom beamed with his tumbler of whiskey raised high in the air. The ice cubes clinked together in the amber liquid.

"He's not Yoruba?" Serena asked, not that it mattered, her family swirled off the continent, but Auntie Louise had been on the hunt with every eligible family and here her daughter had chosen a different tribe.

"What? You told me not to limit myself." Bethany turned to her fiancé and stroked along his cheek, cupping his chin, love glowing in its near-blinding light. "Igbo men have so many fine features."

Conner leaned toward Serena and whispered, "Does this make sense to you?"

"You know humans love to find differences. Think of it as she's a lawyer originally from Chicago—"

"Isn't she?" he questioned.

"Well, yes, in a way, but he would be a cowboy from Dallas. Both 'Merican, but there will be subtle cultural differences." Serena sipped on her melting frosty cocktail. "It's not ideal, but not nearly as devastating to the family, as well as you or my mom."

"I'm so glad to hear," he said. Eventually, Conner's family accepted Serena, but the first few meetings were tense when he brought the girl with the tawny skin tone home.

"That's is why we chose to just come here," Bethany said. "I'm second generation out and all the traditional stuff, ugh. I love a good Vera Wang or Alexander McQueen gown. I want the white wedding dress so I can show my figure."

"And I want whatever my bride wants," Don beamed. "I told Ms. Louise I would happily pay the bride price, but she will not yield."

"Bride price?" Conner asked. "Wait, did I miss something?"

"Oh, you didn't pay Uncle Andrew for Serena?" Bethany asked. "Sinful. Please, my mother only wants him to pay so we can do all the introductions, gifts, meals. I don't have a year or the patience to allow Mama to create ceremonies to sell me off like a prize heifer."

"Was I supposed to pay your father?" Conner asked. "Like a dowry?"

"Yes, technically your parents, aunts, uncles, important cousins," Serena stated and Bethany stood arms wide before the alcohol made her tumble to the side and fall in Don's lap. "We all get together and you basically refund the cost of raising me to my dad. But it's okay."

"That doesn't sound okay? How much was I supposed to pay? I mean, is there a tally somewhere?"

"Yes, Conner," Serena said, her eyes devoid of any actual emotion. The bored and annoyed look he understood to mean she was being sarcastic. "My dad has every receipt from the moment my mother went to prenatal visits."

"Itemized and separated because honestly, I'm not sure I should have to pay for the I-Carley paraphernalia since you basically became her."

"So, no Princeton tuition reimbursement either?" she joked.

"Yeah, hell no." Conner let out a sigh. "But your dad does like me, right?"

"Of course, he loves the man that made his one chance to walk a daughter down the aisle occur in a chapel two doors down from a strip club."

"Why do I suddenly feel like we need to renew our vows on a much grander scale?" he asked.

"Because I'm a master manipulator," Serena said, laying a chaste kiss to his lips. "My love, there is nothing about our wedding I would redo. It was perfect for me."

"And that is all that matters," Bethany said. "Which is why if my mother doesn't want to take my fiancé's dowry payment that is on her. I'm gonna get me a she shed or something for our backyard."

"Uncle David is here, isn't he?" Serena asked a bit of worry in her voice.

"Of course, but you know he will show up in his own time," Bethany replied.

"We all know our tasks," Abaeze said. "Donald makes sure everything his bride wants she gets, and the groomsmen make sure nothing distracts from the day. That way, the bride believes he can pull it off."

"Most of the groomsmen," Bethany grumbled, and Don laid a kiss on her temple.

"What's the matter?" Serena questioned.

"One of our groomsmen is late and my lovely bride is worried about her ceremony."

"It is not that," she sniped. "Honestly, I wish he wouldn't come at all. Balanced or not, he brings the temperature down in the room."

"Dearest," Donald said, trying to bring the party back around to where it should be. "Emma is not upset, so why are you?"

"Enough of this. Conner, the next round is on you as payment for your lovely bride to her family," Bethany said, leaning in with glassy eyes. "Better late than never."

He chuckled a bit since all items were included in their stay and no bill would be presented beyond the resort fee. Bethany had removed her crown and soon was pulling her girls, Serena included, up from the table to dance. Making the bartender turn up the music that had been but background noise. He watched, voyeuristically as his wife's hands were raised above her head and her body began to bend like a snake, charming him from across the room. A few of the women grasped hands and pulled themselves together before spinning out as if it were a big band song playing and not the latest pop hit.

Overall, the mood was joyous as the men joined in, coming to the women to join in the movement. Serena's body pressed to his as she grooved in his arms. Conner's hands explored her body, the curves of which he studied as if she were his thesis. How many years, how many times had he stayed up late or woke before her? Not wanting to move, basking in the feel of her against him. Staying in the moment. He made games so addicting that people, who fell asleep while playing, woke and continued where there were when they lost consciousness. And yet nothing compared to the draw of his woman. Nothing kept him up more at night or fueled him to do more each morning. To be more.

He held her tighter as they danced, his arousal needed to be hidden from others. The only thing separating them were the thin linen of her skirt and the cotton of his shorts. Turning, his head dipped and the sweet taste of strawberries and rum brushed along his tongue, their mouths fusing in ways better meant for a private suite, but they did not relent. Alcohol, heat, and talk of love swam in the sea of music. Pheromones stripping away any inhibition, their coupling became more and more eminent with each passing second until he feared he'd be overwhelmed and go further than he should.

Panting, the two broke from the embrace, gazes locked in the knowledge that only came from years of being with a person. There never had been a real break from their honeymoon. Yes, they worked, purchased a home, and created a life together, but years later he couldn't tell the difference between the moments after he said, 'I do' and this moment. His head became light when he was in her presence. A high no medication could mimic.

The moment fierce in its need to move forward, heart pounding he took steps within lockstep like a pair of tango dancers. His foot moving forward with hers stepping back. Moving to the edge of the bar and glancing over his shoulder, he saw others were all lost in moments too.

Conner smiled down at his bride as warmth mixed with lust, readying for a night to rival all others.

"Don't let me interrupt," an unfamiliar voice said and once again Conner glanced back to see a man with his roller bag at his side standing by Joey and Emma. The couple instantly broke apart, and Emma's lips formed a thin line as she stepped toward the newcomer.

"Patrick," whispered Emma. She cleared her throat. "You made it."

The smile patently false since Conner had seen the real one for hours now and Emma was far from happy. A chill began eking its way over the group like a glass had tipped and the contents were spreading across the floor.

Joey had gone to the bar and was gesturing for another drink. Even the sub-tropic heat could not stop the cold drifting over the area from the man's arrival. How an outdoor bar could have the air sucked from it confused Conner. Somehow this man, wearing a Jets ballcap, a button-down shirt and tie, as if he'd come from a courtroom and not a long plane ride, accomplished the task.

"What? I thought I was invited."

"Of course, my man," Don said, crossing the room and clapping up the stranger who had locked his arm around Emma's waist.

"What just happened?" Conner asked quietly.

"I don't know, but I think we should stop stealing air around here," Serena replied.

"Agreed." Conner intertwined his fingers with Serena's.

"Thanks for keeping my woman warm, Joey." The man's sardonic tone had Serena's would be escape coming to a hard stop.

"This doesn't concern us," Conner whispered and prayed his wife wouldn't insist on filling her cup with the tea about to spill everywhere.

"Hush," she admonished, but tucked in tight to him. The voyeur in her wanting to stay and watch the live-action reality TV show drama playing out in front of them.

"Anything for a brother," Joey replied, toasting the man with no familial resemblance.

Joey had relaxed features, more stout than muscular. Both

were decent looking, but the stranger had a shaved head, with a black beard and pale skin in comparison to Joey's olive coloring. With a long blond hair pulled back into a man bun, Joey had been laid back all night until now. The squaring-off men had Conner tucking Serena behind him. Her hands were soon on his shoulders and he knew she was on tip toes trying to see around him.

"Hey, hey, this is a happy occasion," Abaeze said, waving at the bartender to set up a full round of drinks. "Let us celebrate the happy couple."

"We're glad you were able to make it, Patrick," Don said. "We couldn't have had a wedding without you."

"That right, Emma?" Patrick asked.

"No one else could have walked me down the aisle." Emma's words were so false it was as if a weight was now hanging on all of those in the crowd as they trembled from her lips.

EIGHT

I WENT YESTERDAY, DOESN'T THAT COUNT AS MY EXERCISE FOR THE MONTH?

Sharp stings on Serena's ass were not the way she expected to wake up. The quick smacks were anything, but gentle. Amplified by the headache from one too many drinks. Weren't the resorts supposed to water down the drinks to give the illusion of a good deal?

"Nope, not today. You promised me, Mrs. Love," Conner's voice broke through the thick fog of the night before.

"Promises get broken every day," she mumbled. "Haven't you ever watched election coverage?"

"You're not a politician," he replied as he tried to flip her over in the bed, but she held tight to the sheets, not ready to open her eyes. The light of day would need to wait until at least noon. Breakfast buffet be damned. Jet lag was one thing, Bethany trying to drink the college Greek society under the table was another, and Serena wished for a more traditional dry wedding.

"My wife never breaks a promise to me," Conner said, the obvious guilt trip being packed up all ADHD style in the luggage of her brain.

Had she? Very little was clear anymore. There was a lot of touching, rubbing, her auntie calling her out while comparing poor Bethany as a failure in comparison. How did one talk out of both sides of their mouth and not choke on their words? Serena's mind was tripping too much to contemplate what Conner was saying, and she knew he wouldn't stop this onslaught to let her sleep. Maybe she'd promised him some sort of sexual favor last night and completely forgotten it. Lord knows her body ached in remembrance of what happened when they returned to their room. Determining the promise couldn't be that bad and might even be fun she rolled over only to see the man standing in running shorts and a t-shirt. That wasn't the worst part, he was holding her sneakers.

"Those are for adventure-style hikes," she said as words trickled into her brain from their day trip from before. "Yesterday was a fluke brought on by a need to build up an appetite so the breakfast was not wasted."

"Or," Conner reasoned as he held them toe up in the air, his fingers curled into the back of them. "They are for morning runs."

"Jog," she corrected, scooting up in the bed and pointing at him. "I would have never said run. Jog I'll accept, but don't you put words in my mouth, Conner Love."

"Look here stumpy, if you jog I'll be practically walking."

"It is not my fault your legs are twice as long as mine. I ate my beans and everything growing up, it just never worked." Serena pulled the sheet up to her chest and crossed her arms.

"Or you run, I'll jog. I remember that you said I'll accompany you on a jog, which would mean you accepted that you might have to run."

"Ugh," she moaned, grabbing a pillow and covering her face with the downy softness. "How much time do I have?"

"Five minutes, you've been stopping me or letting me go solo for two weeks now." He tossed the shoes on the bed next to her.

"I went yesterday. Doesn't that count as my exercise for the month?"

"It will get rid of that headache."

The sound of pills inside plastic rattled as another thump landed next to her leg. Moving the pillow just enough to cut her eyes down to the crisp white sheet, she was able to see the bottle of pain relievers a moment before a bottle of water landed next to them.

Resigned to her fate, she took two pills and swallowed them down before arching her back in a stretch as she pointed her toes. Rolling out of bed, she made her way to the bathroom and took care of business. Cracking her neck as she moved it from side to side.

"I'm getting old," she called out into the main room as she slipped on a pair of shorts and a tank top. "You'd think my bones were old, dry wood on a pyre the way they snap and pop."

"Pyre, you trying to get all Ivy league on me?" he teased from the other room.

"Whatever, Norse God, you know your people loved those things," she replied and poked her head around the corner to catch him stretching his quad by lifting his foot to his ass.

"Hey, we were practical. Do you know how hard that ground is in winter? Toss old Uncle Lars in on a pile of logs, rub a few sticks together, two problems are solved."

Finding a binder, she gathered her braids into a ponytail, then only pulled halfway through so they created a loop-like bun style. "Two problems?" she questioned, while finding the tags on the back of her shoes to help pull them over her heels.

"No digging," he said holding a finger up before adding a second. "And fighting the cold of winter."

"You are sick and twisted and know that's not true," she countered.

"It could be. How would I know?" he shrugged. "My family wanted to forget our past so much we changed our last name when we tripped and fell on Plymouth rock."

"Tumbling all the way to the Midwest as you did."

"Exactly," he replied. "You're the one with traditions. Heck, even your mom puts bacon on your turkey at Thanksgiving, very British of her."

"What did you say about being practical?" she teased, then held up a finger. "It helps with the flavor and juiciness of the bird."

"Second?"

"I could steal bacon and not try to slice off a piece of turkey before she served it to our guests."

"I highly doubt that was the reason the British do it," he replied. "But I don't understand most of their traditions."

"It's not a bad thing," Serena said as he tucked a key card into the pocket of his shorts. "Having traditions, but it seems each generation had to add another layer. When you go back centuries, it gets taxing."

"But you still asked your mother to bring her wedding outfit," he pointed out.

"I didn't have time for them to weave me my own," she said, feeling tears pinpricking the corners of her eyes. Maybe she shouldn't have come to Bethany's wedding. They'd been to a dozen of their friends, and she never felt the tug for anything more. "Besides, in a way, I was honoring both sides of my family."

"How's that?" Conner said as they took the side stairs down to the ground floor and walked out to where the cabanas were set up overlooking the beach.

"The outfit was Nigerian, but wearing your mother's dress is the American tradition," she said as they passed the sign stating the beach itself was not patrolled by the security for the resort.

Simply stated, a swim or walk and you were taking your own life in your hands. Like a swim at your own risk warning because no one will come down the stone steps to the beach to help you. The Atlantic Ocean rolled in over the sand littered with seaweed being picked apart by coastal birds. Cool air blew in with every wave of water, making their jog less oppressive than the heat they found when more inland. Hard packed sand had a bit of give from the water as they ran along the edge of the ocean. To their right, the resort stretched out. A line of cabanas, villas and hotel suites no more than three levels up. Bars were beginning to awaken as music drifted over the stone wall that separated those vacationing from those living in the area.

A few dogs were lazily stretching out along the stone work, finding a cool spot to rest from their life on the streets. Though they were far from the spoiled pups you'd see in the city, they were tame in a way. Knowing a set of mournful eyes could get a few bits of meat thrown their way.

The resort spread a mile and half along Cofresi Beach and she wondered how many laps Conner was going to make her take that morning. She also didn't want to tell him the fresh air was clearing her mind and rushing blood was spiking endorphins. No reason to let him know his exercise, instead of therapy, was working for her. When she glanced at his face, she could see he was working things out in his mind.

"Any chance you want me to help?" she asked.

"With what?" he replied with a smirk. "A loan to pay your— what did you call it? A dowry?"

"Bride price," she teased back.

"You know, considering how much time I've spent examining your body, I have yet to see your sales tag."

"Play nice and I might show it to you some time."

"Promise. I'm getting that your family accepted not having a big wedding," he said. "Especially since I wasn't going to be able to talk my parents into doing anything beyond sitting in the front row."

"But," she prodded as they reached the end of the beach in front of the resort and turned around to return back down the beach.

"But you think the reason he gives me the side eye at dinners is because he's waiting on my payment."

"My dad?" she laughed. If nothing else, it let her slow up and stop for a minute. Rubbing the stitch in her side and attempting to recover by holding her hands above her head. "Okay, first, bride price traditionally involved goats, drinks, some food. Honestly, the more I learned about it, the more it was about breaking bread and getting to know each other's family over tossing shekels across a table."

"But really, why do you think your uncle wasn't down there with our group? At least until Auntie Louise left?"

The few times she had been around Uncle David the man had been quiet and reserved. There was always an air of duty over the actual want to be in the room when it came to him. With her parents, she understood why she was an only child. They'd traveled the world, saw unwanted children discarded, and though they spoke of adoption they never did. Between work and keeping up with her, they never saw the reason for more kids. But with Bethany, it seemed as if Uncle David was there because he'd made a choice years ago that trapped him. There was a harsh resentment between him and Louise, one that made Serena question traditions. He'd paid the dowry on the rushed wedding, it didn't mean anything beyond duty.

"Trust me, the last thing my father is looking for from either of us is to cash him out," she said as they began to walk along the beach. Dodging the waves as they went until one came in a bit faster than she could move and the cooled ocean water soaked her, thankfully, open-weave sneakers.

The cool inched its way up her legs as she squished with each step. Having already been ruined, she allowed the waves to crest at her ankles.

"Are you done torturing me?" she asked as a dog limped its way toward her.

"Don't do it or I'll make you run up and down this beach seventeen times."

"But—"

"Nope, I told you I am not rushing you to a hospital after you get a rabies bite. I'll just put you down before you turn into a zombie," he said holding her hand a bit tighter so she couldn't reach out and pet the stray.

"But she's so cute." The dog sat with sad eyes and matted fur. "What if I gave up the Vlog and opened a dog rescue? Bring vets down here, have them fixed, and bring others home. We can do that instead."

"Uh huh," he said, giving little credence to Serena's latest plan for world domination one puppy at a time. "Keep it moving."

Up ahead, Derian was kneeling by a set of rocks. "Derian," Serena called and waved. The teen stood, stared directly at Conner and Serena then took off running in the other direction. "That's weird."

"Maybe he was torturing puppies and didn't want you to catch him," Conner teased.

"Right, because that's exactly—"

The world swirled around Serena as she braced herself by grasping Conner's arm. Breath rushed from her lungs and no matter how clear the sky or fresh the air she couldn't find a way to capture it again. Derian hadn't been playing with a bunch of rocks or torturing puppies.

"Turn away," Conner said as he stepped between her and the vision of the man lying on the beach, his face concaved in to the point she could barely tell who it was.

"That's—that's— I mean we were just—"

"Step away," he said and she saw him waving to one of the guards sitting on the steps who turned his head away. "Jesus, come on man."

"He's dead, isn't he?" she said, trying to make sense of the caved-in face of the crumpled body on the beach. "And Derian."

"Hey, we don't know what Derian was doing," Conner said, walking her toward the closest steps and once again waving over someone.

"How can I help you, sir?" the man asked once they were officially on the resort property.

"There's a man over there, he's dead, he's been killed, can you please call someone?"

The man glanced down the beach and Serena's gaze followed. Salt air comingling with the sour smell of death and rot. A gust of wind captured some fallen leaves and a green baseball hat tumbled its way down the sand coming to rest just feet from her with the letters J-E-T-S emblazoned on the top.

NINE
WOULD THAT MAKE ME TYNE DALY?

"Did you know the man?" Detective Espinal asked as Conner sat at the edge of a big cabana.

The man stood on the sandy faux beach created to allow people the safety of the resort without losing the beach atmosphere. Even with the rock wall keeping the private resort from the public beach, there was no chance of missing the waves crashing below and the ocean on the horizon.

Like those who were used to the heat, Detective Espinal had no issue with wearing a suitcoat, though he wasn't sporting a tie, his canary yellow button-down shirt was crisp and the brown wingtips he wore weren't any worse for the wear. Unphased by the sandy location, the man with a thick crop of black hair, salted a bit on the side, stood easy on the uneven ground. Wire-rimmed glasses had lenses that transitioned in the sunlight. Conner had noticed them getting darker when he stood out of the shade of the cabana, blocking Conner from seeing the judgment in the Detective's eyes.

The initial shock of finding Patrick on the beach had Serena numb beside him. He knew the look. It appeared when she checked out for a bit. Eyes, normally soft and warm like cattails, were glassed over as she stared straight ahead. She was a mix of emotions threatening to burst once her mind had settled. Each time her head tilted to one side or the other she was processing. Figuring out, or at least attempting to solve the mystery before her.

Only that wasn't her job. Which meant he would need to get her to focus on anything beyond Patrick lying dead on the beach. The police would handle the situation and he knew he would have to stop the calculations running through Serena's brain right now.

"We only met him briefly last night. He arrived late to the party," Conner said as he slipped his hand around Serena's and noticed her eyes narrowing. "My wife and I stayed for another round of drinks then went back to our room."

"What was the party for?" Detective Espinal asked.

"My cousin's wedding," Serena's voice was barren as the words pushed their way into the empty space. "She's getting— was getting married on Valentine's Day."

"Was he the groom?"

Serena shook her head, and Conner could see the tears at the corner of her eyes.

"No," Conner said. "He was a groomsman."

"I see, we'll need to speak to the whole wedding party," the detective said. "And do you know his name? There was no identification on him."

"Patrick," Conner said, internally questioning if Derian would have picked the guy's pocket. "I don't remember his last name."

"Poor Emma," Serena softly said.

"Emma?" the detective questioned.

"His girlfriend. I think that's what they were to each other," she stumbled to explain. "Not sure if it was more."

"Who is your cousin?" the detective asked with his hands wide, a pen locked in between fingers in one and a notepad being clutched by another.

"Who's ready for spa time?" Bethany's voice called out and Conner turned to see her with her arms held high in the air.

They dropped a moment later when she read the area. Since the body was cordoned off on the beach below, the staff was keeping morning resort goers from coming down to the area with the cabanas. There were only eight, but they were big enough for a party of twenty to sit comfortably. Each with a view of the ocean and the only place where you could see the area with the body. Then again, clean-up was important and there was only so much of a place you could hide from the guests. Maybe Patrick had been moved by now. Who knew if and what they used for forensics on the island?

"Serena? What's going on? We have an appointment," Bethany said as she tried to get past one of the staff members who obviously was not usually tasked with security duties. "Excuse me that is my cousin."

"The bride?" the detective deduced.

"What was the first clue?" Conner grumbled as he took in the woman with her hair pulled into a mess of curls on top of her head with a smaller tiara today, instead of a crown. Something told him she might have brought a few dozen for the long weekend.

Detective Espinal called out a few words in Spanish to the staff member and waved Bethany over.

"What is going on?" Bethany said with a bit of a pout.

"Madam, I'm sorry to inform you that a part of your group has passed away," the detective said.

"Passed away," Serena spat. "He was murdered."

"Murdered? Who was murdered?" Bethany asked, her eyes widening a bit.

"Patrick," Conner replied. "We found him on the beach when we went for a run."

Bethany glanced over her shoulder to the bridesmaids gathered in the gawking gallery with all the other resort goers now becoming irritated their day was being disrupted. The women were all in camis, some in shorts others in wrap skirts. Their eyes hidden by bulky sunglasses, not that they could tell by what was happening now that Patrick was gone. No way to gauge anyone's reaction beyond Bethany's and hers was confounding.

"Patrick works with my fiancé, and I've only met him a handful of times. He's who you should be talking to." Bethany pulled out her phone and her fingers flew sending a text. "These two don't know him at all. We have an appointment. This situation didn't shut down the spa, did it?"

"I don't believe so, but this is an active—"

Bethany's hand flew up to stop the man from speaking more, the flash from the diamond engagement ring was near blinding when it caught the morning sun. Conner rubbed his eyes to clear the spots as she answered the phone.

"I don't know what happened. They shut down the whole beach," she said once she'd answered the phone. "There's some detective here. Can you please come to answer whatever he needs so I can get what I need done?"

She nodded a few times. Pointing at the phone, Bethany angled it away from her mouth.

"My fiancé Donald, will be down in a few minutes." Bringing the phone back so Don could hear her. "Okay, baby, I love you so much. Thank you for fixing this."

"We need to speak to all of you," the detective insisted.

"We're getting a massage first," Bethany informed him. "Then mani-pedis. I guess you can ask us while we get those, but I insist you leave us alone so we can enjoy our massages."

"Seriously!" Serena exclaimed, coming out of her mental police board pinning together clues. "You want to go to the spa right now?"

"Patrick was a fourth groomsman put in by Donald and I barely knew him beyond a party thrown by his firm." Bethany's excuse was flimsy at best, but par for the course when it came to her. "Besides, our day is paid for and I'm not throwing away money over a man who couldn't bother to even assure us he was coming. I'm sorry he died, but I don't see how it has anything to do with me."

"What about Emma?" Serena asked.

Bethany turned to the gaggle waiting impatiently on the other side of the human barrier.

"Oh my goodness, she's such a sweetheart, too. This will be heartbreaking for her, I'm sure." Bethany's eyes, for a flicker of a second, became mournful. "She's really going to need the spa day."

"Why don't you go with them," Conner suggested and leaned back a bit just in case Serena lost her shit and smacked him. "It's either that or back to the room and stare at walls which will drive you crazy. I'll wait here for Don and see if I can help anymore."

"We have your statement, Mrs. Love. If I have any follow-up questions, I know where to find you." Detective Espinal walked with Bethany over to the women and Conner finally had a moment.

"How can she think about a manicure?" Serena blanched. "She should be…I don't know…at least shocked. Shouldn't she?"

"I'm pretty sure it will hit her soon," Conner said, struggling to find his own sincerity. "Or it will when she comes to the realization her bridal party is now unbalanced."

Emma dropped to a crouch, face in her hands as the detective then knelt and comforted her. Her head shook, revealing a darkened set of bruises on her neck even the best concealer wasn't able to hide.

"Who could have done this?" Serena asked, and a jolt of fear ran down Conner's back.

"No, Serena, I get that is who you are, but let Detective Espinal handle this."

The last thing he needed was Serena trying to piecemeal an investigation together and messing up whatever the professionals were doing. He loved a good mystery, especially when there was a puzzle involved, but that was no way to spend their Valentine's weekend.

"There's a reason they have signs posted on every set of stairs going down to the beach," Conner said. "And why every store downtown had a man sitting with a loaded shotgun."

"Store security—"

"Really? You're gonna play that game with me, Serena. We both know what we saw downtown was more than a rent--a-cop with an outdated can of mace and a case of imposter syndrome." Taking her hands in his, he pleaded with his wife. "He probably wandered down on the beach after we left and was attacked. They took his wallet and remember he had his luggage with him last night. That's gone too."

"Conner, you think I can go get French tips and pretend I didn't see a dead guy on the beach? One I actually spoke to."

"Yeah, that would be a stretch," he said with a conceding sigh as he ran his hand over his face. "But you might get some good gossip sitting in the room being pampered and drinking mimosas."

Serena chewed on her bottom lip, her eyes shifting from disillusionment to processing his words. Taking them in as they mulled around in her mind, he could see her contemplating his proposal.

"I'll stay back here with the men and we can come together when you're done."

He had no intention of paying any attention to the investigation. The murder had nothing to do with him, and there was no way he was going to be pulled into what had happened. In fact, he was going to look into changing their tickets and getting out of the country as long as it didn't make them appear as if they were suspects. Damn. How do the guilty act versus the completely oblivious to the situation? What did he know? The guy made everyone at the party roll their eyes and prepare to go to bed. No one, not even the bride, wanted the guy here and yet he was part of the wedding.

Stop it, he scolded himself knowing he was just as likely as his wife to travel down the road of what-ifs and who-done-its. They'd gotten involved in the past, and he wasn't about to do it again. He promised himself that not every puzzle needed to be solved. If there was anything to be broken down and discovered, it was who hacked into his system and cost him hundreds of thousands of dollars.

"Go on," he said, standing. Conner extended his hand to her and helped her rise from the cabana. "Go, be Harriet the Spy or whoever it is you want to be."

"I could put on a cardigan and be Cagney."

"Would that make me Lacey? Wait, would that make me Tyne Daly?"

"If you're not up to it…"

A fire ignited deep inside him. The gauntlet laid before him as he fought every competitive bone in his body to say no.

"Don't—" he warned, not wanting to fall prey to whatever challenge she had for him.

"Fine, but I'm at least going to find out why they all hated him."

"Who hated who?" Detective Espinal asked as he approached the Loves again.

"Nothing," Serena said as she took the bottle of water that had been brought over when they first sat down.

"If you know anything that could help us, we would appreciate finding the person or persons responsible," Detective Espinal said.

"There were too many people last night, and we had been drinking," Serena said, waving him off. "I'm not even sure what I thought I saw."

The man eyed her. Even through the transition lenses, Conner could see the mistrust of a man he was sure had seen a few things.

"If you think of anything, the front desk has my information," he said. "When are you done with your vacation?"

"We fly out on Sunday," Conner said, praying they wouldn't end up in Cárcel de Rafey.

TEN
EXPERTS HAVE BARRIERS

No matter how hard the masseuse would rub there is no way Serena could wipe the image from her mind of Patrick on the beach. The black of his suit pants and his knees, bent a bit, from a distance resembled any other beach rocks. Sand dusted, smoothed edges from a mix of higher tides and the wind coming off the ocean.

His fingers were what caught her eye. Slightly pinker than the taupe of the sand. Palm up, the fingers were frozen, with a bit of a curl as if he'd been holding something in his hand. Only, it wasn't that. Constriction, first, then the bloat of death. He never made it to that, thankfully. They might have never known who he was, then again if it weren't for the JETS cap she couldn't have recognized him. Face smashed, creating a bowl with his nose in the middle like those serving dishes with a spot in the center for dip.

Her mind was racing, trying to check off what could have happened. A gun would have alerted the guards, even in the middle of the night with loud, violent waves crashing against the shoreline. This was pure rage and a heavy object. Maybe a rock, there were plenty of them along the edge of the beach big enough to do the deed. A shiver tore through Serena, making her body jerk in the chair where she sat in the lobby. All of it too much for her. No one noticed when she tried to play off the movement and it was then she remembered she was supposed to be listening in on the gossip.

Only the women weren't chatting it up about the lost grooms-men. Bethany had informed the front desk that Emma would not be receiving her massage, but she should be back in time for her mani-pedi. Lord knows if she wasn't Bethany would lose her mind if all the bridesmaids weren't matching. Perfectly polished and quaffed for the day. The simplicity of a beach wedding was crashing up against the perfectionist who never had so much as an errant clown at her birthday parties. All celebrations involving Uncle David and Auntie Louise were coordinated like a Russian ballet. In Serena's family, her father and her Auntie Olivia were the ones who blew off minor issues. If it was God's will to have the electricity go out in a black out, so be it. We would light candles and move on.

As much as Bethany tried to push against the training her mother drilled into her, there was little doubt whose blood ran through her veins. A checklist was being reviewed and the only discussion being had was whether or not to cut Emma out completely or promote a guest to groomsman.

When Bethany turned to Serena, batting her thick fake lashes, Serena turned to see if someone was behind her.

"What?"

"The wedding was set for five attendants," Bethany said. "There's a symmetry to the whole thing."

"You're not suggesting Conner step in as a groomsman."

"Donald and he got along so well, sure he hasn't known Conner as long as he had Patrick, but it wasn't as if they were dear friends."

Had she put Patrick in her wedding to balance the pictures? Honestly, Serena couldn't understand why she was the only one to have a visceral reaction to the loss of a human being. Bethany only seemed upset about her bridal party not being picture perfect. As if the timing of his death was the issue not the fact the man died. How inconvenient it was of Patrick to be killed before the wedding and not after all the pictures had been snapped.

"Emma could be a flower girl," Serena suggested, her belly knotting at the idea of tasking Conner to be slid in place of a dead man.

"Or," Bethany prodded, then waved her hand. "Never mind, that giant you married couldn't balance it out, plus he wouldn't fit in Patrick's suit."

Why was it she liked Bethany again? Was Bethany her favorite because they were the closest in age? Auntie Olivia's children were in grade school and Uncle Simon, her mother's younger brother, had kids who were entering high school. Proximity in age and the fact they lived different and distant lifestyles had to of muddied her memories of Bethany. Right now, the reasoning for favorite status was slipping from her mind as her cousin's selfishness was hitting a level higher than expected. Why was no one trying to figure out what happened to Patrick?

Conner thought it was absurd when it came to her trying to follow clues. Leave it to the experts, but experts have barriers, legal and otherwise that she didn't possess. Those lead to mistakes and mistakes can be forever.

"I suppose I could kick Emma out of the party," Bethany said with a sigh. "I'm not really friends with her. She was there because of Patrick."

"He did say something about being the only one allowed to walk Emma down the aisle."

"That sounds like something he would do," Kaitlynn, one of the bridesmaids, said. "Sorry, I shouldn't intrude."

"No, do," Serena prodded, praying she'd get a nugget of information.

"He's overly protective of her," the woman said as she and Bethany exchanged dark glances. "I would say it was sweet, but then again I'm not really one to send hourly updates to the men I date."

"Hourly, it was more like every fifteen minutes when he

wasn't in court," Bethany scoffed. "Her choice to be with that type of man, well, we are not in their relationship."

"Maybe it wasn't her choice," Kaitlynn replied. "Maybe she wanted out."

"Serena," a woman called and Serena pushed up from the chair to follow her. "You are getting the coconut sugar scrub massage."

"Okay?" Serena glanced over to her cousin and the brides-maids, minus Emma.

"With all your traveling, I figured you needed a little extra skin care," Bethany said. "Trust me, I had one yesterday when we landed and my skin is so smooth. Planes can be so dehydrating."

"Wait, you already had your massage?" Serena questioned, more because she was worried she'd miss the mani-pedi interro-gation if the women weren't being put through the same thing she was.

"I had one yesterday, I'm getting one today and I have two more scheduled. I want to be as relaxed as possible. Especially now with all this Patrick business." Bethany rubbed at her neck as if there was a huge knot that needed to be buffed out. "I swear my spa add-ons are probably the same price as the whole trip, but it's something I know I need to get through."

"Serena," the woman prodded and Serena followed her in the back to a room, slightly clinical with a massage table, cabinets and a corner shower stall. "My name is Isabella and I'll be doing your treatment today."

The room bright from natural light streaming through a frosted glass wall she hoped was thick enough to not be seen through. The woman told her to strip down, underwear and all. What had her cousin signed her up for? Serena had experienced massages in various countries and with all sorts of special features. Hot stone, aromatherapy, and reflexology. But she'd never had to be fully naked with only a bonnet for her hair.

Stripping out of her clothes, she laid on the table and the smell of warmed coconut filled the air. Isabella's hands worked their way into the tightened muscles of Serena's neck. Granules of sugar adding a layer better than sand scratching at her skin, but at the same time the coconut oil made it smooth. Working her way down Serena's body, she was lulled into a hovering unconsciousness where she was unable to move, yet could feel and hear everything. At one moment, Serena worried she'd been drugged in some way until the woman hit a spot on the side of Serena's foot and her eyes shot open.

"You okay, Missus?" Isabella asked.

"You found a sore spot, I guess," Serena replied.

"Oh, you had fun last night." The woman giggled a bit. "This spot is often tender here."

"Why is that?"

"I do reflexology massage also, and this is assigned to the liver," she said, pressing in harder with her knuckle.

A sharp stab to her foot jolted up her leg and Serena clenched her teeth for a moment before a sense of relief washed back down her body. The toxin released in some way in her body as the woman returned to rubbing and moving around the whole foot.

Thirty minutes later, the woman was done with the massage portion of the treatment and Serena was confused a bit since she was covered in oil and sugar. The bonnet for her hair now made sense. The moment the shower was turned on, her being naked made sense as well. The fact the woman was standing with the shower door open ready to help Serena wash herself was the strange part. Slipping off the bed, she discarded the sheet on the bed and stepped in the glassed in shower. Letting the woman cleanse away all the granules. Awkward at first, Serena was grateful for the assistance because there was no way she could have gotten all the grains off her body without the removable shower head and Isabella angling the spray.

Bethany was right, her skin did feel amazing and smooth. She hadn't noticed how rough it was until this moment when she got dressed and ran her hand over her silken skin of her arm. Digging in her purse, she gave a generous tip to Isabella then left the room where another woman was standing just outside the door with a champagne flute. The orange liquid with bubbles at the top was offered to her as well as a bottle of water.

"Serena, it is time for your mani-pedi."

Serena followed, sipping her mimosa because the water bottle wasn't open and with two hands full there was little she could do. Hopefully the pedi part of her treatment would hit that liver point on her foot again, while the fizzy orange juice was refreshing the last thing she need was more alcohol at ten in the morning.

Rounding the corner into a bay of tables and relaxing pedi chairs the women of the bridal party were all in various stages of their treatment. Emma was back. Red-rimmed eyes, a bit vacant as she stared at nail polish colors with her own champagne flute being held in front of her with two hands.

Auntie Louise had joined for this part of the treatment and was having acrylic nails applied at the moment. She gave a slight nod to Serena, but no other acknowledgment was needed for Serena to cross the room and give her Auntie a kiss to each cheek as she sat with her hands extended on the table.

"Morning Auntie," she said.

"What a morning," Auntie Louise let out a gasp. "And you found the poor man."

"Mama," Bethany admonished, then cut her eyes to Emma.

"No, it's fine," Emma said as she sat, never choosing a color, but then again maybe she'd only been waiting her turn because Bethany had already chosen for the bridesmaids. "They won't let me see him. They said you identified him."

Serena took a long swallow of her mimosa before proceeding. "His hat really."

"His hat? That's all they found?"

"No," Serena replied. "His hat was the final clue, the man on the beach—Patrick, well he—"

The whole room had stilled, even the staff, who knew how to

avoid conversation as well as they knew how to listen in. All were waiting for the description of the dead man on the beach.

"You know, I better find a color to match the dress I got yesterday," Serena said making her way to the rainbow color rows of polish.

"Was he upside down? How did you not know?" Emma asked. "We got in a fight, I told him to sleep on the beach because he wasn't sleeping with me. I figured he'd get a room. This place can't be fully booked, right? Even with it being Valentine's Day weekend. I mean, it's so massive."

"What were you fighting about?" Serena asked, not really expecting a response.

"Joey, he says Joey tries to take everything from him. Cases, clients, paralegals, but he wasn't going to take me," she replied, before taking a sip of her mimosa, then finally settling down the glass she was using as a shield. "As if that was the only reason Joey—"

"Morning ladies," Detective Espinal came in with two other plain-clothed detectives with him.

One male, one female, both had their badges locked onto their belt and unlike Detective Espinal who wore a suit coat, these two were both in button-down shirts and slacks so their badges were on display. More importantly, so were their weapons. Serena hadn't noticed the men sitting in the doorways when they'd went on their tour until Conner had said something to her. Strange how that worked. Her tunnel vision only focused on the main subject at times, while other moments she noticed the slightest things. Like Emma running her finger just inside the rim of her glass, then bringing the same hand close to her eye.

Tears triggered and flowed down her cheeks. Coating them in what Serena began to see were false shows of emotion.

"We just need to get a few quick statements," Detective Espinal said with his hands up. "I assure you we will be out of your hair in no time."

"I hope so. I'm not sure what we could say beyond the fact

Patrick showed up late, and I went to bed," Bethany said, her long fingers resting on a rolled hand towel to prevent her from having any strain while the polish is applied. "Katelyn and I are sharing a room."

"Until the wedding night," Katelyn giggled. "Then I lose my roommate for good. Hopefully, find a new one that will snuggle with me and watch sappy movies."

"But you can't share the brownies with them," Bethany said. "This woman makes homemade brownies that is to die for."

"What kind of brownies?" the female detective asked with an arched eyebrow.

"Not those kind," Katelyn assured. "They have a caramel swirl in them. Super fudgy."

"Honestly, do you think we have anything really to share with you?" Kaitlynn number two asked, deftly brushing back her golden hair without damaging her newly polished nails while her feet soaked in a bubbling basin. "Half of us are lawyers, and the other half—"

"Are sleeping with one," Katelyn the red blurted as if more than their names were similar, their brains seemed set on the same wavelength. "Sorry, but it's true. Outside of Serena here."

"And Auntie Louise," Serena rebuffed. "Unless Uncle David took a second job."

"No," Auntie replied. "Your uncle has his hands more than full with his duties at his family business."

"Well, there you go. No one will say anything more on the advice of counsel," Chelsea said as she slid her feet into the warm water of the foot soak. "Besides, is it really a loss? I mean, everyone knows Patrick was—"

Emma's head shot up and her lips pursed.

"What? You know it too, like that was your first fight." Chelsea leaned forward a bit, the camisole she wore made both male detectives have to turn away from her very ample breasts nearly bursting from the top. The deep caramel skin glistening in a way Serena wondered if she too got a sugar scrub massage.

"Come on, Emma, we all know you were just holding on through this weekend to not ruin Bethany's wedding. Shed those tears somewhere else."

Detective Espinal's phone buzzed, and he stepped to the side. His words quick as he spoke and all of the detectives showed a body language saying they had a lead. A good one. And it wasn't in the spa.

———

Conner gathered his phone, and laptop then headed down to the dining area where they were interviewing people. It wasn't his place, but he was told to stick close if they needed any more information from him. What could he say beyond the guy shared a drink with him, shifted the relaxed vibe and then was dead in the morning?

Donald was still being interviewed at a table. He gave a quick nod of acknowledgment to Conner as he went in search of a table. The other groomsmen had gathered at another table and were sitting dumbfounded. In wet suits, Joey, Eric and Evan had all been recalled from a scuba lesson and not given time to change. Coffee or juice in front of them at another table with a uniformed cop assigned to stand guard.

Instead of Patrick, Conner turned his focus to the more pressing matter at hand. Ones he had to deal with because there wasn't a police force that would do anything to help him unlock the mystery. Logging into the resort's network, he routed through his personal VPN and then called up Huey.

"Aren't you supposed to be drinking something with a paper umbrella in it and being lazy in a cabana?" Huey asked when his image, slightly pixilated and delayed, came on the screen.

His mouth not matching the timing of his words, and his eyes weren't glued to a different screen in front of him. A fact that caused Conner to twitch a bit and his fingers flew on the keyboard, hoping to clear up the connection and remove any delay.

"Josh said this was a real vacation this time," Huey continued, his game controller coming into frame and the headset he was wearing had the mic arm up so those in the game he was playing wouldn't be part of the conversation.

"You saw Josh?" Conner asked, as the image cleared. A slight hiccup in the words from the delay to making it live had him unsure if he missed something.

"Nah, you know all us lovely peons message each other to gossip."

"Right." Conner shook his head. "Any traction on who broke in?"

"How clear is your signal?" Huey asked, putting the controller down and turning the camera away from him, toward the bay of screens before him.

Lines of code were on some, others had first-person games in various stages and then just for good measure, Huey was streaming a movie. Guess you don't need meds for ADHD if you over-stimulate yourself daily. Who said men can't multitask?

"Clear enough, in fact it may be a bit too clear? Who's Natasha?"

Huey quickly minimized the screen with a chat going that had pictures. "You don't need to see that."

"You know Natasha's probably a dude with bad B.O. and an addiction to *Hot Takis*."

"Now, why do you have to say that? She could be a girl with bad B.O. and an addiction to *Hot Takis*."

"You think you'd get that lucky?" Conner teased. "Finding your soulmate like that?"

"Don't worry. She's not getting my codes or passwords. I'm just sending her thousands of dollars a month for no good reason beyond her loving me deeply," Huey joked. "Plus she knows a guy who's a prince that needs me to help transfer money."

"Of course." Conner laughed. "All on gift cards."

"It would be crazy to do it any other way. That is how I pay the IRS right?"

Conner could hear the keyboard clicking on the other end of the line and watched as the programming genius disseminated code across the screen. Breaking it out in separate windows until there was one clear avatar, middle finger raised, with a cracked heart spinning on the tip.

"So, basically, you're saying this is personal," Conner said as he tried to break down a list of enemies.

"You screw anyone on your design? I know not lately, but early on maybe?"

"Not that I can think of," Conner said. "They were all my ideas and programming."

"No glitches you farmed out?"

"My first game was a basic solitaire," Conner said. "I sold it to Looper Games. Every once in a while, they hit me up to do an upgrade, but that's it."

"What was your first solo?"

"Tinker," Conner said, the game was a basic fix-it-style game, tied in with solitaire, tic-tac-toe, and a memory game to earn points. Last he checked, no one had gotten to the top three levels, so he hadn't thought about that game for years.

"People still play that?"

"Hey," Conner said a bit rebuffed. "It's a good earner, last I checked no one beat it."

"Reeeaaaally," Huey said, and Conner realized he was going to have to add levels now. No way would Huey let that stand.

"In your spare time have you been able to trace this virus at all?"

"Yeah," he said, flipping the screen back toward Conner. The guy was guzzling from a clear cup with neon green liquid and ice. "But unless you have an enemy in outer Latvia—"

"Did you say Latvia?" Conner asked as his mind tripped through enemies from the court.

"You know it's a bot, I went through seventeen countries to get there."

Jokes about common scams aside, Latvia was a bit too close to home for Conner to dismiss the hacker's chosen dead-end spot. Even if the former Soviet block country fit the profile.

"Yeah, well you're not finding Natasha's harry ass there, it dead-ended right?"

"Well," Huey leaned back in his gaming chair and took another drink. "Yes, but why? Does Latvia mean anything to you?"

"You're slow on the uptake, aren't you?" Conner said. "I played basketball there for three years."

"Why?" Huey's face screwed into confusion.

"They paid me to," Conner said. "Send me what you have about the—"

"*Por favor*, no," a woman cried behind him. Spanish words he didn't understand continued to flow with a tone of pain and anguish unmistakable in any language.

Glancing over his shoulder a woman in a chef's coat that all the staff in the kitchen wore was pleading with Detective Espinal as she held Derian back. Protecting him the best she could, angling herself to block the uniformed officers from putting cuffs on the boy who was obviously her child.

"Huey, I'm gonna have to call you back," Conner said, closing the laptop and walking over to the scene. "Derian, what's going on?"

"You know this boy, Mr. Love?" Detective Espinal asked.

"Yes, he helped me and my wife out yesterday. He's a good kid."

"You were lucky then, since this good kid was seen on tape with the victim," Detective Espinal said as one of the officers yanked Derian from behind his mother.

The child showing his youth. His face was one of a baby, not trying to be tough, as his mother's cheeks were streaking with tears. No longer the kid on the street who could take on the con artists. Derian was petrified as all the predictions from the adults Conner and Serena had encountered came rushing toward him. The kid was destined for jail. Only there was no way Derian overpowered Patrick. The man had to of had a foot of height and at minimum a hundred pounds on the Derian.

"Was he killing him on the tape?" Conner refuted.

"I'm not at liberty to discuss that with you."

"He isn't, is he?"

"Mr. Love—"

"Why do you have him in handcuffs?" Conner asked, frustration mounting in the blatant 'he did it' bullshit routine he'd heard repeatedly with no evidence since he'd met Derian.

His mother pleaded with the detective in Spanish. Her hands grasped the lapels of his suit coat. Detective Espinal grasped her wrists and shoved her away.

"Hey man," Derian spat in the one burst of strength he had him.

"Why not sit him down and ask him questions like you have the rest of us?" Conner said. "Right here, his mother can see what's going on."

"I do not need to explain my methods to you." the detective rebuffed. "This is not America, we do not follow your rules. Here we punish the guilty."

"He didn't do it. I know this kid." Conner held his hand up to stop the detective, as if he had some right to do so.

"So do we, he's a charmer." Detective Espinal's head tipped a bit, indicating the uniformed officer needed to leave and Derian's mother dropped to her knees. Her head in her hands sobbing, as others from the kitchen came out to console her. "Your friend is dead, you should be happy we've captured the man responsible. Now you can continue your vacation with some semblance of peace."

"Man?" Conner blanched as his stomach bubbled and acid crept up his throat at the injustice of it all. "The kid probably hasn't even had his first wet dream. Are you kidding me?"

"Don't let his youth fool you, Mr. Love. He's been in cuffs more times than you can probably count."

"I can count pretty damn high," Conner replied, chest out and jaw clenched.

Derian had been on the beach looking at Patrick's dead body, but there was no way the kid had anything to do with it. This swift, make-the-tourists happy response, was going to destroy Derian and end up with him either dying in jail or coming out a different person who would be ten times more dangerous than people thought he was at the moment.

Conner knelt beside Derian's mother, tightness in his chest forming with every painful sob and cry out from the woman. The love she exuded and professed to her son as they marched him away tore at his heart. The officer's grip was tight and completely encircled the kid's willowy bicep.

"Can you speak English?" Conner asked Derian's mother and the other kitchen worker who'd been consoling her.

"I can," the other woman said.

"Tell her I know he didn't do it," Conner said and as the woman began to translate and Derian's mother wrapped her arms around his neck. The hug so tight and furious he nearly lost his footing and had to sit flat instead of kneeling. "And ask how can I help?"

Derian's mother released his neck but took his face in her hands. It was then he saw she couldn't have been much older than he was. Her life was on a track where she tried her best with a child she loved with all her heart. Glancing down to a name badge, he listened as Wilmarie's words were a mix of sobs, steady, but clear in her needs.

"A lawyer," the translator said.

"Really, with all those words a lawyer was all she said?" he questioned.

"What she asked for isn't really possible. She asked for a lawyer who would believe he was innocent. One who would fight for him." The translator Amayah explained. "I only know one lawyer in the city who does that and he wouldn't take this case."

"Why not?" Conner asked, and a supervisor came over causing Amayah to return to the kitchen like a cat that had been shooed by a broom.

"I'm sorry if this scene has upset you Mr. Love, Wilmarie will be returning to her job now," the man in a tie and button-down short-sleeve shirt explained then snapped in Spanish to the woman whose face dropped in concert with her hands. "Can I get you anything from the kitchen? We could heat something up for you. This has been an unusual morning, and I hope you do not see this as a poor reflection of our resort."

"No," Conner said, pushing up from the ground and dusting off his shorts. "A bottle of water would be great, thank you."

"And thank you, sir."

Conner returned to the table and saw Serena walking toward him. Her face was drawn as she approached with her sneakers dangling from her freshly manicured hands. Feet bare and toenails painted a pale blue. "Hey, baby what's wrong?"

"It feels wrong we're going ahead with the wedding," she said, sliding into the seat next to him. "No one, not even Emma, seems that upset their friend died. One of the Kaitlynn's even insinuated no one cared and it saved Emma the trouble of breaking up with him. Bethany is self-centered at times, but this is extreme."

"Did you talk to her about it?" he asked.

"I couldn't get her alone." Serena reached over and took his hands in hers. Unlike the normal warmth, he was met with chilled palms, the ones she tended to get when her mind was anywhere but where it should be. "When it is just me and her she's different. I've always hated her putting on this show when others can hear. I swear the two of us would play, she would be a bratty little cousin, but sweet at the same time. And true, not this false persona of the queen of the world. I'd hoped she would have grown out of the need to do it in public. It has to be exhausting."

Amayah brought him a bottle of water and placed it on a cocktail napkin. The clear plastic distorted the writing but it wasn't the resort logo, it was a handwritten note and being passed to avoid the glare of the supervisor standing watch.

"Wilmarie is like her son, a dreamer, wishing for things that aren't possible." Amayah turned and went back to the kitchen.

"What was that about?" Serena asked as Conner slipped the napkin from under the bottle making sure to not smear the ink from the condensation of the bottle.

"Derian has been arrested."

"What? Why? How?"

"You're just missing who and when," Conner said as he rubbed his finger over the mouse pad for his computer and brought it to life.

"That too," Serena said. "How could they think that kid had the strength to kill Patrick?"

"Well, Detective Espinal believes it, and he just took the kid into custody." Conner leaned in closer, unsure of how near the supervisor was when it came to listening in. "My gut tells me this is a quick put away the bad guy no matter who he is situation."

"Then we have to help him," she said, leaning back in her chair and crossing her arms. "And hiring a lawyer isn't going to be enough."

"Don't," he said. "You know getting too involved will only damage the case, not help it."

"Well, if you're not up to it." Serena batted her cattail eyes at him, knowing he couldn't resist a challenge or the deep velvety pools.

"Baby, please."

"Conner, we saw how everyone looked at Derian as if he were nothing. One second from a jail cell and now they've put him there. Does he seem like a vicious killer?"

"No, but—"

"But what? We can't let him go to jail for this. It isn't some petty thing," she reasoned. "He's not going in for a scared straight come to Jesus night in jail. This kid has been written off for years."

"Detective Espinal did say we weren't in America, their laws are different here." Conner shook his head. Wondering if a teen could be charged as an adult. Would there be a death penalty? How swift was the justice system in the Dominican Republic? Questions needed to be answered even if every part of him wanted to stay away from the case he couldn't allow Derian to be written off and flushed down the system. The idea was enough to turn his stomach and eat at his sense of justice. Derian was trying to make it in this world, the money they spent to have him take them around was a pittance, even without his business or Serena's trust fund. Unlike others who would gouge and use the fact tourists didn't convert money quickly in their head to get a bigger tip, Derian had been honest. Helping them understand and taking the Loves to places with vendors who appreciated the sales, but weren't trying to double or triple prices.

That's not a murderer. Although anyone could be pushed, he couldn't see Patrick attacking Derian, no matter how frustrated and Derian would only fight if cornered. All of which meant the kid couldn't have felt trapped on an open beach. He was more of a flight type of personality. Run, hide and wait for the danger to pass. All of that culminated in Conner's outrage increasing and the need to right the wrong being done to the young man before too much damage was done.

"You know when they were in the spa they left abruptly," Serena said, her eyes narrowing a bit. "I mean, one second they're questioning the bridesmaids and next thing I knew he got a phone call, and they left."

"Were the women saying anything incriminating?" he asked.

"That they were either lawyers or sleeping with one so not to expect anything from them," she replied, setting Conner back a bit. "At the same time, throwing Emma under the bus for fake tears."

"I guess they have video," he replied. "But I didn't see any cameras pointing toward the beach, did you?"

Serena leaned forward, resting her crossed forearms on the table, her eyes moving around to see the security, while blending into the surroundings and high enough most people could miss it, she didn't. Each camera was focused on the resort itself. Even the ones on the steps were pointing in, not out.

"No." She shook her head. "What's on the napkin?"

"An attorney's name," he said as he typed the name into the search engine.

His office information came up, followed by pages and pages filled with local articles about his wins. Even with Conner's current financial loss, it was nothing compared to what Derian was going to lose. No matter the cost, Juan Diaz was obviously the best in town and at this point they needed someone who understood the laws.

"We can reach out to him, but we're going to have to bring him more than our opinion."

Dialing up Huey, the screen soon filled with his best partner in cybercrime.

"Hey boss man," Huey said. "The conga line come by?"

"Yeah, hey back trace my signal."

"Really?" Huey asked his smile broader than it should be.

"Just my signal, I'm going to drop the VPN for a moment, and I need to you figure out the server here. I want you to break into the surveillance and get me everything for the past twelve hours."

"How exactly do I bill this?" Huey joked.

"Oh Huey," Serena said, leaning into camera view. "Since when do you charge us for having fun?"

"Everyday, Serena." Huey beamed back. "Ready to leave Conner for a real programmer?"

"When your game skill reaches his, call me," Serena retorted. "You know I love a good puzzle."

"This one of those puzzles?" Huey asked. "Or did the two of you get caught doing something you shouldn't have and I need to bury the evidence?"

"Guess you'll find out if you can get the video," Serena challenged Huey's hacking skill much like she challenged Conner.

"Dang, say my manhood is child-sized," Huey bemoaned. "That would be less painful."

"Goodbye Huey," Conner said and ended the call as Serena reached out to the attorney to make an appointment.

Resigned to having to wait, and not wanting to be around for the clean-up, they headed back to the room. Passing the groomsmen and Donald who was signing his statement as the men sat, having not been interviewed. All confused, except for Joey, who seemed relieved and ready to move on with his day.

"This is so surreal," Serena said as she dropped her shoes and collapsed on the bed.

How had it only been hours since their run that morning? It felt as if it had been days. Conner hadn't even showered afterward, and both of them were still in their running gear.

"I need to restart my brain," Serena said, pushing up on her elbows. The curve of her body made him wish she had other thoughts on how to hit the button to clear out her mind.

Crawling over her, his body dwarfing her diminutive frame, he leaned in for kiss.

"Seriously," she said, turning her head to the side causing his lips to make contact with her neck.

Not a bad place to land. The sweet smell of coconut on her skin mixed with a new flavor when his tongue stroked along the column of her neck. Much like the whole shoot for the stars and ending up on the moon. Only this moon was shoving the astronauts off into space. Her hand to his chest, she pressed hard, and he flopped to the side next to her.

"What's going on with Gaming Love?" she asked, and he groaned.

"Nothing, it's fine," he replied, never wanting to pull her into his problems unless he honestly believed she could fix them.

Rolling on her side, she laid her arm on his chest then rested her chin on the arm. Serena's eyes pulled him in every time. She knew exactly what to do when it came to him. A simple look and he was done.

"Can you think of anyone I wronged in Latvia?" he asked.

"You did break that one guy's nose," she pointed out.

"That was in a game, no one holds on to that," he replied with a slight yawn. "Huey tracked the hack to Latvia. He was thinking it was a bot farm. Maybe I'm wrong. Just find it random that it traced to Latvia."

"Agreed, seems a bit too coincidental." She let out a light sigh. "Did you steal anyone else's bacon bun?"

"That was not stealing. You were behind me in line."

"Lies, lies, lies." Serena became animated, pushing up and spreading her arms wide. "I claimed it when I walked into the shop."

"Strange," he replied, wrapping his arm around her waist and pulling her closer, capturing her lips in a quick kiss. "I don't remember it that way."

"And this is why you can't remember who you wronged in Latvia," she joked, then returned to serious conversation. "How bad was the hit?"

"Financially? Haven't heard back from Amy. Too many variables. Just because credits were given doesn't mean that person would have purchased them instead. Moving up levels, less ad revenue. It could be a month before I actually know," he said. "Hey, it's a tax deduction, right?"

"Sure," she said rolling her eyes as her phone dinged from a text message.

The heat from her body leaving him made the conversation between them worse. Reality of someone hating him so much to destroy him financially. The crash into the system had no benefit for the hacker unless he got three times the fake crypto currency created in the game app. Even then, it was a game to get people through, not an adventure one, just a basic puzzle to solve before the next guy.

Conner hadn't slipped into the games where actual money could be won. If that had been the case, then maybe he could understand the reason. Even hacking for the pure thrill of 'can I do it' didn't seem as if it were an option in this equation. This was personal. A shot across the proverbial bow that had him now questioning any slight, both real or perceived that may have occurred between him and another person. Who had he wronged so much?

"Bethany said she arranged for us to all be at the same reservation tonight," Serena said, holding her phone in her hand. "I guess I can bring my pre-wedding gift to her."

"This means I have to get dressed and showered, doesn't it?" he said.

"Was that not on your to-do list today?" she questioned. "We're supposed to go to the lawyer's office in a few hours and my love, you need a shower."

"Like playoffs need a shower?" he questioned with a grin.

"Final game, triple overtime, need a shower," she replied, stepping toward him.

"What about you?"

"I had a shower." The smirk on her lips was unmistakable. "The masseuse made sure to get all the sugar scrub from my body. Every—inch."

Conner's mouth dropped open. The visual was erotic and enough to drive a man wild. "She did what?"

"Well, first," Serena began, her hands gliding over her clothes, catching the bottom of the t-shirt and exposing a sliver of her belly. "You know I was completely naked. No bra, no panties."

"You're evil," he growled, popping up on all fours.

Serena turned her thumbs on the waistband of her shorts as

she stuck her round booty out and wiggled her hips. "Scrubbing every inch of my skin."

Kneeling on the edge of the mattress, Conner reached for her and pulled her into his arms. Her back pressed to his front as his hands slid over her belly. Too much was between them. The cotton of her shirt and his own. When his lips found the column of her neck, he was once again hit with the smell of coconut. The taste of a warmed macaroon. Sweet, soft and so tempting.

"You should feel my legs," she teased, and his hand glided over her exposed thighs.

The skin satin, smoother than normal, and every part of him wanted to explore, taste, lick, touch.

"Shower," she stated as he gripped tight to her thighs and pulled her onto the bed.

"Five minutes. You won't even notice what I'm doing," he teased, rolling her so he was on top of her. Bundling up her shirt, he kissed right above her belly button and her skin rose.

"Tempting," she said as she scooted back on the bed. He may be bigger, but she could wiggle her way out of anything. "Shower."

"Join me?" he offered. This shower was large enough for two. "You did say that you wanted one in our home."

Her eyebrow raised, and he nipped her knee.

"If you're not up to it…"

"That's my trick," she whined as her body gave way to his.

ELEVEN

NO ONE WANTS TO VACATION IN A PLACE WHERE THEY CAN GET KILLED

The resort management tried everything to stop the Loves from leaving in a taxi. Citing they could help, wondering where they were going and why they weren't taking them up on transportation from the resort.

"We thank you for your concern, but honestly it's none of your business," Conner finally said as they passed through the armed gate and slid into the backseat of the taxi.

The route was familiar as they made their way back down to the center of the historic district. A sign hung from the upper balcony of one of the double-storied buildings. Creaking from the older iron holder as the wind blew along the column and greeted them on the nearly empty street. As if tourism or the elements were the only reason for street noise.

The eerie quiet made Serena's heart thud in her chest and echo through her body to the point where she wondered if Conner could hear the accelerated thumps as they approached the door to the attorney's office. One of the few without a guard sitting post. The stairway, narrow, with cracked plaster and worn wood steps led to a fairly modern design at the top. Turning the handle on the frosted glass door with Juan Diaz Esq. painted in gold letters she wasn't sure what they would be walking into.

A secretary greeted them warmly. "Hola."

"English?" Serena said, her nerves making her the ugly, rude American instead of the diplomat's daughter who knew proper behavior and Spanish. There was no reason for Conner to be excluded from the conversation.

"Of course, hello, how can I help you?"

"We called earlier about a meeting with Mr. Diaz," Conner said. "The Loves."

"Oh, right," the woman said, her smile bright in the small vestibule of a room. "I'll let him know you're here."

"I thought it would be bigger," Serena said as they sat in the only set of chairs allowed for waiting.

A small table had kids' puzzles, books, and toys. In the far corner, a potted plant appeared to be fake and nothing about this place screamed the best lawyer in the city. All the accolades they'd found had her believing they would be going to the modern part of Puerto Plata with glassed in buildings. Maybe they didn't have that area, but she knew being a tourist locals tended to never highlight those. History and beaches brought people to the country, not a world they could see in their own hometown.

Conner shrugged, his phone in hand, as he attempted to watch the surveillance videos coming through from Huey. A slow and tedious process due to low signals and the size and number of files.

"Mr. and Mrs. Love," a beautiful woman said as she stepped into the vestibule. Her ink black hair smoothed, with just a hint of a curl toward the ends as it fell a few inches past her shoulders, but somehow framed her oval face. "I'm Ana Peña, Mr. Ruiz's paralegal. How can we assist you today?"

Conner and Serena stood, a knot formed in Serena's stomach, making her fear this woman wouldn't let them back into the main office once they spoke. At this point, they barely had an appointment. They were offered a moment squeezed between clients, yet no one came out and no one was waiting.

"We were looking to retain Mr. Ruiz to represent a friend of ours," Conner explained.

Ana clasped her hands together and gave a curt nod, not moving from her spot that blocked the entrance to the hallway. "I apologize, Mr. Ruiz currently has a full client list."

"Then why did you take our call?" Serena asked. "Surely there had to be an opening or you wouldn't have even entertained fitting us in."

"Our secretary did not inform us you were tourists. We do not deal with foreign nationals."

"Our friend is Dominican," Serena could hear the pleading in her voice, maybe it was the quotes she'd read while Conner showered, but Mr. Ruiz had an unyielding record when it came to false acquisitions. "And a teenager. Please, give us ten minutes to explain the situation. We read the press on Mr. Ruiz and feel we know what kind of man he is."

Ana pulled in her lips and breathed in deep. "Fine, ten minutes, no promises."

Walking in the back, the air staled. A mix of the normal mildew that happens in warmer climates no amount of dehumidifying can stop, old leather and wood filled the hallway. No matter how modern the glass desks or fresh paint in the office it couldn't remove the historical aspect of the place. Why should it? For Serena, she embraced the past. The architecture built at a time when every bit was done by hand, not machine. Crown moldings with slight imperfections because no human could be as perfect as a robot router. At least they hadn't removed those in the renovations done to the place. When she sat in a cloth-covered chair across from Juan Ruiz a strange comfort came over her from the mix of modern while still celebrating his heritage in art and custom shelves filled with law books.

Ana sat to the side of Mr. Ruiz's desk with a notepad in hand.

"Mr. and Mrs. Love are here about a Dominican national, not themselves."

"I see," Mr. Ruiz said, steepling his fingers in front of him. "Is this some sort of adoption thing, because I don't do that."

"Why is it that all we hear is what you don't do?" Conner asked, his eyebrows knitting together. "When you don't even know what we want."

"No reason to waste my time or yours," Mr. Ruiz said, then let out a long sigh. "But maybe I've become hardened over the years. There are many lawyers in the city that will happily take your money and work with you."

"Maybe we want someone who would do more than work with us," Serena said. "We need someone will fight for our friend."

Mr. Ruiz spun his hand in a beckoning motion and the Loves relayed the story. Their suspicions and the need for the teenager to be at least released on bond. Ana stopped taking notes halfway through the explanation.

"They won't do that," Mr. Ruiz said. "Not on a murder case. And I'm sorry to have wasted your time, but we tried to warn you. When the resorts and tourists are involved, money is changing hands to calm fears. No one wants to vacation in a place where they can get killed. Mugged, they'll take, but a murder, especially like this one. The police and court are going to push through a verdict like a greased pig to slaughter."

"Derian is a good kid," Serena explained. "A little wild, but physically there is no way he could have done this. Doesn't anyone care a child's life is on the line? Not to mention a murderer is walking free."

"Caring isn't the issue," Ana said. "This would be an embarrassment to the police if we pursued another option. Honestly, by now this Derian has been offered a deal and probably told to sign so he can get out in ten years. Earlier if you want to pay for it."

"Pay for it?" Conner questioned.

"If this goes to trial it could be six months before he goes to court, we've had some as long as five years. There is no..." Mr. Ruiz's eyes told he was searching for the correct word. "Right to a speedy trial in the Dominican. Pleading might save him time in jail. Most public defenders are as over-taxed here as they are in America."

"So this kid is just lost?" Serena said, her gut tightening and throat burning from the hard lump in her throat.

"Unless you find evidence and an officer who is willing to listen," Mr. Ruiz said, shaking his head a bit. "One, I hope you can, but the second will be a hard sell."

"If we can, will you present it?" Conner asked. "You know the system, you know the judges. Or do you not care about justice?"

Mr. Ruiz leaned back in his chair. A slight tap filled the space like a metronome from Ana bouncing her pen on the tablet in front of her. Nervous habit or her way of focusing the man, either reason had both Loves counting the seconds from the challenge laid down to the man whose record said he did care about justice. He was one of the few in the country who did. Articles went on to describe how he'd been wrongly imprisoned not long after Mr. Ruiz had passed his finals in law school. It took three years to prove this, and he swore to work on cases to create better conditions and the legal system as a whole.

"Reach out and tell them I am assigned to this case. Any chance your little tour guide told you his last name?" Mr. Ruiz asked.

Serena and Conner exchanged glances.

"I didn't think so." He drummed his fingers on the desk. "Cofresi beach murder, aye, aye, aye. What have you brought me into?"

"We'll investigate at the resort," Serena assured.

"Good, because they will not let me in to do that. I'm assuming there will be no issue with my retainer?"

"No," Conner said.

"Fine, Ana will see you out and take that, I will be in touch. You said you're leaving on Sunday."

"We're supposed to be yes," Serena said.

"Then we'll make sure you know the long-distance code because arrests are quick, but justice is slow."

Serena and Conner left the office. Standing outside, they searched for a taxi to wave down. The feeling of dread weighed heavily in Serena's heart. Instead of an ally, she couldn't help seeing Mr. Ruiz as a cog in a machine with tines broken off. Conner stood behind her, his hands rubbing the shoulders that should have been putty after the spa, rather than the hardened, tense bricks that they were.

How could they leave the island with Derian behind bars? She didn't think she could. Part of her wanted to search for an apartment to rent until this nightmare was over. Right was right and this whole situation was nothing but wrong dressed up with a crooked bow.

"Maybe we could bribe him out?" she thought out loud.

"Then they would grab another innocent person and stick them in his place," Conner surmised. "And I know you like the kid, but I'm pretty sure you wouldn't be able to leave anyone behind bars that didn't deserve it."

"Could too," she challenged, though the words were false and both of them knew it.

A taxi rolled down the street and Conner flagged it over.

"Can we go back to Carlos' first? I'm just not sure I can return to the wedding prep with no acknowledgment of the dead groomsman just yet."

"Sure, but he's gonna wonder why we're there and not eating."

"I can drink," she replied. "Lord knows I need something."

Ten minutes later, they were at the beachfront with Carlos chopping up fish on his grill top again. "Loves," he called to them. "Back already, that resort food has nothing on me does it."

"No," Conner said. "It doesn't."

"Another round of tacos?"

"Ceviche," Conner replied. "Not sure we're up for a whole meal today."

"And two Coronas with lime." Serena sat on a stool, elbow on the bar top and head resting on her upturned palm.

"Mrs. Love, something wrong on this sunny day?" he asked, his smile honest and pure.

Setting the premade cooled appetizer before her, he retrieved a few lime slices. Popping the metal top to the beer, he placed the limes on the mouth of the bottles.

"Derian was arrested," she said, pressing her thumb on the lime to slide it down the neck of the bottle and absently dipping a chip into the ceviche. A bite of fresh shrimp and veggie dip refreshing in comparison to what was offered in the resort. Her stomach grumbled a bit and she realized she'd only had a mimosa so far that day.

"Oh, man, what for?" Carlos said, moving the food grilling around to avoid burning.

"Murder."

The ding of Carlos' metal spatula chopping the grilling meat silenced as the man mouthed a few words in prayer, then crossed himself before continuing to cook. After serving up a set of tacos to a man at the other end of the bar he returned his focus to the Loves.

"He do it?" Carlos asked. "On accident, of course. That kid is too tenderhearted to want someone dead. Even if the SOB deserved it."

"No, he's a scapegoat," Conner said. "At least we're pretty sure that's what he is."

"You check with his little friends?" Carlos asked. "I tell him not to run around with them, they'll only get him in trouble. Those guys, they make me nervous most days."

"We were thinking the cops just wanted to sweep away a tourist murder," Conner said. "But tell us about these friends."

"Neighborhood kids mostly, but I know he's gotten caught more than once when they were stealing." Carlos shook his head and let out a sigh. "Half the time Derian didn't know what was happening, and they jetted out of a store. He was stuck standing there, transfixed on a display of packaged pastries. Not willing to tell on his friends he served a few days and his mama had to pay a fine."

"Any chance you know where we could find them?" Serena asked.

"Stay out after dark," Carlos warned. "They'll find you."

"No," Conner said, squashing any chance of her doing that. "Not gonna happen."

"But—" she rebuffed.

"No." The word harsh and deliberate. There was no mincing words. "Don't tell me about your mad self-defense skills. He said friends, plural. No."

"Yeah, it's usually about ten or so together," Carlos said, then glanced around as if checking for prying ears. "But there's a big boss man, he comes out once in a while."

"Let me guess," Conner said. "Not to help the youth."

Carlos shook his head and Serena set down the chip she'd been holding. Her belly was empty, but she couldn't eat. If they were processing things, trying to figure stuff out, she'd be stuffing her face. Fueling herself. Right now, it seemed hopeless.

TWELVE
YOU HAVE YOUR TRICKS, I HAVE MINE

Conner wasn't exactly sure how he could casually ask Joey if he was sleeping with Emma. It was evident there was bad blood between him and Patrick. To him, jealousy was always a strong motivator when it came to murder. Then again, thinking back to the night before, Joey wasn't the only one who'd been less than thrilled that Patrick had arrived.

"Glad you were able to catch that last flight out," Don said, his face not matching the sentiment. "Here we thought we were going to have to pull a man from the crowd to escort Emma."

"No one," Patrick said, his eyes dark as the words fell from his lips like a warning to all in earshot. "Walks Emma, but me."

"Right, right," Don said as he waved over the bartender to get Patrick a drink. "You need to catch up to us old man. We've already lapped you a few times."

"I'm good," Patrick replied, holding his hand up to stop the bartender from pouring. "Someone needs to make sure everyone gets to their correct beds tonight."

"Guess that means I'm good to drink," Emma said as she wrenched herself free of the man.

"The case all tied up?" Don asked, pulling out a chair for Patrick to sit and join the group.

The man's eyes stayed on Emma with Joey at the end of the bar. His gaze locked on her every movement. While hers stayed downturned as if even an absent glance could set off an explosion.

"Yes," Patrick replied. "As well as it can be considering. I'm surprised you can focus on this whole wedding thing with all you left at the office."

"Life is more than the office," Don said, a smile drifting toward a slightly tipsy Bethany whose eyes were starting to droop a bit, but nonetheless was stunning to the man set to marry her. "Do you not have plans for the future?"

"Of course," Patrick said, still not fully engaging with the table because Emma hadn't moved from the bar. "What are you having them do? Distill the sugar straight from the cane?"

The snap made Emma's spine stiffen, and nearly everyone at the table shifted from the harsh bark.

"Not everyone wants their drinks served straight up," Joey said his hands extended with a beer bottle in one. "Maybe she's more complex than you give her credit for, has a more refined pallet."

The challenge did not go unmet. Patrick stood, sending his chair flying backward as the metal cried out across the pavement. When his head cocked to one side and jaw tensed, everyone took note. "Trust when I say I know exactly how complex and yet simple she is. Everything about her, I know."

Men in the group were all silently communicating. Abaeze leaned a bit forward, ready to leap from the chair. The bartenders and evening staff had come to a halt. Testosterone oozed in the air like a humid fog, choking those around as the two men stood, refusing to give ground.

Unthreatened, Patrick shoved his hands in his pockets and spoke. "Don't I." His voice like a knife slicing the air as Emma turned on her heel to face the group.

"Even better than my mother," she said, the air escaping Joey's lungs as if he'd been shot by Cupid's wayward arrow. Missing his heart completely in the processes.

Patrick tucked Emma under his arm, holding her close. The claiming her like a trophy was obvious, only it felt as if she were bought and paid for, not earned. Owned, in body only.

Serena rested her chin on Conner's shoulder. Her hand clasping his bicep. It didn't matter if she had self-defense training. He tended to be what she clung to when she was uncomfortable. Though he understood the need to stand one's ground when it came to protecting your woman, Emma was showing signs of a woman wanting to get away. Conner had mistakenly put her and Joey together by the way they had been acting, then again between the two men, one made the woman smile while the other had her cringing in a way that made him think she'd seen the back or front of his hand more than once.

Big weddings were one thing, but why bring drama and chaos when all could be avoided by choosing to not include an attendant? This flirtation wasn't a first-time thing. There was history there and no matter what it was, tension had broken the joyous occasion and he could tell his wife wanted to leave.

Arriving back at the resort, one would think nothing had changed. Laughing could be heard amidst the splashing at the pool. Kids were still running around and when they got back to their room a message had been left telling them they would be dining at the Indian restaurant on the resort.

Serena sat on the settee, her right foot tucked underneath her left leg, the map of the resort in her hands. The booklet designed like a passport had her flipping between pages, then glancing at the clock.

"We're going to need to find a shuttle," she said. "The restaurant is in another section of the resort."

"I noticed you didn't eat at Carlos'," he said, digging through their luggage for an emergency granola bar and passing it to her before sitting on the coffee table across from her. The metal and wood creaked a bit under his weight, but he was confident it wouldn't give way.

"I'm not hungry," she said absently. "All of this has my stomach churning."

"How about we break it down and go through the videos

Huey sent?" he offered. They would download faster and clearer on his laptop, anyway. What little he could make out on his phone was useless.

Her eyes perked up a bit.

"But," he said, knowing she was running on half a beer when he handed her the granola bar. "You need food or I'm not going to pull them up."

"Like I don't know your password," she said with a wink, but took the bar. "Ugh, why didn't we get tacos to go. You knew eventually I'd get my appetite back."

"Poor planning on your part," he said, retrieving his laptop and moving to sit next to her, extending his legs to rest on the coffee table. "You know I'm a lacky following you around."

"Of course, I'm the brains," she said, taking a bite, then holding her hand over her mouth as she spoke with a mouthful of granola. "Way to suck up."

"You have your tricks, I have mine."

Trying to figure out the best angles, Conner used the little passport map booklet to download files with location codes that matched prime spots. Huey had gone above and beyond when it came to stealing security footage and with the acreage, buildings, beaches, and facilities on this particular resort Conner understood why the time-share tour would take half a day.

The black and white image showed Patrick checking in at the front desk, his rolling luggage at his side. Conner moved to a shot of the bar and moved the cursor to a spot about ten minutes later.

"How did Patrick know where we were?" Serena asked. "Everyone seemed surprised to see him there. Did he call someone? Or message? He couldn't have, because people would have known he was coming."

"Was everyone surprised?" Conner asked.

"It seemed that way," Serena said.

"Let's go back," Conner said.

Moving back to the check-in he saw Patrick getting his key and then turning in the lobby. He stood, scanning his phone. His thumb swiping up on the screen. A chill ran through Conner as the man on the screen's jaw tightened. Patrick's irritation evident as his mouth twisted and hands clenched around the phone.

A concierge approached him, offering something as he pointed to the man's luggage and was shoved away as Patrick stormed off. A moment later, he returned to the frame and held his phone screen to the petrified resort staff member face.

Words stumbled out of the kid's mouth as his hands spun. Patrick's rage and annoyance obvious as another staff member approached and reviewed the image. He then pointed out of the lobby, hands giving directions to the bar.

"Was Bethany posting all night?" Conner asked. "You think it was some social media post?"

"Maybe," Serena said, pulling out her phone and scanning the major photo-sharing sites. "What's the time stamp on this?"

"Nine-thirty-seven," Conner said.

"Let me follow the tag train. Lord knows I don't follow all of Bethany's friends."

"Anything?" he asked, his leg bouncing a bit in anticipation.

Serena was the social media guru. A necessity to maintain her followers. She would take a day or two each month and plan out posts using a site that would auto-post for her. Linking to all the hot apps and making sure to at least be interacting with those who are interested in finding the most beautiful and fun places on Earth. Recently she had moved up in the search engines as one of the top spots when people typed in travel. All of it garnered her attention from more than the random vacationer.

Glancing at Serena's phone, he saw her scrolling through a myriad of images. Swiping up and down. Then stopping when the images were from the flight or arrival. The zoomed in picture of a fancy drink or sunset weren't going to help anyone know where on the resort the group was. Especially with a timestamp hours before his arrival.

"No," she said, the disappointment evident in her voice. "Can you zoom in on the phone when he's holding it out?"

"Really?" he said, shaking his head. "Let me see if there's another angle."

Serena chewed on her lower lip. "You'd think every picture would have tagged Bethany or Donald."

"There might be a hashtag," Conner suggested. "Then again, maybe not everyone isn't as in love with your cousin as she is with herself."

"Ugh, if I search for DR or Dominican Republic I'll get thousands of unrelated shots. This is insane." Serena tossed her phone to the side. "Okay, so he saw a picture and made his way down to the party. Then what?"

"What if it was a message?" Conner asked, backing up the video again. "All those images you brought up on Bethany's feed were group shots. Girls together, guys being guys. The only couple shots were of Don and Bethany."

"True." Serena leaned in closer to the laptop as he backed up and played the video at half speed.

"What's this?" Conner asked, the movement of Patrick's hand from the counter to his pocket abrupt.

"You see something?"

"Maybe," Conner said, pointing to Patrick placing his hand on his pocket. "Think about it, why would he pull out his phone? We don't have mobile keys and he doesn't seem like he's a big see where I am in the world type of a guy."

"For only hanging out about a half hour with him, I'd have to agree, his priority was Emma."

"Exactly, which means if someone at the party thought Emma was doing something she shouldn't…maybe it was a text with a quick couple shots of her and Joey."

"But if no one knew he was here," she began. "What would be the point?"

"Maybe to get him here," Conner said, returning to the footage of bar and backing it up. "Think about it. Bethany was irritated already that her bridal party wasn't going to be balanced out."

"Was she? I thought that was a new thing."

"I overheard her speaking with Don about the family he had flying in for the wedding," he explained, remembering the discussion going on to the side of him when they thought he was part of a different one.

Knowing what was going on in his peripheral was necessary in basketball. The slight squeak of rubber from the shoes of a teammate coming around his backside to set a screen and allow him to take a shot undefended. Words triggered him too, but when he played internationally tones of voice keyed him into things since he didn't always understand what his teammates or opponents were saying.

"She was wondering if any of them would fit or be willing to step in if Patrick ended up not coming. Don assured her that he would get Patrick here and everything would work out."

"You think Don took a picture to get Patrick to get his ass on a plane?"

"I don't know," Conner replied, unsure of the man's loyalty. All of the bridal party confounded him beyond Abaeze since he was family and maybe one of the Katelyn's. The redheaded one who was the maid of honor. The rest seemed as if they were mere acquaintances. Don did ask if Patrick had put a case to bed, so it was obvious they worked together.

He needed to figure out which of the files was for that area. Although some were labeled *lobby A* or *pool twenty,* most were numbered and not in sequential order. A still image in the file-sharing portal wasn't enough for him to easily tell between a bar on this side of the resort or another. It wasn't like this had three-sixty technology where he could swoop through and see the whole area without moving to a new file. Closed circuit wasn't for actually stopping crime. Only finding out what happened. Who knew how many hours of video they would have to review to find what the police believed was incriminating. Maybe Mr. Ruiz would be given access.

"I need to get ready," Serena said, a bit resigned. "I'm sure we won't be out too late tonight, so maybe we could review then."

"Giving up already?" he teased.

"No," she replied. "But I do need to do more than toss on an outfit. I'm the sole representative for Andrew Isola's family. My Auntie Louise was more than happy to remind me of my duties when I picked a color for my nails."

She flipped her hand around and wiggled her fingers. The robin's egg blue made sense to him, considering the dress they'd found the day before for the wedding. But he wondered what the other women got, maybe French tips like Serena had mentioned. That would be the classic beauty he figured Bethany would insist on.

Serena went to their luggage and pulled out her makeup bag. Three dresses were laid out on the bed and she walked along the edge, her mind running through her steps when it came to dressing up. They had a limited wardrobe since they had been working, Even now her halter top with high-waisted cotton pants would qualify for a casual Friday in an office. The sandals made it so the belled-out pants seemed to be practically a skirt. Only at this moment, his focus was on the waist and now nicely her round ass stuck out.

When she picked the outfit and slipped away into the bathroom, he returned to the files, creating a folder to dump the ones he believed were from areas that weren't relevant. Not totally deleting them because one never knew, but there were places he figured weren't important. At least not to him in this moment.

Playing the video at the bar, he noticed in the bottom corner of his screen a still image for a video focused on the pool adjacent to the bar. Clicking through, he let it play and got up to get a notebook and pen. Returning to his laptop, he marked important times. When Patrick arrived. When it seemed he'd gotten a message. No reason to watch before then and creating a timeline was important.

Tearing a few pages, he marked the start and finish and laid them out on the table in front of him. Skipping ahead, he caught sight of a Kaitlynn, the blonde one had wandered from the bar toward the pool. Taking a few selfies with the crystal blue of the water, now dark, but reflecting the moon on the water. Or maybe it was one of the lamps outside the pool. Either way, Kaitlynn's body language switched, and he watched her eyes narrow. Her phone in one hand, her fingers moved to the screen in the telltale sign of her zooming in on something toward the bar area. Marking the time on his notes, he moved back to the bar and hoped he could see what brought her ire.

The view in the bar was obscured by the group, all dancing. Conner had a problem not getting lost in the vision of Serena in his arms. Their height difference faded away when she was in his arms. Only in pictures did he notice how much he had to lean over for their lips to touch. His hands dangling in the middle of her bare back. The outfit she'd worn the day before was open and exposed the back of her.

His memory providing the music and the front of his body warming from the memory of her pressed to him. Serena's head lolled back to look up at him and between the two of them was a fuzzy figure of two people standing close enough it was hard to discern one from the other in the gray of the recording. But it was the same place Joey had camped out at the bar when Patrick arrived at the party.

Clicking on the image, he attempted to zoom a bit and there was no denying if Joey was the man in the fuzzy couple his head was buried in the woman's neck. Her hair long, like Emma's draped down over into the open space. Checking the time stamp, it matched perfectly with the camera from the pool. If there was another angle, he could prove Kaitlynn was taking pictures.

"Conner," Serena's voice cut through his need to find the missing corner piece to link the puzzle together.

Glancing up, he saw she'd taken her sister locks and braided them together, tucking the end back up and under at her neck. One of the thicker locks she wrapped around her head like a headband. Her dress made him do a double take. Never in a million years would he think Serena owned a sheath-style dress. If he didn't know better he'd wonder where his wife went and the corporate businesswoman came from.

"Where did that come from?"

"I tuck it away just in case."

"In case of what? A court appearance. Do you have a power suit coat to go with it?"

"Stop it," she admonished, her unease at the starched clothes obvious. "It's a formal dinner."

"On a resort," he replied.

"You don't like it?" she said, twirling around, the tightness of the skirt limiting her ability to move.

"Are you comfortable?"

"Not really," she admitted. "But you know I have to represent the family."

"Serena, I promise this isn't sexual," he said, holding his hands up in surrender. "Strip. Put on a flowy skirt or a sundress."

"I do have this one," Serena said being reserved in her response, very unlike her, as she crossed the room and picked up a skirt that was peach at the top and faded into blue like a sunset over the ocean. The gauzy fabric translucent with a slip built in underneath. "There's a matching top."

"Since when do you worry about representing the Isolas?"

"I don't know. Auntie Louise gives me these looks and I feel five and unable to hide behind my mother's skirt." Serena sat on the edge of the bed, her back straight from the dress that had her locked in place. "Like this is who I'm supposed to be. My father is an ambassador and I'm a flighty travel geek. I should be working like my father for the government or in some high-rise building where I have a corner office. Hell, I got a degree in foreign relations and public administration."

"Outside of me not paying your father—"

"I don't have a bride price," she admonished as he closed the laptop and walked toward her.

"That aside, your father has never so much as scoffed at our adventures." He sat next to her on the bed, she leaned on his chest. "Since when do you care what Auntie Louise says?"

She shrugged. "You think this is how Bethany feels all day, every day?"

"Probably, and that's why she's having this destination wedding she can't let go of because how could she return to her job engaged and not married."

"You should have seen them today," Serena said. "All being primped and so caddy. I still haven't figured out how anyone beyond Katelyn the red made it into the wedding party."

"The blonde one?" he asked.

"No, get it, Katelyn the red for the redhead that was her room-mate in undergrad," Serena said. "I needed some way to keep them straight. Why?"

"Because the blonde might be our messenger."

THIRTEEN
LIFE IS A SOCIAL MEDIA POST

The joy of being married for Serena always came from Conner knocking her back to reality. Her free spirit was never snuffed out, but it was put in its place over the years. This meant she wasn't really sure when her self-doubt would creep in and tell her to stop. Though most times it included her family.

What did she expect from a man who never questioned why she was vacationing in Latvia? The getaway when she studying abroad for a semester in college. A break had her heading north from the college in Italy where she had been taking classes. Hopping on a train with little more than a direction to guide her. Connecting to another when she didn't like the look of the station. The quiet, quaint town of Valmira, with its mix of historic and modern only a few steps from each other, won her over as she found a hostel to stay for a few nights.

Boldness had been a mask she wore, but Conner let it be her reality. The shadow behind her made each move more authentic as she searched for who she was. Their marriage had been an overshot trip back to school. An Atlantic City runaway marriage would have made more sense since she had been going to college in Princeton, but she wanted more sun than the coastal city could provide in early May. Vegas it was. Much like her riding a train until she liked the station, flying to Vegas made perfect sense and Conner came along for the ride. Indulging her to the point they were making a midnight call to her parents where they begged the two of them to wait for them to make their own way to Vegas.

Maybe her parents thought the twenty-four-hour cool-down period would change their minds. Making promises like her mother bringing an outfit and her father wanting the simple task of walking her down the aisle. She was their only child, and it would have been selfish to deprive them of this one important moment in her life. So, Conner wasn't the only one who indulged her, but much like when her parents were around protecting her from family members' judgment, he was her shield.

The ankle-length skirt moved with her, making it feel as if she were in a cloud that randomly kissed her bare skin. Conner slipped his hand in hers as they walked toward the shuttle that would take them to one of the other parts of the resort, closer to the Indian restaurant. In her other hand was a gift bag with Bethany's pre-wedding gift. Her slight meltdown in the room had her hoping for a few moments alone with Bethany. Everyone needed someone to say it's okay to scream like an uncouth monster and over the years Serena had been that person for her cousin.

They weren't the first to arrive and Bethany was on full bride mode with a crown of colored jewels. Her outfit was closer to the Nigerian heritage in style, but something told Serena her hair would never be covered by a gele no matter what Auntie Louise believed. Maybe that was why she was wearing a buba and Iro to dinner. The blouse and wrap skirt were as bold in color as the jewels in the crown.

"Ah, Serena." Auntie Olivia reached out with both hands. Golden bangles chimed along her wrists. "I was told you were here."

"Auntie, when did you get here?" Serena questioned as her aunt clasped Serena's hands then came in to kiss her on each cheek. Olivia was closer to Serena in age than to Serena's father, making her feel more like an older sister than aunt. The Isola children had been very spaced out. No two attended the same school at the same time growing up.

"This afternoon," she replied with a smile as bright as the sun and with two of her three children hanging on her skirt, as if all the commotion was too much for them.

The oldest, Wisdom, was nine and had always been a shy child. Sitting on a bench in the corner in a starched button-down and dress pants, the young man appeared to be trying to melt into the wall and disappear as he sat next to his father. Uncle Emmanuel was engaged in conversation with the men who were waiting for the table and allowing the child to be unattached.

Joy and Grace were five and three respectively, and the skirt clingers. Not that Serena begrudged them a bit. Dressed as pure princesses themselves, with fluffy skirts and sparkling shoes, the girls each had their hair smoothed back with a headband and the poof of their natural hair creating a halo behind them. Grace, the youngest, was sucking on her thumb, her dark eyes engaging with every bright and shiny thing that crossed her path. Watching as the people piled into the space waiting on their table.

"These two are going to be flower girls, aren't you?" Auntie Olivia said, as she urged the girls to move forward and acknowledge their place of honor in the wedding.

Serena knelt to be at eye level. "Let me guess, Grace is going to toss gummy bears," Serena said and Grace giggled and twisted her pointed foot on the ground. "And Joy, aren't you stunning?"

Joy reached out and grasped the pendant Serena had purchased in town. The blue stone nearly filling her palm.

"Be careful," Auntie Olivia warned, slipping her finger down the chain of the necklace to make sure Joy didn't tug and snap it. "You like your cousin's necklace?"

Joy turned her eyes up and nodded to her mother, never removing her thumb from her mouth.

Standing, Serena smiled at her aunt. "I need to give Bethany something. You've met Conner, haven't you?"

"Oh, yes, I believe once or twice, but never for enough time," Olivia said.

While Conner enjoyed the distinction of being a wallflower most days, he was able to pull off the charming gentleman when necessary.

Bethany stood among a few of her bridesmaids. One of the Katelyn's, Yvette and Chelsea. She smiled as Serena approached.

"Bethany, can we step outside for a moment?" Serena asked, enticing her cousin by holding the giftbag at the end of her fingers. "I see a few people aren't here yet."

"Presents." Bethany beamed and stepped forward. "Of course. Donald," she waved. "I'll be right back."

The man gave her a loving smile as she and Serena stepped out of the lobby and Serena instantly noticed the difference in volume. All the talking by guests had created a stereo-level hum in her ears and once out in the open, it was as if she'd stepped away from a live concert into a library.

"So, what is so special about this gift that we couldn't open it in front of my friends?" Bethany asked, her hands out and fingers curling repeatedly in a gimme-gimme motion.

"Are they your friends?" Serena asked sincerely, then waved away her question. "I don't mean to judge, Katelyn and you are adorable. Like two wild girls on vacation."

"Too many months apart," Bethany confessed. "We get together a few times a year, but this last one I've been bogged down working eighty hours a week and any free time I try to spend with Donald. I guess we missed each other. Is it bad that I'm loving bunking with her again? I swear it's like when we were undergrads, but we don't have to sneak the liquor past the resident advisor."

"Not at all." Serena smiled at the innocence of it all.

"Okay, present." Bethany extended her hands, the manicured acrylic nails beckoning for the present to be passed off.

"I got this on our tour of the island. I'm not sure what traditions you are going for American, Nigerian, Bethian."

"Bethian, I like that." Bethany pointed and wagged her French-tipped finger. "That is probably the best description. I'm making my own rules for once."

"Well, I got you something new and blue," Serena said and passed her the bag. "Not sure if it will go with your dress."

Bethany pushed aside the tissue paper and removed the box where the necklace had been placed. Nodding her head toward a bench, they moved and sat down. With a creak, the white velvet lid was lifted to show the larimar and silver necklace.

"It's pretty versatile. You can lay it on your chest from shoulder to shoulder. With how long and elegant your neck is, you could wrap it around a few times to make a choker. Then again, it can also be wound around a few times on your wrist," Serena explained. "Or even around your flowers, I guess. Maybe it's stupid, but this stone is only found in the Dominican Republic and when I travel around I like finding things exclusive to where I am."

"My dress is strapless and this will be perfect," Bethany said. "I brought some diamonds, but none of them would do me justice compared to this. And this is almost the same shade as the bridesmaids' dresses."

Serena's heart warmed from the approval and the fact Bethany was not on the full Vegas billboard, bright and glowing personality. "You doing okay? We haven't had time to really talk."

"Tell me about it," she replied. "Mama is driving me crazy, but then again it's a day ending in Y, so what do I expect."

"Where's Uncle David?" Serena asked remembering the moment her father slipped his arm around hers and walked her down the aisle. Tradition crashing against her need to be non-conformist. The simple gesture she never planned on having, not wanting the transfer of property from father to husband, suddenly meant more to her than any rite of passage before. Now she cherished the memory and was hoping Bethian style wouldn't deprive her cousin of the same.

"He was in there," she said. "Mama has more than enough personality to take over a space. Daddy never needs to speak. I don't want that for Don and I."

"Your family, your choices," Serena said, patting Bethany's hand.

"Is it hard?" Bethany asked, sincerity in her eyes. "Not just going with the flow? I did everything right, well, sort of. Grades were always a struggle for me, when I got my denials from Harvard and Yale for law school I was relieved. Then mama insisted I find a place to go to law school. She'd raised me to be a lawyer and I am one, but I feel like my life is a social media post."

"Sunshine, rainbows and glitter," Serena surmised, knowing the pressure created by the constant need to have the perfect image portrayed at all times. "Hiding the fact you're exhausted and in a job not a calling?"

"Don doesn't care about that," she replied. "The pressure is off my shoulders when it is just him and me—do parents not understand what they do to us? Oh, look who I'm asking. My mother is the Isola stand out, demanding attention all the time."

Adjusting her crown, Bethany's gaze turned up, and she slumped back on the bench.

"Dear Lord, have I become my mother?"

"No..." the word eked out of Serena, who couldn't hold back the truth of it all. "Maybe a little, but only the good parts."

"Liar," Bethany admonished with a slap to Serena's hand.

"You think she has middle child syndrome?" Serena joked. "Like our grandparents forgot about her, so she turned her life up to eleven."

"Eleven?" Bethany questioned.

"Sorry, Conner loves weird movies," Serena explained. "Look, I don't know much, and trust me when I say I have doubts all the time, but if I'd learned one thing from being an old married woman it's this. As long as you are happy where you are in life, everything you want will come to you. If our parents approve well, that's a bonus. But we can't live for them. We need to live for ourselves and the family we are making."

Bethany wrapped her arms around Serena and held tight. The hug crushed in the vice-like grip.

"I hate you," Bethany said when she released and brushed her finger under her eye. "Please say my make-up is still flawless."

"Could it be anything but?" Serena replied, taking Bethany's face in her hands and turning it from side to side. "Did you get industrial strength to combat the heat here, Jesus woman?"

"Yvette has a machine, she does airbrush makeup on me every morning," Bethany said, swiping at Serena. "You think Don will notice if I move her into the spare bedroom after we're married?"

"Probably, you'll have to tuck her under the sink in the bathroom."

"Oh my God, Serena." Bethany laughed and grasped Serena's upper arms, squeezing hard. "I'm getting married."

———

Although it would mean they wouldn't currently be in the Dominican Republic, Conner wished the Isola's had only had two children. Auntie Olivia was a lovely woman. Her brother and his father-in-law was a decent man. Auntie Louise was another story and he was glad once they were seated at dinner to be at the opposite end of the table from the woman. Not quite lucky enough to make it to the overflow table sadly, but that's what family relations got you. A place at the main table.

Once Donald's family arrived, their group of a little over a dozen had grown to nearly thirty between the arrival of Auntie Olivia's family and Don's. The group took over a whole section of the restaurant as the staff, Dominican, but dressed in Saris and tunic-like coats. Serena learned the proper names when they went on a temple tour in northern India, but Conner had little brain space for fashion knowledge. For his wife, it was learning a culture which he feared might be an addiction stronger than crack and considerably more expensive. At least she was smart enough to make a living at her passion.

With so many finger foods the communal feel of the meal was perfect as plates of samosas, naan, and kababs made their way to the table. When the main dishes of butter chicken, makhmali kofta, and a wide variety of curry infused dishes balancing vegetarian and meat perfectly. For a moment, Conner had to remember he wasn't in Delhi. The mix of spices melding together as well as the family communing together brought the sounds and smells of peninsula country to life on an island a half a world away.

The only sour-faced one at any table was Auntie Louise. Conner wondered if it was because Donald's family wasn't having as big of an issue of the non-traditional nature of the wedding. Maybe they were enjoying not having to pay a bride price.

"What's so funny?" Serena asked.

"Huh?" Conner replied, then realized he had been chuckling a bit. "Bride price, I was thinking about that again."

"Really?" Serena shook her head. "Do you need me to call my father and get a dollar amount?"

"After all these years with the late fees and penalties, I'm afraid to ask. You think he compounds the interest daily?"

"He'd be a fool not to," she said, dipping her naan in mint sauce before taking a bite. "Honestly, after all these years I'd hope you'd negotiate a discount."

"You have taught me some mad bartering skills."

"Never accept the first price," Serena wisely advised. "Trust me, they want to sell more than I want to buy."

"See, that's where your father would have me trapped." He nudged her with his shoulder. "I'd get stuck paying double."

"How does all that work?" Katelyn, the redhead maid of honor asked. "Sorry to eavesdrop, but Bethany never really brought up her Nigerian side in college. I thought she was just another girl from Milwaukee."

"My father wasn't big into it either," Serena said. "Letting this one off scott-free and all. I guess our grandfather wanted them to assimilate, while our grandmother was the one who passed the heritage stuff on to us. Traditional weddings are a long drawn-out process. Honestly, I don't think Bethany has the attention span for one of those. Then again, neither would I."

"Long?"

"Like days. And the buildup is a lot of meals like this, but with gifts between the families," Serena explained. "Those happen months before the ceremony. Discussions on timing, if the two are a good match, not only the couple, but the families themselves. All of the wedding is planned between all the family members, even the date."

"Oh." Katelyn the red's mouth rounded to a perfect O of confusion.

"Maybe you could help us catch up," Conner suggested. "Since we weren't brought into the planning session, we are flying blind with the people here. We get you and Bethany best friends and all."

"Yes, she called me the moment Don asked her to marry him," Katelyn the red boasted, the badge of honor had Conner wondering if she wanted a sash saying *first to know*.

"Exactly, the most important people," Serena followed Conner's lead in stroking the ego of the maid of honor to get her to spill. "But the other bridesmaids, what's with them?"

"Right? You see that too?" Katelyn leaned in closer. "Yvette, I get, but the rest I was shocked when she gave me the lowdown. I mean you're her cousin and she talks about you all the time, but these other girls are Don's friends. Bethany never really had a lot of girlfriends to begin with."

"Really?" Serena questioned.

Bethany acted like the type of person who would have an

entourage, then again that was the social media image Serena spoke of.

"I've never even met these women before," Katelyn confessed as if it were a sin. "Or the men, for that matter, though I have to say Don's best man is making me think I might need a trip to Nigeria myself."

Katelyn glanced over at Abaeze, then away with a blush of pink filling her cheeks.

"Anyway, from what Bethany said, something about this big case at Don's firm and the pressure from the other associates is insane. They've all been trying to take it from him and the only way he could protect all his work was to rope them into the wedding. Either that or she would need to postpone, and I guess that wasn't an option for her."

"She's not pregnant, is she?" Serena asked. "It wouldn't be bad if she was, it's just I don't remember hearing anything about this wedding until a few days ago."

"If she is, it isn't why they are getting married," Katelyn said. "Bethany had this crazy thing since college about Valentine's Day. A boyfriend broke up with her freshman year like three days before and from then on she vowed when she got married it would be on Valentine's Day and she'd never be alone again."

Serena's face contorted into confusion, before she shook it off and returned the smiling, *that's totally normal* look she'd been sporting for most of the trip.

"Didn't Patrick say something about a case when he showed up?" Conner asked Serena, moving away from the subject of the rushed nuptials.

"Oh him," Katelyn the red rolled her eyes. "I don't mean to disparage the man, especially when he can't defend himself, but he stayed behind to try to take Don's case. And after Bethany put that Emma into the bridal party because he refused to leave her in New York by herself. As if she couldn't just be a plus one."

"He seemed protective of her," Conner said, as he poured more wine into Katelyn's goblet.

She smiled and took a long sip, the alcohol adding to the pink in her cheeks as it slipped down her throat. Evident in the loosening of her lips.

"Protective, please," she scoffed. "He had her on a short dom-style leash. I'm not saying they're into that kind of stuff, but really, who can't go twelve hours without seeing their significant other? I mean, does that even make sense? Like break down, unable to work type co-dependence. He was screaming at her so loud on the phone at the airport when she was flying out with us I could hear it and she wasn't on speaker."

Katelyn the red took another drink, her eyes bouncing between the two Loves. "I'm sorry, are you two like that? I know you guys are travel buddies and work together."

"Actually, Conner has his own business, and I have mine," Serena assured. "And trust me, he enjoys when he's not tasked with being my camera guy."

"A bit too much," he confessed.

Katelyn giggled. "Well, that's what Bethany and I have been talking about. How Don will get buried in a case for weeks at a time and when they come together, it's like no time has passed. She's so busy, I'm surprised she even met Yvette in her building."

"You did say she knew her, didn't you?" Serena said.

"Yep, she's a neighbor in the condo—" Katelyn got small, bending closer to the table and the two Loves leaned in to listen. "Next to Don and Bethany, don't tell Louise, they've been living together for about six months, right after they got engaged. See, that's why I say she's not preggers, they've been together for a while now."

Serena gave Katelyn a wink and sat back. "Do you know, did Joey just meet Emma? Or is there more?"

"The other Kaitlynn told me all about that," Katelyn the red said as she finally added a few bites of food to the alcohol in her belly. "Kaitlynn was part of the firm and now she casually dates Evan. Guess she left after Patrick took one of her clients and the managing partner basically told her she needed to do more and Patrick hadn't done anything wrong."

"This firm sounds like a viper pit," Conner said, wondering how people worked in an environment that toxic. Cutthroat businesses were one thing, but in the same office, he wouldn't be willing to put up with that.

"Makes me think my job in event planning is a cake walk," Katelyn said.

Conner wondered if Bethany really was her best friend or if the maid of honor was a means to an end when it came to planning this wedding. "Well, all I know is Emma was a late bloomer, like a tomboy in high school that all the guys thought of as one of the guys."

Conner wondered if the alcohol was going to lead them down a winding trail to Patrick's killer or a gossip blog with as much relevance as the debate over a dress that appears blue or gold depending on the device you are viewing it. An interesting side note in a world of real issues. Like Patrick's killer and the fact they were dining at a fine table, with delicious and perfectly spiced food while Derian was in a cell petrified about what was going to happen to him.

He knew he had to stay attentive to the woman's wandering tale about the wallflower becoming a ten and drawing all the men to her. But all he could see was Derian in a corner praying the men decades older would leave him alone and the kids a few years his senior wouldn't try to explain the power structure in the prison on his face.

"After that party, she was with Patrick and Joey was friend zoned," Katelyn said and Conner shook his head knowing he'd miss an important part of the story. "But I guess he's moved out and into the possible zone."

Emma and Joey were at the overflow table and the trio all glanced back to see them talking close. Sitting on the corner allowed them a way to be a part, but not of the group. Their body language telling of the want to be alone and the fact they might pass a plate of butter chicken on to the next guest, that guest was getting little else from them.

"Not that she was the first thing Patrick took from Joey," Katelyn said when they refocused on the food in front of them. "Kaitlynn is far from the first attorney Patrick stole clients from. Joey was his favorite, the man gets the best clients, whales really and Patrick treats—well treated him like he was his own personal procurement officer. Guess Emma decided she didn't like the alpha anymore. All that testosterone does get old after a while, especially from a man who wouldn't even let her shower alone."

"What?" Serena questioned and Conner's mind flashed back to their arrival shower.

"She's staying next to Chelsea who says Emma spent an hour in the shower the last night. I guess Patrick usually washes her. Like some damn child, every shower. If she dared to take one without him he would flip out because his job was to make sure she was clean."

"Every shower?" Serena asked the question, confounding Conner in the same vein.

Once in a while is natural, but every time. That is beyond excessive and more important was very controlling.

"Guess she took one by herself last night in rebellion. She was crying about it during the mani-pedis," Katelyn pointed out. "She had been sitting next to Chelsea. Guess she felt guilty about defying him."

Or guilty because she killed him, Conner thought, a notion shared between Serena and him if her glance in his direction was any indicator.

"What about Eric?" Conner asked, thinking Don, Joey, the other Kaitlynn, and even Emma, all had motive at this point.

"Same I assume, but who knows. I think Don actually is friends with Eric, or maybe that was Evan." Once again the trio's eyes turned to the overflow table where the men, dressed nearly identical even though Eric had a blond, *Abercrombie* wind-blown way hairstyle and Evan sported a clean shaven, bald head with a dark goatee. The ying-yang, black and white twins were in near lockstep, even the way they moved.

The tink of a knife on the edge of a glass caused a hush to take over the room. Even the diners on the edge of their group stilled and turned, maybe from curiosity, to see what was about to be announced or to find out how a group this large and diverse had come together in clear celebration.

Uncle David was standing, his face stone as usual. Conner wondered if he'd ever heard the man speak. In the eight years since he'd met Serena, he'd only been around this part of her family sparingly. The transient life they led didn't really bring about big family Christmases or Thanksgivings watching parades and football.

Although his family had done that when he was growing up, he hadn't missed the gatherings in his adulthood. The shelf life of most of those events was about two, maybe three hours before alcohol or old unresolved issues would surface, causing a break-down of family unity. Lines were drawn, allegiances proclaimed and all Conner had wanted to do was disappear to a room where no one was around or he could work on dribbling.

The man wore the abgaba, a four piece traditional outfit. Loose fitting upper part resembled a jacket and tunic combined. Pants were of the same silken fabric, comfortable and made of a rich wine color with golden trim. The squared off cap topped the outfit, his body stiff as if he were a statue at the end of the table with all eyes focused on him.

"In a few days, my only child, my daughter, the baby who completed my family will be passed on to another." The voice, deep, rich and slightly cracking as Uncle David spoke. "I have now dined with Donald's parents. Showing me the respect and honor for both myself and my beautiful bride of more years than most at this table have been alive."

Serena took Conner's hand in her own, squeezing as he slipped his other arm around her waist and rested it on her thigh.

She scooted in her chair practically to the edge, the two lovers coming together in this, most precious moment.

"Our children push against our traditions. My daughter is one of the best at the practice."

Auntie Louise pursed her lips, but gave deference to her husband by lowering her eyes.

"There is only one tradition my daughter would respect. This is my blessing on her marriage." Uncle David raised his other hand, finger extended, and wagged the digit. "If I do not approve, we will have had a wonderful time in the sun, but she will return to her home and job as a top attorney. Unmarried."

The room became hushed now. No plates being moved, no food being brought to lips or errant kisses on a lover's bared shoulder or neck. Bethany's eyes widen as if her father would for any reason disavow this marriage. Auntie Louise's face appeared a bit satisfied. She hadn't been happy about the way the marriage was being put together, but would she have her husband lay the death blow?

Uncle David raised his glass and waved his hand for each of the guest to join him in his toast. "May your marriage bring you blessings by the dozens."

FOURTEEN
THIS IS LIKE A FREE PEEP SHOW

Although they had taken the shuttle to the restaurant, there was a trail they could take to get back to the room. Serena needed the fresh air. The quickest route would be the beach, less winding around buildings, pools and bars. It was soft on her bare feet, which were irritated by her sandal straps. But she knew her husband, while he didn't think Derian had killed Patrick, that didn't mean the beach was safe. Especially at night, when the lights of the resort face in, not out. It would be over a mile. Which meant a longer walk, on cooled concrete and tiles for her.

Mr. Fitness morning run wasn't going to complain, even if he was in his dress shoes. Slipping off her strappy sandals she locked them over her index and middle finger. Dangling them by her side as they started on the path. Waving to others as they loaded in the first shuttle. The older group went back to bed. While the rest of the party was going to continue the debauchery of youth at one of the bars with dancing.

"Katelyn was chatty," Serena said once they were out of earshot.

"Yep, sadly, a bit too much," Conner replied.

"Too much?" Serena questioned, because that should never be

an issue. Information was needed to solve this case. While Conner may enjoy putting together a puzzle with no picture on it, only a solid color. They didn't have that type of time if they were going to help Derian.

"Let's see, now our suspect pool has, geez I don't even know how to do the math. Who didn't want Patrick dead? That might be a smaller number. Hell, at this point Uncle David is a suspect because his daughter's happiness is his goal and Patrick irritated her."

"Let's be realistic," Serena said, noticing all the pools were a different style and the one they were currently by had a bridge over the center so she had to walk over even though they could have gone around. Sitting on the stone arch, she set her shoes next to her and tried to suss this all out. "Joey, obviously, but now I wonder if Kaitlynn saw a bit of revenge."

"Blonde right?" Conner asked as he sat across from her on the bridge. The low arch causing his knees to be practically shoulder-high when he sat, and she wondered how uncomfortable he was.

"Yes, you want to keep walking?"

"No, this is good. The pool light is bathing you in a blue glow, it's kinda cool."

"Alright, weirdo."

"There's a game with a goddess that floats, legs crossed with blue waves behind her," he said. "Got to the highest level on that one."

"So you could see the goddess," she teased.

"Yep, this is like a free peep show." His crooked smile warmed her belly.

"Focus, Love," she barked with as much gusto as she could, mocking his coach from Latvia. "We've got to get down to business."

"Yes, boss," he joked. "Heck, at this point we can't rule out Emma or Don."

"Don?" she balked. "Is this the Uncle David theory? He would do anything for Bethany?"

"You heard Katelyn, the man stole clients. We both heard Patrick goad the man when he got here about leaving a case behind."

Serena buried her face in her hands. At this point all they were doing was adding, not subtracting from their work. Tomorrow was their last free day. Then the wedding and they'd be on a plane out of the Dominican. At this point she wanted to hook up an IV of coffee to her vein and pull an all-nighter to cut through the muck.

"It's going to be okay, my love," Conner said and she felt his hand rubbing a circle between her shoulder blades, the heat of him beside her instead of across from her soothing.

Wetness covered her palms, and she realized the tears of frustration were flowing. "All I can see is Derian crouching in a corner with some homemade shiv in his hand."

Conner pulled her up into his arms. "You're probably right, I was seeing him without a knife, should have known that scrapper would make one."

"Ugh, why couldn't it be pinned on some random guy we didn't know?" she questioned. "I could have blindly accepted the arrest as fact and be impressed with the police work."

"No, you wouldn't," he countered and snagged her sandals. "The way everyone is acting about Patrick would have your nose wrinkling and eyes narrowing."

She gazed up at him, and he nodded his head toward her.

"Like that," he said, and try as she might, she couldn't relax her face. "Baby, you have a lot in common with Mr. Ruiz. You have a need for justice, no matter how messy."

A phone buzzed in Conner's pant pocket and he dug it out, then passed it off to her. With big pockets come big responsibilities like lugging all her stuff around. With a quick swipe across the screen Josh appeared. His face showed he was beyond annoyed.

"Tell me you're not involved," he said, not even giving her a chance to say hello.

"Good evening to you too," she replied, a bit confused.

"You know I haven't seen any new footage added to the Love on the Run folders," he added. "And as much as I would like to believe you and Conner are actually vacationing and kicking back I've worked for you longer than a week, so I know better."

"His scrunched-up face isn't nearly as cute as mine is," Serena said and angled the phone toward Conner, who was leading her through the resort and away from any people that were milling around in the cool seaside air.

"Huey told me about your little..." his voice dropped to a near whisper before coming back to full volume. "Hacking adventures...and then I, being curious, happen to take a peek into what is happening where you are."

"I told you we should have uploaded those videos we took. Especially at Carlos' beach bar because then Josh would have been busy trying to copy his recipe," Serena said.

"You know what happens when he gets bored," Conner replied, making Josh's face twist more in frustration.

"There were five murders in Puerto Plata since you've gotten there. Which one has you committing a felony?"

"Is it a felony to hack a resort's CCTV?" she wondered aloud. "We'll need to check with Mr. Ruiz."

Conner grasped her hand and angle the phone toward him. "A man named Patrick."

Josh turned his head to the side then refocused on them. "Patrick Dugan?"

"Sure," Serena said and realized they never did get that far on the whole introduction with any of the guests.

"What can I do to help?" Josh asked. "Because lord knows if you two don't have back up you're going to end up making your-self the prime suspect."

"They already have one," Serena said with a hard sigh as they chose to take the stairs to avoid losing signal. "And that's the problem."

"So you aren't the guests who discovered the body?" Josh

said, clearly reading an article neither of them had seen. "Because you, Serena Love, have two radars. One for delicious street food and the other is for dead bodies."

"Oh man...our signal—low, you—cutting in—out I can't hear you," Serena said, skipping her words as she spoke.

"Right, so you don't want my help?" Josh offered and Conner took the phone from her.

"Patrick's wallet was stolen," Conner said.

"Bank records, credit cards, you know some day they are going to protect those better," Josh said, needing little instruction from Conner. "Huey and I will get back to you and see if we find anything."

The phone went back to her apps, and she clicked the button to turn the screen black. "That is a felony," she rebutted as she snatched the phone from Conner. "He's a good assistant. I'd rather not have to train a new one."

Conner waved his key card over the lock, and they stepped into the room.

"Want to order snacks?" he asked, toeing off his shoes and kicking them across the tile floor. "We could sit out on the balcony, maybe overlook the crime scene or part of it."

"If all those people hated Patrick, and he knew it, why would he agree to be part of the wedding?" she questioned as he powered up his laptop and gathered his notes.

"People enjoy torturing others," he surmised. "Think about what we've learned. Patrick was a bully in every sense of the word. Keep the enemy closer than friends. Isn't what that phrase basically says."

"I bet Patrick would catch flies and rip their wings off when he was a kid," she said.

"And squeezed the toothpaste in the center of the tube," Conner teased.

"You know, he left the toilet seat up every time." Serena pointed and Conner glanced over his shoulder as if he were completely innocent of the crime punishable by death in her mind. "Kaitlynn was trying to set him off taking those pictures, wasn't she?"

"Appears so," Conner said. "The more I reviewed the video, there was no other explanation. I wonder if she'd been sending him pictures the whole time? That might explain the blow-up at the airport."

"Unless he really was that upset she was flying off and leaving him," Serena replied as a shiver tore through her body at the thought of not being allowed to be away from a man. As much as she loved Conner, space was a necessity. The only time he got irritated was when she put herself in danger, even then he wasn't so much mad as worried about a situation that could occur.

"There's no way to know without talking to Emma, and something tells me she'd lie at this point."

"We need to get ahold of her phone," Serena said waggling her finger. "That would prove at least part of the case."

"I wish we could find Patrick's, but I bet that's been jail broke, stripped down to the base model and sold twice by now."

"What if it hasn't?" she reasoned. "I know you could do all that in like twenty minutes, but who's to say whoever took it could? Especially if he has the wallet app on his phone making it so they could swipe and pay, they might find it a better way to make money."

"Good point. We'll see what Josh and Huey come up with."

Serena stepped out onto the small balcony with its two metal chairs and a wrought-iron table. It reminded her of a set her mother called an ice cream social table. Little round seats with straight backs, perfect for posture, not comfort. While it was a good view of the cabanas, pool, ocean, and bar, she couldn't see the beach. More importantly, no matter how willing Conner was to sit out in the fresh air, he'd bust more than his back trying to sit in the chairs more suited to Joy and Grace than grown-ups.

Stepping back inside, the condensation on the glass door obscured the world just a few feet away. Even the palm tree was little more than a blob of green in the corner of her window. Although seeing the real deal wasn't that important compared to the video. By now, the resort was cleaned up and in some ways, they seemed to be the only ones interested in what happened less than twenty-four hours ago just beyond the rock wall.

"No go?" he questioned.

"Since when do you turn me down when I say let's lay in bed instead?" she teased, slipping off her skirt and making Conner's shoulders straighten. "Down, boy, I just want to be comfortable."

He whimpered like a puppy, but she knew the puzzle of Patrick's death was eating at him as well. Passing her two pieces of paper, a pen and notebook as a hard surface, she shifted under the sheet and propped up the pillows behind her.

With a few quick clicks, they were back in the video sharing cloud and clicking through the thumbnail images. Some less unique than one would think. Although the pools were all in different shapes, there were only subtle differences when it came to behind-the-scenes areas and more importantly where the bars were.

"That one," she said, pointing to a view of the cabanas where the faux beach was.

Conner started the video, dragging the cursor closer to a time when Patrick arrived. While he seemed focused on the time stamp she was watching as the jolted movement of people appearing and disappearing, trees blowing and more importantly a security officer moving over to the top of the stairs in the upper left-hand corner of the screen.

"Wait," she said and Conner paused on the empty area. "Back it up."

With a few quick clicks back, he landed at the spot where the security guard was blocking the top of the steps.

"Why is he there?" she questioned.

"I can't see," Conner said, moving the mouse over to zoom in a bit. A blob was lower on the steps. "You think that's a person or people?"

"It has to be a group," she said, and Conner clicked the play button. Her hand covered her mouth with a hard gasp as the guard lifted his gun, pointing at the group and hands rose in surrender.

Another person ran into view, his hands waving, and they could only assume he was calling out the guard. The weapon lowered as the smaller person ran through the sand. Turning his head back toward the bar area, his face in full view. Her heart raced as she watched Derian stopping the guard and slipping down the steps with his friends and becoming absorbed into the blob at the edge of the screen.

"I hadn't seen him last night," Serena said, swallowing back the feeling this was the reason he had been tagged with Patrick's murder.

The gesture was innocent, the guard moved back to his post without any fear as he put his weapon back on his hip, but they could see him watching the kids walk away. Conner clicked the mouse, moving the video further along, and soon Derian was back. Talking to the guard, his hand extended toward the bar adjacent to the kitchen where his mother must have been working. The discussion more animated than it needed to be and soon both of the Loves sat back. At the top of the right side of the screen was another set of steps from the beach. With the guard distracted, a group of kids made their way up the stairs and onto the property. Quickly disappearing from the camera's view as Derian, his gaze mindful, moved on from the guard after getting approval to return.

———

"Sneaking his friends on the property couldn't be enough to convict him, could it?" Conner questioned. The video had paused with Derian walking in the middle of the cabanas. Glancing at the time stamp, there is no way this was irrefutable evidence. Especially since this happened thirty minutes before Patrick even arrived at the resort.

Serena pushed play and let the video run. "Here's what we know, the quickest way to get down to the beach from where we were is one of these sets of steps," she said. "Whatever happened, Patrick must have gone down these steps at some point. Either on his own or was dragged."

"I doubt he was dragged," Conner said. "Even in the highest tide, the waves don't reach the steps, which means there would have been drag marks unless a person stole one of those rakes they use in the morning to smooth out the sand."

"That's true, and you're the only one strong enough to carry him," she said, and he shook his head.

"You do realize me tossing your little butt over my shoulder is not the same as Patrick. A fully grown man."

"Are you calling me short?" she grumbled, crossing her arms.

"No," Conner said, turning his head to the side before saying, "The American Medical Association might."

Serena nudged him hard enough he had to brace himself by reaching out to the wall. A move he used when holding back defenders in a game, but splayed fingers weren't holding a ball away this time.

"Is the guard there all night?" Serena wondered aloud, tucking her legs underneath her and sitting kindergarten-style. "I mean, really, when you think about it, this one guard has to watch both sets of steps. He's told to not stop anyone with one of these wristbands from coming on the property."

Serena held up her arm, the plastic band Conner had gotten so used to he forgot it was even there was bright orange indicating they were guests, but not members. The plastic strap with a white locking clasp could be easily cut but was waterproof and loose enough it slid around the wrist easily.

"Patrick was in a suit coat, but at night after being tossed from his room by Emma—"

"If she really did that," Conner rebutted. "She said she did, but only the two of them know for sure."

"Or three of them," Serena countered. "What if Joey was there?"

Seconds clicked on the screen and Conner pressed the fast-forward button to make it four times as fast. The movement quick enough to get through the evening, but not so fast that they would miss any major action.

"Can you grab your laptop?" Conner suggested. "That way we can line up the bar and the cabanas. Watch them at the same time and see who left when."

"Good idea," she said, uncurling her legs and bouncing out of bed.

Her blouse hung perilously at the crest off her butt cheeks. The glorious globes tempting him from across the room when she stepped or stretched. An unintentional peep show reminiscent of a burlesque dance, where feathers moved around and allowed slivers of skin to tease one's imagination. When she bent and picked up her backpack his mouth watered and he had to adjust himself in the bed.

"Quit looking at my ass," she commanded, not turning to make sure he was doing it.

"Who said I was?" he challenged and moved his gaze to the video that was now hours ahead of where it had been and quickly he stopped the video to back it up.

"You did," she replied, laptop held tight to her chest like a notebook, and turned on pointed toes. Though short in stature, Serena's legs were exquisite. He only wished there were more of them to explore. They were perfectly tapered and when she was on pointed toes, the thickness of her thighs made his fingers itch to hold them. "Have I ever told you when you look at my ass you make a little whimpering noise?"

Conner's face heated up thinking he wasn't that much of a sex-starved teenage boy, was he? Had he always been this way or was Serena a special case?

"Wow, it really is that subconscious," she mused and climbed back into bed.

"Are there any other noises I should know about?" Conner asked.

"See, here's my dilemma," Serena said, holding her hands out in front of her like the scales of justice. "Do I tell you? Or continue to have a superpower?"

Her hands moved up and down as if the weight of the knowledge was worth more than sharing the little eccentricities he had.

"Fine, then I'm not going to share your quirks."

"My quirks or your kinks? Which is it? Because something tells me much like your little whimper, you get excited by my quirks." She reached up, taking his chin in her hand and trying to turn his head toward her, but he held firm. "Oh, don't be like that."

Her voice was sweet and in a sing-song in tone, weakening his resolve as always.

"Nope," he said, trying to be strong. "You can't just turn my head and take what you want. I distinctly remember you having them remove obey from our wedding vows."

"Did I demand a kiss? Nope, I was going to take it like the raging sex-driven animal that I am," she rebutted as her hand dropped from his chin.

"Oh, well, in that case…"

Conner slid his laptop to the side and turned. Curving his fingers, he brushed them along her cheek and her head curved into the caress. Stretching her sensual neck and exposing the little spot he knew sent fire through her body. One sweep of his lips and her flesh would rise, a second would elicit a moan and if he pressed his mouth in the crescent-shaped arch between shoulder and throat, he wouldn't be the only one letting out a whimper.

The movement was fluid at this point, the lovers so knowledgeable of the other and yet up for a discovering new way to tease and tempt the other. Only this wasn't the time. Bodies on fire, wanting to push through the fog of hormones he took what he could, understanding their kisses needed to wait. And still, as his hands roamed and hers clawed at his back a few moments couldn't really be that distracting, could it?

Blood pumped through his body as his heart raced in his chest. She straddled his hips, knees bent, and when she pushed up, her breasts were perfectly aligned with his face. His hands clutched the globes he'd coveted from afar and she tilted his head upward. Claiming his mouth with a passion he found he expected when she was in the mood to prove a point. And being a gentleman he was more than willing to accept her way of seeing things no matter how long she wanted to show her side.

A knock at their door had him moving to the side as she nibbled on his ear. "Wrong room," he called out only to be greeted by another knock. "You know how to say no in Spanish?"

"No mas," she offered, her breath rushed and fingers tugging at his shirt.

"Isn't that no more?" he questioned.

"Yeah, no more knocking," she practically growled.

"No mas," he called out and received a third knock. Serena sat back and he shook his head. "Hold this thought."

Slipping from the bed, he headed to the door, sex denied rage having him ready to yank the door open and give this intruder a piece of his mind.

"Look, wrong room—" Conner quickly tucked his lower half behind the door and poked his head out voice cracking as he greeted their guest. "Hey, Mr. Isola, we didn't think you were coming to the wedding."

"My business wrapped up early and I have a deputy ambassador for a reason," he explained.

"Daddy?" Serena's voice called from inside the suite, the sound of her feet on the tile pattering around wasn't helping Conner lose the excitement that should have been tamped down the moment he saw his father-in-law's bald head standing outside of the door.

The man was barely five-foot, dark as midnight with the

same cattail brown eyes his daughter had, and petrified Conner's six-seven frame as if he were a giant. Serena pushed Conner aside and gave her father a big hug. Her skirt thankfully back in place. When she stepped back, she held her father's hands in hers.

"Where's mom?"

"Choosing which room we will stay in," he explained. "They insisted we have a small detail with us and so we required two rooms."

"Doesn't one have a king bed?" Serena asked.

"You'd think so," her father replied, then tilted his head to the side. "Is there a reason why your husband has become a floating head?"

Serena glanced over her shoulder and scanned Conner, cutting her eyes in the *what the heck are you doing* look?

"Sorry," Conner said, opening the door wide and inviting Mr. Isola inside still slightly blocked by the door as he glided into the space. Serena followed her father and smacked Conner in the chest when she walked behind him. "What? I can't just toss on a skirt."

Her eyes cut down to his hips and a smirk lifted the corners of her mouth.

"Daddy," she said, skipping a bit as if she were closer to five than thirty. "What made you change your mind?"

"You have met your aunt more than once," he explained as he sat on the settee and eyed the rumpled bed. "We are practically in the same time zone for once, and Bethany is one of my favorite three nieces."

Conner smiled at the diplomat who never took a break when it came to covering all his bases.

"I'm so thankful you came, and I know Bethany will be so happy." Serena plopped down next to her father.

"I see you two are working as usual," he said, pointing to the open laptops on the bed. "Aye, aye, aye, your mother will be most displeased."

"Mom?" Serena questioned and glanced to Conner who was as confused as his wife. "Why would she be upset?"

"Work is, but one aspect of life, my child," he explained. "What have we missed since the bride arrived?"

"Don's family," Conner said, sitting down on the edge bed as far from Mr. Isola as possible without being rude.

"And," Serena's voice became solemn. "One of the groomsmen was killed."

"Aye, aye, aye." Mr. Isola tsked, shaking his head. "How is the couple? Is the ceremony going to happen or have I made the trip to visit my favorite son-in-law?"

Conner's back straightened, falling into the diplomat's words, much like what others had done. Fear crept up his neck, wondering if Mr. Isola going to be wanting a little alone time him, if so he would need to figure out what else is part of life before that happened.

"It is happening," Serena said. "Bethany's head would explode if anyone told her no."

"Is that a family trait?" Conner teased with a wink only to receive a hard look from Mr. Isola.

"We weren't really working," Serena said, breaking the tension.

"Weren't you,?" The man's eyebrow raised and Conner got the feeling the extra he wanted was a grandchild.

"A young boy was charged with the murder," Serena explained, then a pleading note was added to her voice. "But Daddy, I swear there is no way this boy could have killed Patrick."

"Ah, I never should have let those security officers give you a sticker badge when you were younger." Serena's father shook his head and closed his eyes. "You know there are positions at the State Department that could allow you to play Nancy Drew."

"Here I thought it was Harriet the Spy," Conner joked, and Mr. Isola smiled.

"Her too."

"Dad, that's not why we're looking into this. Someone, more than likely in the wedding, probably murdered this man." Serena knitted her fingers together. "I can't let it go."

"Do you know why they insisted I have a security detail when coming here?" her father asked.

"Because you're their favorite and the world wouldn't know what to do if you got so much as a paper cut," she teased, drumming her hands on his knee.

"No." The firm line of his lips were the exact ones that first sent a bolt of fear through Conner's body when he met the man in Vegas outside of the chapel. "This island's crime rate is high."

"I know, but—"

"There is no gray area here, Serena Anaborhi, it is not my place to tell you no." Mr. Isola's gaze shot to Conner who got the message sent across the room with precision. The mantle for her care had been passed to him and he was failing in his duties. Like he had any chance of success with the woman who had been allowed to do what she wanted her whole life.

"Me?" Conner said a bit out of shock and dismay, his finger pointed directly at his chest, in a knee-jerk reaction. "You've met her, right?"

"Yes, and sadly, any man who tried to take control of my wild daughter would be left in a lump on the floor clinging to life," he admitted. "Best you can do is try to keep up."

A knock at the door released Conner from the conversation as he jumped up and opened the door to see his mother-in-law flanked in a protection detail.

"There a reason they abandoned their primary protectee?" Conner asked the woman, dressed in a light cardigan and simple skirt. Ash blonde hair styled in the helmet of a diplomat's wife.

"He's slippery," she explained and their room was becoming crowded as the woman came in with the two men uncomfortably in suits that would stand out on the resort where even the staff wore polos.

"Drew, I should have known when you got her room number

you would come here," Mrs. Isola said, then placed her hand on Conner's bicep. "How are you doing, Conner?"

"Better now that I have you to protect me," he said, realizing he wasn't flattering her, he did feel a bit less pressure with her to block for him.

"What have you been doing to this poor boy?" Mrs. Isola asked, smacking her husband in the belly with the same backhand her daughter possessed.

"Me?" Mr. Isola became innocent as he stood, hands out as if he hadn't pushed grandkids and locking down his daughter in less than three minutes of conversation.

"Right, right," she admonished, tugging on the tie he wore before giving her husband a light peck on the lips. "Innocent of all charges, I don't believe a word. Serena, how are you holding up with Auntie Louise?"

"I'm still standing," Serena said, accepting a hug from her mother that ended in her mom taking her face in her hands and his wife whining a bit. "Mom, I'm not a little girl."

"To me you always will be. And this hair." Her mother shook her head and turned Serena's head to the side where she'd tucked the mix of braids and locks underneath the larger braid. "It's getting so long. I wish I had your patience. I swear anytime my hair hits my shoulders I have no idea what to do with it and just chop mine all off."

Serena beamed, the acceptance from her parents tended to make her glow brighter than the North Star.

"Alright, well, these kids don't want us bothering them." Her mother glanced at the bed and grimaced. "Hmm, well, either way, it's been a long day. Your father insisted on working the first half of the day or we would have made it for dinner."

"Oh, and you would have loved it," Serena gushed. "Indian food."

"Naan? There was naan, wasn't there?" Mrs. Isola shook her head as if she had been denied one of the world's greatest delicacies instead of a piece of flatbread.

"With mint dipping sauce."

"Drew, pull rank, make them open the kitchen. It's not even nine, so it has to still be open," Mrs. Isola commanded then turned to the security goons hanging at the back of the room toward the door. "Do you two fetch and retrieve?"

"Um, we could," the shorter of the two men, even though both were over six feet tall, replied double checking with his partner. "There isn't a policy is there?"

"Was there butter chicken?" her mother asked.

"And samosas, with this curry sprinkled on the veggies inside I couldn't quite place," Serena said.

"That's it. Now it has become a necessity. I'll need at least eight of those bad boys to figure it out."

"Or I could ask the chef," Mr. Isola offered only to be waved off by his wife.

"What would be the fun in that?" she teased and he placed his hand on the small of her back, leading the woman three inches taller than him out the door and on to their next location.

Conner feared for those in the area if food was not present when they got there. The click of the door had him snagging his wife around the waist and pulling her to the bed.

"Where were we?" he asked.

"Um, trying to save Derian," she pointed out. "Really, my parents are here."

"Your parents were practically scolding us for not having enough sex," he pointed out, and Serena's eyebrows knitted together.

"They were not," she admonished, smacking him in the chest.

"Right? That's why both of them scowled at the bed with the laptops in it."

"That was about overworking," she said, her focus bouncing between the sheets, the hallway to the door, and the settee. "Wasn't it?"

"Work is only one aspect of life," he said. "Your mother would be displeased. Did you hear her sigh when she saw the bed?"

"No," Serena's honest innocence warmed his heart. "Why would they want—oh, no, they wouldn't want—would they?"

Recognition crashed against her consciousness in the same way it had him. Her parents wanted grandkids and she was their only child. All of it rested on her shoulders.

"Unless they say it to us directly I'm going to ignore the idea. Besides, it couldn't happen right now, anyway."

"Are you challenging my abilities to perform?" he asked, a bit rebuffed by the accusation as he puffed out his chest like some lowland gorilla set to pound on his pecks.

"No," she said with a smile. "But even you can't fight the pharmaceutical precautions going on in my body."

"And here I thought it was dumb luck," he said, flopping back on the bed.

"And here I thought you weren't that dumb," she replied, booping him on the nose, then opening her laptop.

FIFTEEN
WHO GAVE YOU CAFFEINE?

The black and white of the screens burned Serena's eyes. A good movie set in the forties without so much as a bit of colorization was fine. That was in focus, there was drama or comedy. This was a blurred-out image, pixilated and shaking at times when the wind blew off the ocean hard enough to rock the cameras. Pinching the bridge of her nose, she staved off the headache before yawning and going in search of water.

Conner's eyes were barely slits at this point. The exhaustion hit him as a light snore drifted from his pillow, the video playing in front of him showed the closed-down bar. Outside of the random dogs and cats wandering in search of dropped food, there wasn't any action on his side of the resort. She pressed the spacebar to pause the video and Conner snorted.

"I was watching that." His words were less than a mumble as he rolled to the side and grabbed another pillow.

She had caught his laptop before it was smooshed under the weight of the man who might be confusing her with the pillow in his arms.

Setting it on the dresser where the TV was, she wandered to the bathroom when the full-length mirror caught her eye. Her hand slid over her belly, smooth, only a small paunch that could be hidden most days and required her to slouch to make it appear. Stepping back into the room, she snatched a throw pillow from the settee and returned to the mirror. Stuffing the pillow over her belly and under her shirt, right at her hips, and stood sideways.

The vision was unsettling, and she tossed the pillow across the tile floor. She and Conner had been together for nearly a decade, but their life wasn't missing a thing. There wasn't a huge call to create another human being. Bethany may be selfish, but so was Serena, in a way. Her heart wasn't sure she could handle what Wilmarie was going through with Derian.

Right now she was feeling the crush of the poor child's future and she'd barely spent a day with him. If he had been her child, she wouldn't know what do to with herself. Would she be crumpled in a ball sobbing? Or would she be planning a daring escape? Running to a lawyer was one thing, but actually having to save her own child? The thought sent a chill down her spine and her body jerked like she was having a seizure.

She wasn't ready or willing to add to the Earth's population. That was for the Auntie Olivia's of the world. The ones whose hearts were pure and sweet. Who like to spend time on cold mornings building a fort or evenings coloring the sunset with a girl who insisted the sky was green, purple, and had polka dots. A mother shouldn't be the one coloring the sky that way and daydreaming of saving people who've been wronged.

Hours of watching the grainy video had done nothing, beyond giving her a headache and moving the moon outside the window. The sun would be up in a few hours.

There wouldn't be an early run on the beach for her and Conner today, but now she thought more about Patrick lying in the sand. His body slumped in the way it was and more importantly his face concaved, with blood pooled around what was left of his nose.

The attack couldn't have happened hours before he was found. There was no way that animals, especially the wild dogs and cats, while tame enough to approach a tourist, they would have been gnawing on the freshly beaten man. All night long the animals wandered onto the resort but were shooed out by any staff member. While the face was destroyed, it hadn't been devoured. A blood pool would take a long time to dry, but none of the splatter seemed to have been hardened or congealed.

"Patrick was killed while we were on our run!" Serena exclaimed, covering her mouth quickly and peering around the corner to see Conner hadn't stirred.

Timing wise they'd spent about thirty minutes max, he may have been killed a bit before then. Had she passed him? Her brain tripped along slowly, but her focus was on Conner. This had been time for them. She wasn't searching out a good location or getting lost in finding a local special spot to shoot. Working or not, they found time for each other. She might as well be a horse with blinders in a parade, being marched by Conner.

Walking toward the stand with the TV, she saw a figure, no, an object, entering from the edge. It was the rolling luggage Patrick had, she remembered thinking that the shape was odd. Like a jet pack, angled in at the top. She had wondered if it had a zipper or was it touch controlled. Pressing start on the video, the luggage moved and when it was at the edge of the faux sand the extension handle was lowered. The man, no the boy carried it by the smaller grip as he walked across the sand. His head glancing back to make sure he's not caught. Was she looking at Darian? It had to be.

Once by the stairs, he passed the luggage off to someone below. Then Derian crosses over the sand, making his way back to where she assumed his mother was prepping for breakfast. It wasn't him sneaking a friend on the resort, it was his theft of the bag. Shaking her head, she carried the laptop over to the settee and sat. Replaying the action, wondering where Patrick was. This was hours after he was supposed to have been kicked out of the room by Emma.

Why would his bag still be around? More importantly, who did Derian pass the bag to? Mr. Ruiz was right, this wasn't America. Going to see Derian in jail wouldn't require an approved pass or an attorney. And when the sun was up, she was going to see Derian in jail. Until then, she would move the video ahead. She watched as others came to their posts. Using the rake on the faux beach. Cleaning up whatever had been blown onto the area.

There was no rush in the area. Even when it got to the point where she and Conner were crossing down to the steps. Their run set to start. Strange how large he was next to her. In a dark alley, she would be petrified if a man towered over her like he did, but never once did she fear the man.

Broad shouldered, biceps for days, even with his trim form. The years of basketball and other sports sculpted him into a statue she wanted to study, climb and do nefarious things with. Instead, they became best friends with benefits, making her wonder if the man, opposite to any she'd ever been attracted to, had made a deal with Cupid himself. Everything about Conner Love was in contrast to what and who she was. Maybe it was their ability to complement each other that was important then.

Her parents were like that. Her father was metered, calm, and patient. Willing to compromise, but not break his beliefs. Always willing to help others in need. Where her mother could be a bulldozer when necessary. Storming through life to make sure the world was the way her father needed it to be. Never taking credit publicly and allowing him to shine. Her quiet compassion was enough to make Serena wonder how big the woman's heart was.

Conner stretched in the bed, his feet dangling a bit off the edge before he curled on his side. She watched his side rise and fall with his breaths. How did she fit in bed with that man? She curled into him. That was how. Lying next to him so most nights she couldn't tell where he ended and she began.

Waking with a hard jolt, Conner pawed for his laptop in the empty bed. His brain reminded him that he was supposed to be watching a video and the last thing he remembered was heavy eyes he couldn't stop from closing. Then suddenly it was as if he were trying to bench four fifty and his arms were lowering faster and faster until the bar was across his throat. Choking him as the man set to spot him laughed.

The laughter was what woke him. Panic setting in as the pressure on his Adam's apple caused him to choke and struggle to gulp air through a constricted opening. Above him, the shorn head of a man watching, but not helping, as Conner tried to shift the bar to his chest or unevenly press with his right arm. The fire from burning muscles, tendons, and ligaments was all fighting a fruitless battle of will as the oxygen depletion made darkness touch the edges of his eyes. Vision focused on one face, the one above him, the one that was supposed to be spotting him, and more importantly the one who tossed a few extra plates on the ends of his bar.

He couldn't get words out, if he could they would be choice curse words. Instead, he used what little strength he still had left in his tank to roll the best he could to the side only to barely move an inch. Anything to shift the bar away from his throat and soon others in the weight room noticed the struggle. The words being yelled were tunneled and distant. When the bar rose, the first hard inhale of breath came with it as fire burned through his starving lungs like tissue paper being lit.

Ronnie, a teammate, had shoved his spotter to the side and was helping Conner sit upright so he could find his breath again. Two other guys had lifted the bar and placed it on the hooks that held it up, and the coach came over.

Words were being barked in Russian or Latvian or some other former Eastern block country's language. The coach's tone was unmistakable as his spotter, a newer player on the team argued a point.

"Weak American," his new teammate spat. The man was a center, with the same long arm issue Conner had.

The shorter person's arm made it so they could throw up hundreds of pounds a dozen times, but Conner knew his body. His arm length made the four hundred and fifty pounds more to him. Lifting it three to four feet up verses two, to two and a half. Athletes understood this and adjusted accordingly. This man with a wingspan of close to seven feet should know this. Even with the thick biceps and stock body. The man was a good five inches taller than Conner, that's why they had been paired by the training staff together. No other player was close to the man's height.

Maybe it was the lack of oxygen, the watered-down alcohol of the last few days, or mix of travel convoluting his brain and making it so he couldn't remember the man's name. All he could recall was the guy was traded or cut the next day after only being part of the team for less than a week. The new man had been under the delusion he would be the starting center when he showed up. Even with the height difference, Conner could still beat him on the tip and he wasn't giving up the starting spot just because the man could block most shots without jumping.

A high-pitched screech of metal was followed by the shower spray turning off. Jarring him into the here and now. The Dominican Republic, a resort, and his wife would be coming out of the bathroom in a towel and bonnet to protect her hair soon. Still, the bothersome thoughts of this 'teammate', barely an acquaintance, who he only remembered because when he thought he was going to die, the man's hard jawline and piercing gray eyes were sharpened in his mind. As if killing Conner would earn him a starting spot and not a jail cell. The twisted sociopath might have gone on to have a career on another team, Conner didn't know since he had retired at the end of the season and married Serena. Now he'd need to search files to get the name of the guy. Or send a few texts to the teammates he had stayed in touch with that might remember him. Huey asked if he had any enemies, this was the only man he could see as that angry. Could he hack? That was something they would have to investigate.

"Oh, you're up, good, get dressed," Serena said as she crossed to the luggage and dug out a pair of clean panties.

Shimming them up her legs and under the towel she had wrapped around her chest. Unhooking the tuck at her breast, she pulled a top out and slipped it over her head. Braless, the deep plunging V of the top landed a few inches above her navel. Her breasts draped by the gauzy material, with a quick tug of shorts, she buttoned them at her waist and then released her long locks from the silver bonnet she'd worn in the shower to keep her hair from getting wet. Strange the behaviors one got used to over the years. The little eccentricities he knew and now watched with fascination over the years. Simple things, like the shower cap he had always been confused by over the years, now made perfect sense. The way his wife would apply lotion to her legs, feet, and arms. At times, even applying the cream over her belly when he never thought of anything but hands needing a layer of moisture to avoid cracking. Did all husbands marvel at the extra time and care their wives put into themselves, or was he the only one?

"Hello, Earth to Conner," she said, clapping her hands. "You with me?"

"Yes, always, sorry, I was—"

"Distracted, I heard the whimper, and I promise, after we go to jail and talk to Derian we can make time to practice making babies we're not about to create."

"Whimper? Again? Damn," he said, shaking his head and crawling out of bed. "I really am a simple man."

"Yes, but it makes it easy on me," Serena said, her right foot on the chair as her hands glided over her calf, turning her skin from smooth to shimmering from the lotion.

Making his way to the bathroom he took care of business and then rubbed his stubbled chin. The light beard came in evenly for once, maybe he was growing up. When he was a teen ,the broken patchiness of it made him shake his head in frustration.

"No time," Serena called from the other room as if she knew he was contemplating taking time to shave or not. "I'm leaving with or without you."

Knowing his wife, there was no chance of stopping her from going solo, so he gave up any attempt. He'd shave before the wedding, between now and then there would be no time unless they found the video showing Patrick being killed. Resigned, he stepped out of the bathroom and was greeted by his wife holding a pair of shorts, underwear, and a t-shirt. He may wear the pants in the relationship most days, but Serena did pick them.

"I called a driver," she said. "And my father has already contacted the local ambassador to get us the case information."

"How long was I asleep?" he questioned, glancing at his phone that said it was only a little after seven.

"Too long. By the way, I saw Derian stealing Patrick's luggage. Or someone's," she said after they left the room. "But I watched until we came back up after Patrick was found dead and he didn't go down the stairs."

"Then how did he get there?" Conner asked as they moved toward the front of the resort. The manager watched them with a disapproving look on his face as they moved into the waiting car.

"I reviewed the resort passport, and there are twelve places to get down on the beach. Depending on which part of the resort you're staying."

"Did you sleep?" he asked, noticing she was speaking very quickly, which tended to happen when she had slipped past the exhausted state and moved into the manic lack of sleep.

"Yeah, no, but I did find the videos and gave the guys directions."

"Directions? Huey and Joey I assume?"

"Yes, I gave them points of reference images so they knew

who and what they were looking for in the video." Her eyes were wild and her hands were flying, moving like she was creating shadow puppets of the email or discussion she had with the two men.

"Who gave you caffeine?" he questioned. "Or was it straight jet fuel?"

"I was thinking about Patrick's face," she said, her fingers joining together to create a circle. "His nose was fine."

"Was it now?" he said.

"Yes, and have you ever seen a rock with a perfectly concaved spot in the middle?"

"In a cave," he said and she had a full-body shiver. Tight places weren't exactly her favorite, especially when they were dark and she couldn't see the way out. "But it was underneath a stalactite that had probably been dripping for centuries."

"And was big right?" she reasoned. "Too big for someone to grasp and smash into someone's face."

"Yeah, I guess so."

"What have we seen with openings like that around the resort?" she questioned.

"Ashtray?" he said with a shrug then realized that was at a place in Malaysia they had visited. The ones here were black and had the opening to toss your butts in to extinguish them. "No, that's not right. At least not in our area."

"Even when we wander through the resort, that's a no. But we do need to figure out what has that shape. I doubt a bowl would do that type of damage," she replied. "Besides, it would have smashed into a dozen pieces."

"Unless it was metal? Or rock."

"You see any of those?" she questioned, then her brows knitted together. "Wait, I did. It was like a pharmacist uses."

"A mortar and pestle?" he questioned.

"The bowl part," she replied. "Wasn't our guacamole served in one last night—wait two nights ago."

Once again, her lack of sleep had the days melding together in her mind and he would need to break down her timeline for her at some point. Right now, he was just trying to keep up with her racing brain.

"So someone stole the guacamole bowl and killed Patrick with it?" The idea of it had Conner's brain tripping over the unlikeliness of the whole idea. While the mortar could be palmed, it was a force thing. The necessary power to reach a velocity, even with rage powering it, was astronomical.

"Kaitlynn was coveting that dip the first night." Serena's eyes were narrowing and her lips became thin.

"Yes, and I worried you were going to take her out if she didn't unass the bowl."

"There are few things in the world you cannot be a glutton with," she replied. "I can, but others can't unless I've gotten my share."

"How did I not lose a finger that day in the bakery?" he mused and received a backhand to his chest.

"You're lucky you're cute," she replied as they pulled up outside the prison.

Their driver eyed them in the rearview mirror as if they were crazy. Maybe they were. Who comes to a foreign country with beautiful beaches and instead visits a cement-walled jailhouse with barbed wire circling the top? Tourists were supposed to stay oblivious to the crime and dark places of a resort town. Even if the town had over a hundred thousand people, they were supposed to pretend living close to water made it impenetrable to the bad that happens in other places. Much like his hometown. Small, isolated, and in a bubble. More like small, isolated with the residents wearing a bubble to block out what was happening right around them.

"You want I stay close?" the thick Spanish accent of their driver with kind eyes and knowledge of the city allowed him to sympathize.

"Not sure how long we're going to be," Serena said. "I would hate for you to lose fares."

"It's early," he said, holding up his phone. "Pings not too much."

"Thank you," she replied as they slipped from the backseat onto the sidewalk. "If you can."

The man nodded, but drove away, possibly to a nearby neighborhood or restaurant.

"Hopefully he's staying close," she said, then turned to see the line-up of people outside of the gate. The shift in her mood hurt his heart. Yes, they'd be standing in line for a while, but that wasn't what made her eyes sad.

"You okay?" he asked as they made their way to the back of the line.

"There isn't a suit among us," she said, glancing at the line in front of them. "This is family trying to see a loved one."

"Maybe the lawyers are all in the courtroom," he replied, hoping to help ease her discomfort.

The line moved quickly, but when they got to the front part of him crept into unease. Security was tighter at the resort. All you had to do was sign in and the guard called the inmate. No one took their phones or even checked the cross-body purse Serena wore. Families were sharing meals at the tables with prisoners dressed in street clothes. Guards ignored or didn't care about what might be passed. Although only plastic utensils were being used, that didn't mean anything. Those could be sharpened and weaponized.

Sitting at the round, plastic coated and wired table, he could imagine they were sitting outside of a Dairy Queen in the summer, if only there wasn't the loud noise of men crying out. Yelling at people behind the gate where, after ten minutes, Derian exited from. Still wearing his school uniform. Hair, mussed and greasy. No longer sporting the Cheshire cat smile on his now split lip.

His eyes scanned the tables in search of who might have come to see him. Passing the Loves, he then bounced back, hope blooming in his lost eyes. The guard pointed toward their table and Derian followed the directions. His already slight frame, near skeletal now. As if more than hope had left his body in the last twenty-four hours. Had he given up once inside? Or had someone destroyed him on his first night behind the iron bars? The innocence of youth lost from a trauma no one should face. Tossed away without so much as a second thought, his life gone before it even began.

"Derian," Serena said, reaching out her hands to his.

His knuckles had cuts and were purpled. None were displaced at least, but the kid had been defending himself. Conner wondered if it was from the other prisoners, guards, or the police. No matter who, they needed to help the teen before he was lost forever.

"We got you a lawyer," she said. "Has he been by yet?"

Derian shook his head.

"Do you know why they think you killed the man?" Conner asked and fat tears welled at the bottom of the boy's eyes. Catching on his thick lashes like a wave held back by sand, not being allowed to return to the sea.

"I stole his bag, that's all," Derian confessed and the tears broke through the dam holding them back. "His phone too, but it was on the bag. I shouldn't have done it. I know, but I didn't hurt him. He was fighting with this girl and got distracted."

"Why were you there so late?" she asked. "I saw you passing the luggage to a friend."

"You did?" Conner asked.

"Yes, sleepy head. I did," she rebutted. "Closer to sunrise."

"I took it earlier and hid it in the kitchen. Mama always makes me come with her to open up the kitchen and take the bus to school from the resort, so I knew I could get the bag before she saw."

"And you passed it off to your friends, right?" Serena asked.

"Yes, there is a shop in town with used items, but—well it's a cover, yes that's what you call it," he said. "We get things from tourists—"

Derian glanced around at other tables with men and boys close enough to get him in trouble.

"All I did was steal a bag. The man wasn't even paying attention. The girl wasn't letting him come up the stairs. His bag was at the bottom and he was trying to force her."

"What building?" Conner asked. At least they'd be able to see the CCV coverage if they knew where to look on the property.

"The Palms, building sixteen."

"That explains why he didn't go down our stairs," Serena said. "That's the next set of buildings over with their own steps. We walked past them on the way home last night."

"Do you know if he ever noticed the bag was gone?" he asked. "And what time was this?"

"Eleven or so, maybe later. I tend to wander a bit," he replied. "My mama works days, but everyone knows me at the resort. I'm like a mascot, I grew up there."

"And no one thinks you would steal anything?" Serena asked.

"Steal? Probably, but only a few say anything," he replied with an honesty Conner hadn't expected. "Besides, people lose lots of things on vacation and if I take an expensive pair of sunglasses, they'll go to the gift shop and buy another pair."

"The natural balance of things," Conner replied, thinking of the animals in the wild that allow smaller ones to travel on them. Helping them migrate in return for them cleaning off other parasites. Only he wondered about the shop Derian spoke of. The circle might be larger than the kid thinks. Those in place could be giving a kickback to the staff at the resort. Everyone allowing just enough to be stolen to not get a bad rep.

"And now you're getting blamed for something bigger to close out the case." Serena leaned back a bit and crossed her arms. "I am so sorry, Derian."

"On the beach, when you saw us," Conner began. "Why did you run?"

"A man was dead," Derian said as if it were an obvious reaction. "I don't know you, not really. And after what people have been saying about me—"

"The only person we believed was Carlos." Conner could see the boy lighting up and Conner wondered if anyone beyond his mother and Carlos had believed in him before.

SIXTEEN
WE'RE FAR FROM CELEBRITIES

"Mr. Ruiz should be coming by to see you," Serena assured. "Tell him what you did. Even the stealing. Especially the part about you getting on the bus at six thirty."

"What would that matter?" he asked, the naivete of a young boy who didn't understand the forensics, she hoped the coroner did. Lividity, blood loss, rigor mortis. All the things that help with timing.

"Trust me, it will."

A guard walked past the table, his gaze cutting down to the Loves.

"We need to go," Serena said, even with her heart aching from the thought. "Conner and I will be reviewing a few things on our own."

"Where's the store you talked about?" Conner asked, and a chill went down Serena's spine.

"It's at the edge of downtown. Right before the locals' section starts." Derian found the spot on Serena's phone and she entered the address into the ride-share app.

Their driver was less than three minutes away and she stood, hugging Derian tight. "Everything is going to be okay."

"If you see my mama, tell her I'm good."

"We will," Conner said, ruffling the kid's hair before a guard came by, snapping at them in Spanish to break apart.

Serena let go, leaving a piece of her with the kid as they were escorted out of the building. Her body tensed from the loud bang of the gates closing behind her. Wiping at her cheeks, the wetness warm as her tears stung the edges of her eyes.

"It's not right. That kid is too damn little to take out Patrick."

"What about his friends?" Conner asked. "We can't count them out. Or say there wasn't involvement. Yes, he got on the bus to school, but then was off it and back at the resort a few hours later."

"I want to shake that kid and say why," she howled as their driver approached the curb and parked.

"You really want to go there, missus?" he asked as they slid into the backseat.

"Yes," she replied, clicking the seatbelt across her lap. "You know it?"

The driver's eyes cut up to the rearview mirror. "They take something of yours?"

"Not really," she replied. "A friend's."

"Expect to pay triple to get it back," he replied, pulling away from the curb. "Being, what? American?"

"What if we told the police it was stolen?" Conner questioned, and the driver let out a laugh.

"They know it's stolen. Even the boxes they pretend their goods come in are stolen." The driver shook his head. "Are you going to want me to stick around again?"

"Maybe," Serena said, feeling they had found the driver version of Carlos.

"Here's the deal, go in, get your stuff and keep it close next time. Little hands are all over the city ready to lift your property."

"What else do little hands do around the city?" Conner asked. "We've heard tell of violence."

"Oh, there's plenty of that too, but not really for tourists," he explained. "Gangs are here too. This spot is run by the traficantes de muerte."

"Death dealers?" Serena translated. "Why would Derian be involved with a gang like that?"

"You think people have choices," the driver said. "Single parent, both parents, doesn't matter. School, no school. Neighborhood. All of it creates a situation that pulls the kids into a wicked place at times."

"You have kids?" Conner asked.

"Yes," he replied. "We live in the country, the only way I could keep them safe. Drive into the city, work this job, and hope when they are old enough they stay at home. Some get out. I did."

"Before or after you joined a gang?" Conner questioned, his hand protectively wrapping around Serena's alerting her to the possible danger she'd been oblivious to before then.

"Before. My mother moved me out when she saw them coming for me," he said.

"How dangerous is this group?" Serena asked.

"The name is like a dog that barks," he replied. "Warning others, but a good scratch behind the ears will make them your best friend."

"Good thing you got your nails done," Conner said.

Unlike other shops, no man was sitting with an AR-15 or shotgun in the doorway. The door, thinner than a conventional one, was open wide. Worn wood had flaking, mint green, paint showing it had previously been yellow and any wood was now gray with age. Tile, with cracked grout that was missing in spots. Unlike most of the stores, this one had a front window displaying random items. None of them sunburnt, showing either care was taken to rotate items frequently or items sold at a high rate of return.

The faster they moved, the less of a chance for a tourist to press charges. Although the sign outside the building showed the tell-tale sign of a pawnshop with the gold bar with three gold balls dangling from it, she doubted people pawned much, considering all the resorts along the coast. If they did, there was no 'where did you get it' question and the way Derian described the place he was to bring items for a leader. Was it protection or actual cash he was given for his task?

"Hello," the man behind the counter said as they entered.

Shelves full of a myriad of items. Along one wall clothes hung on hangers in sections, male, female, kids. Random sizes all vacation wear for sure. Otherwise, the shop was like any other pawn shop she'd been in around the world. Electronics, jewelry, DVDs, and musical instruments. All of which were near pristine condition. On a bottom shelf, the jet pack style rolling luggage sat front and center.

"Is there anything in particular you were looking for?"

"A phone," Conner said, then took his phone out and dialed. In a glass case, a phone vibrated and rang with a harsh beep. "That one will do."

"This one?" the man said, taking the phone out and silencing it. "Is not for sale."

"But it's on display," Conner countered and two young men, in their early twenties, came from around the counter, having been sitting in a way to be invisible.

"A mistake," he replied. "As you can see, I work with young men still needing to be trained."

"Like Derian?" Serena questioned, stepping up with little fear. A habit she had that annoyed her father only slightly less than her husband. Of course, when you have a six-seven man willing to kill for you, you tend to make the move more than you did as a child. "Because your little runner is now locked away."

The man's face stayed statue still. Unmoved by the name he should recognize.

"About fourteen, his mother works—"

"Fourteen is much too young for me to work with," the man stated plainly. "Child labor laws, though manufacturing and tradespeople tend to hire them. I believe children need time to mature."

"The phone was a friend of ours," Conner interjected. "He was killed yesterday on the beach by our resort."

"Accidents happen when you don't know the terrain."

"We don't think it was an accident," Serena said. "And you've got his phone. How did that happen?"

"This phone?" he questioned, holding it up. The movement made the screen bright, showing an oval with JETS emblazoned on it. "We were holding it for someone. This is a pawnshop. That's why the number still works."

"Yeah, I don't think so," Conner said, stepping up to the counter. "The man who was killed isn't really a pawn his property type of guy. None of our group is."

Serena stepped behind Conner, her hand on his waist, but completely aware of the men less than two steps away from her.

"Drugs, sex, even the wealthiest man could have his weakness. Maybe trying to keep up with those around him. Especially if none of them are a pawn type." The man set the phone on the counter. "Now, if you had his claim ticket, you could rescue your man's phone."

"Seeing as he's dead, he won't be coming back," Conner said, then glanced over his shoulder to the man behind him. "You think I have a purty mouth?"

The southern drawl was poorly executed by her husband, but the man behind the counter raised his hand making the enforcer step back.

"Derian's being charged with this man's murder," Serena pleaded. "In that phone, there could be answers to who actually did it. If fourteen is too young to work for you, then you should know it is too young to be in an adult prison."

The man spoke in Spanish to the man behind Serena, unaware she understood every word.

"Derian, is he our in at Cofresi?"

"Yes." The man behind her was solemn. "He didn't say anything about killing a guy, but Jorge said he saw him being arrested."

"That street rat couldn't strangle a chicken if he was starving. You

197

really think he could kill a grown man?" The man behind the counter shook his head. "Him being arrested meant anything he gave us needed to be in the back. How many times do I have to explain this to you?"

"You're right," Serena said. "Derian didn't do it."

The man froze again. His attempt to keep her from the conversation by speaking a foreign language thwarted.

"Your Spanish is good. And here I thought U.S. teachers couldn't do it justice."

"They can't, but I learned on the streets of Honduras, at least more than the immersion school I was in."

"You're Hispanic?"

"American, but my father is an ambassador. Which means, you may have a deal with the cops, but they don't want to be embarrassed on an international level."

"Maybe we should make sure they aren't notified," the man said and Serena's arms were grasped from behind.

Her heart rate spiked. With her left foot, she stomped backward on the man's foot and jerked her right arm forward. Not hard enough to pull free, but she knew to bend her elbow and angle to let the man's own strength help in the hard thrust to his solar plexus. Bony elbows were a benefit as they practically stabbed the man's gut, making him cough as air was shoved from his lungs from the contact.

When the hands released her, she spun on her heels and used the palm of her hand to smash the man's nose. Blood spurted as he fell backward into the shelves sending merchandise tumbling to the floor. When he tried to regain his composure and come for her, Conner stepped between them and pressed his hand into the center of the man's chest.

"Hold up, cowboy, or I'll let her keep kicking your ass," Conner said. "We're offering to pay for the phone. Not demanding it for free."

The man behind the counter called his goons back in Spanish and the one with the misshaped nose glared at Serena as he passed. Fists balled, but not willing to cross the man behind the counter.

"Apologies," he said as the men melted into their respective corners once again, making them damn near invisible like when the Loves entered the store. "My English is not good sometimes."

"I think your English is just fine," Serena said, stepping to the counter and pointing to his hand. "The phone."

"Yes, this is the latest model, like you said, your people are the type to have the latest and greatest aren't they."

"They are," she said. "And his clothes, suitcase and whatever else you have in this store we won't claim as stolen. Sell at will, but that phone I want."

"You have a nice one," he said, eyeing her latest iPhone. "How about a trade?"

Ten minutes of haggling like a nomad trader, mixed in with a few threats from the princess status she held allowed her to get the phone. A few hundred U.S. dollars shorter than she'd wanted to pay since it was a stolen item, but she knew if she called in the police they would take the phone into evidence and that she didn't trust. They needed to see what was on it and bring it to Mr. Ruiz, if it could help Derian.

The last thing the police wanted was a reason to reopen the open and shut case that they could explain as a random act of violence when they presented the case to the Americans. The statistic added to the travel blogs, showing a murder occurred but justice was served with swift efficiency.

Stepping out of the shop, she called for a driver and soon their regular guy pulled up outside.

"Where did you get Patrick's number from?" Serena asked as they slipped into the backseat.

"Really?" he questioned, his face pinching a bit. "Huey, Josh, you think that wasn't dropped in my messages hours ago?"

"Maybe I should have slept." Serena shook her head at the obvious clue she'd missed.

"I'm thinking that spike in adrenaline should get you through the hours of video we'll have to review again."

"Any chance the guys sent you his passcode?" Serena asked as she stared at the screen with a keypad requesting a code to enter. "Six digits that could take—"

The phone vibrated and rang in her hand. Her finger glided across the glass to answer Conner's call, unlocking the phone with a simple swipe of her finger.

———

Some phones required a code or fingerprint to answer, but Patrick had seemed like the type of guy who didn't have time to bother. Why take the extra step? Or more than likely, he didn't even consider doing more because his phone rarely left his hand. Always within reach, as if pickpockets feared him and those in his office wouldn't dare touch the electronic.

The man had a handful of apps, nowhere near the amount Conner and his friends had. And this psycho had a folder with all his travel apps in one. Conner hadn't even created one for his own games, let alone a one-click to stop to all the major airlines, car rental, and hotel chains. At first, Conner believed the man had to travel extensively until he opened a few and saw the man had barely enough miles or points to make it from New York to Hoboken.

Serena was the one who managed all of theirs. Even with her love of the off the beaten track places she still made sure mileage, room stays, and rentals were granted points. If they pulled up and she saw a loyalty program, she downloaded and created an account as if they would never use another company. Everything was managed fully and allowed for a few extra upgrades over the years.

"Kaitlynn was dropping photobombs on him from before the airport," Serena said as she scrolled through messages. "At first it was all girls just wanna have fun, but if you zoom in you can see Joey in the background of every picture."

"That one isn't in the background," Conner said as they saw a smiling Emma with an iced coffee in one hand, her leg crossed toward Joey who was fully engaged in a conversation with the woman. "Or the five after it."

"You think this caused the blow-up at the airport?"

"Maybe," he said, helping her scroll through the images and they both paused. The image intimate, Joey's face was buried in Emma's neck as her hand wrapped around to stroke his cheek. Holding the man closer with her eyes closed. "But I'd be making a call if I saw a picture of this."

"Kaitlynn upped her game," Serena said. "The man wasn't responding."

"No, this is a story," Conner said. "See the timestamps for arrival. She basically made a flipbook for him."

When they pulled up outside the resort, Conner slid their driver a few fifties as a tip for being willing to watch out for the two of them. He knew Serena would be putting a tip on the app she was using, but the man went above and beyond for them.

"Hey, save my profile, maybe I can help you later," the man beamed, tucking away the U.S. bills into his shirt pocket.

"There were a few choice words between him and Kaitlynn," Serena said, still lost in the story unfolding between the bridal party members. "More from her, she knows how to trigger the man."

"Let me guess, calling out his manhood or lack thereof."

"Pretty much," she said. "Also—"

"Excuse me," the current manager on duty called to them as they were crossing the lobby.

"Yes," Serena replied, and tucked the extra phone away in Conner's oversized pocket. A habit she'd picked up years before.

"I was just informed you two are Serena and Conner Love," he said, the smooth, smarmy tone of an overly excited person that would have Serena recoiling in less than a minute. "We did not realize your celebrity status."

"We're far from celebrities," Serena assured and attempted to step away when the man reached for her hand.

Conner took a step back just in case Serena decided to twist the man's hand upward and flip him on his back. There was always a possibility when it came to her and unwanted contact. The only saving grace for this man was her worrying about her vlog. Trolls come in all forms and even with Conner's skill at vaporizing them, it didn't mean they couldn't do damage first.

"Please don't." Serena's smile was syrupy sweet, but her eyes were death rays.

"My apologies," the man said.

"Why am I hearing that so much today?" she questioned. "Maybe because too many people think they can take liberties with me."

"Serena, my love, you need to change your shirt. I see a bit of blood by the hem," Conner pointed out hoping to intimidate the man who'd approached them.

"So there is. That man was grabby too, wasn't he?" she beamed, the pride in her ability shining through her cattail brown eyes.

"We were wondering if you were highlighting our resort?" the man asked. "You haven't taken your tour, but I could arrange for a private one."

"At this point no, we are here for a wedding," she said. The man's face blanched. "Yes, that wedding, with that guest."

"I want to assure you—"

"Don't," she replied, holding her hand up to stop him. "As much as a private tour would be interesting, the most we would be interested in would be your security feed."

"Why is that?" he questioned, distancing himself a bit further.

Conner reached for her upper arm and pulled her aside. "You know we have all the videos," he said.

"Yep, and we have no idea what file number is what," she

pointed out. "He wants something I want something. I don't want to sit in our room all day looking through hundreds of angles, especially in stairways that have zero difference from twenty others. This way, we can cut out hours and get to the meat."

Conner shook his head, exhaustion in his wife's eyes and still her brain was firing twenty levels above him. At times he believed they shared the same brain, their minds so in sync sentences didn't even need to be finished because the thought flowed between them like a well-knitted scarf. Then there were times like this when he wondered if the yarn was unraveling and she was gathering it into a ball to reinsert later when he could handle the information.

"Derian said he was a mascot here," she stated as they walked back to the manager. "But you had no problem throwing him away."

The manager, Alfonzo's face became drawn. "I've watched him grow up here."

"Then you know he isn't the type to hurt anyone."

"I've also grown up on the island. I know anyone can be pushed too far," he rebutted.

"A few minutes, reviewing a handful of videos couldn't be that big of a deal, could it?" she questioned. "You already know which pieces to review since you gave them to the police. I'm wondering about a few other parts. Now that's not too much to ask for, is it? Especially if it helps me see other features of the resort I might want to highlight."

The man waffled a bit.

"Did I tell you World Traveler Channel is in talks with me?" Serena teased and Conner could see no deception in her words.

Much like she wasn't part of Gaming Love he didn't do more than carry her stuff and take some videos for Love on the Run. This, though, she should have approached him about. At least shared the crazy insanely good news. He wasn't sure why the confession hurt his heart. It wasn't so much a betrayal, but tossing it out in front of another person when he wasn't the intended target had his eyes narrowing a bit. Trying to not let his face show his hurt, he crossed his arms and let out a long sigh.

"Follow me." Alfonzo led them out to the pool adjacent to the lobby.

"Hey Serena," Kaitlynn called, waving her hands in the air. The blonde had her hair pulled up in the type of messy bun that was supposed to appear haphazard, but he'd learned over the years rarely was.

The full bridal party was together and turned. He flashed back to their discussion with Katelyn the red the night before. Saying she didn't know which of the groomsmen the blonde was dating. It seemed as if the woman was flanked by Eric and Evan at all times. Maybe there was a little competition going on between the two men. The way they both were so accommodating to the woman.

"Come with us," Katelyn the red said.

Each member, including Don, were in wetsuits. Only Bethany and Yvette were in street clothes.

"It appears your friends are taking our scuba lessons," Alfonzo stated, switching back into salesmen mode. "We could pull up the videos you want and you could join them. Have you seen all the different activities we offer?"

"Yes," Serena replied, and cut her eyes at Conner. No matter the guarantees or the fact Alfonzo would practically wet himself if she documented the 'safety' of learning on the resort Conner wasn't willing to take that risk with his wife. It was more than their thoughts that were one in the same. There were many things he would take a chance with, but losing half of his heart wasn't one of them.

A few folded signs indicated the pool was closed. The pool was blocked off for guests taking certification tests in the water. Along the edge were canisters of air, and a table had all the equipment laid out for one diver. Plastic labels next to each of the pieces for those who were new to the whole processes.

"Don't you want to see the videos?" Conner asked, hoping his wife would move away from the temptation to dive into the deep end of the pool and make her way into the ocean at some point. "Besides, Love on the Run prefers the real to the staged. I know my wife, she'd be more drawn to real, not cherry-picked, adventures."

"Spoilsport," she admonished and slapped at his belly before calling back to the group. "Maybe another time."

"We could offer you an extra week at the resort, gratis," Alfonzo offered as they moved behind a locked gate where a small shack and other behind-the-scenes buildings were at. No longer perfectly painted and fresh in appearance. It was obvious that care and maintenance were reserved for the spots tourists would see.

"This is Nicolet," Alfonzo stated as the woman in the chair in front of a wall of screens turned in her chair. "She's our security manager on duty."

Nicolet's eyes widened a bit at what Conner could only assume was an in name only promotion from Alfonzo. The woman was in a starch white uniform top and black pants. On her shoulder was a patch for the resort with Security emblazoned across the logo. The gold badge embroidered on the left side of her chest held as much weight as Serena begging for access to the videos. No matter what any of them found, it wouldn't allow them the right to actually free Derian.

SEVENTEEN
WE HAVE A CERTAIN SET OF SKILLS

lfonzo left them with Nicolet, bringing in a few folding chairs before he did and giving her the instructions to show them what they wanted. What Alfonzo didn't understand was she knew about him prodding the security officer to make sure to accidentally pull up people having fun in various parts of the resort. Never before had Serena realized exactly how useful her bilingual abilities were. Especially when hidden. Over the years, there were times her mother had hoped she understood Chinese, Thai or Vietnamese so they could get the good stuff when ordering. While Serena had an ear for languages, the Asian post they had was in India. That only gave them both a yearning for a good mint sauce and love of curry in all the hundreds of flavors.

"Why didn't you tell me about the World Traveler Channel?" Conner asked after they sat down and gave Nicolet the building information about where they wanted to start at.

"I haven't even read the proposal really," she admitted with a sigh. "I'm not sure I want to give up the freedom of how we travel."

"But you don't know if you'd even have to."

"Exactly, so why say anything when I don't know the details?" she replied, watching the film skip.

"Because it was an offer," he countered and she turned to see a hurt in his eyes she hadn't expected.

"Your first big game sale, before you started Gaming Love, how close did you hold that to your chest?"

"That was different," he replied, and leaned back in his chair. "One time sale, it was about money alone."

"Okay," she replied with a sigh. "But it led to you creating Gaming Love."

"After the check cleared and the game hit number one in downloads and we realized I got shortchanged."

Her brows knitted together and her belly tightened. Had she been hiding the World Traveler Channel offer? To her it was so far on the back burner it was still in the fridge, but Conner didn't see it that way. Plus, why would she present a thing she didn't understand yet, she would be stumbling. Reading the offer to him at the same time she was to herself. The quick scan of the email didn't have a deadline, like they need to know by Friday or the end of the month. It was a random email probably sent to all the bloggers to see who would bite.

Sure, they'd pointed out a few of her trips individually, but the offer felt boilerplate and was tucked away. The most she did was star the email to circle back and review it if they ever had downtime. If it hadn't been for the murder, she would have looked at it this week. Maybe.

"Honestly, I barely glanced at the thing," she said. "And with that logic, I should ignore the thing fully and keep Love on the Run going by myself."

"Not necessarily," he said. "It would be nice to have a schedule, time off, instead of living each day as a vacation, but still working."

"What do you mean?" she questioned, the tightening in her belly turning into a fireball of fear. "I thought you loved the freedom."

"I do, and there's nothing better than finding an excuse to have you in a bikini a few days a week, it just..." he trailed off his eyes catching a sight of something on the screen that stopped him from finishing his train of thought. "That's not Emma."

Serena turned to see Kaitlynn standing at the first step, stopping Patrick from moving around her. He set his luggage to the side and physically moved her over. Shoving her against the wall and storming up the stairs with her recovering and chasing after him. Was she the one sharing the room with Emma? Could she have been the one keeping him away from her, not Joey? Derian said he was fighting with a woman and distracted. The security guard switched to the lower level video, and they watched Derian walk through, his hand sliding over the handle of the bag, then extending it before slipping out. At first, Nicolet switched the camera to follow the kid.

"No, we don't care about him," Serena said. "Follow the man going up the stairs."

Nicolet paused the video and her fingers clicked along the keyboard in front of her. Calling the next video onto the main screen, she moved it forward. Kaitlynn grasped his wrist and he spun around slapping her face. She stumbled to the steps, her hand covering her cheek with rage in her eyes, her mouth wide, obviously shouting out. Unease crept over Serena in the still and quiet of the security office as Patrick wrapped his fingers around Kaitlynn's throat. Her hands clawed at his wrist to pull it away. The moment passed in slow motion, even with the video playing at full speed. When Joey, Eric, and Evan came into the stairway, pulling him from her and slamming him into the corner as Kaitlynn lay gasping for air and being consoled by Emma.

"Was this shown to the police?" Conner asked and Nicolet paused the image. "Wouldn't pinning the murder on a tourist be better for public relations than a rogue band of teen thugs? Even with a quick arrest?"

"I'm supposed to show you the surveillance," Nicolet replied, not answering the question, pressing the spacebar to move the video along.

The men pulled Patrick past the women and down the stairs. Nicolet moved the video back to the main floor and Patrick pulled away from the men. Shucking them off and gathering himself. Pulling on his hat, smoothing his suit coat. Arguing with the men, blocking the stairway as if the elevator wasn't a few steps away and could get him to the floor he wanted just as easily. Recognition of his missing luggage, the space moments before Derian had smoothly slid by, capturing the handle as if it were calling him like a woman across a dance floor.

Patrick took off and Nicolet had to pull up another video, the breaks in between were worse than reality TV promos. The promise of a fight or some major revelation only to go to a commercial break and then come back to someone else's story-line. While she didn't want to slow down Nicolet in her retrieval of videos, she wanted to know why she wouldn't expound on Conner's question. There was violence and obvious hatred in that stairwell and the focus is on a young man stealing a carry-on bag. None of it made sense.

Nicolet followed the trail of Patrick chasing after Derian. The kid did leave out a few details, like he'd actually been caught for just a moment, but threw the bag over a wall. One he would have access to at some point in the day and Patrick wouldn't. The busted, bruised and cut knuckles might not be from the prison, but instead from the man tossing him around like the rag doll he was. Slight, underweight, but scrappy. At over six feet, Patrick couldn't chase after the kid who knew which bushes to disappear into and duck under. Getting away, Nicolet continued to focus on Derian and Serena covered the security guard's hand to stop her from moving forward on the video.

"Why are you showing us Derian, when there were three men ready to kill Patrick in the stairwell?"

The woman's eyes filled with tears, silently they slipped from the corners, her breath halting as if holding in the air could somehow stop time, take her to a new place and allow her the escape she so desperately wanted.

"You know him, don't you?" Serena asked, keeping her voice low and soothing.

"He lives in my building," she confessed. "His mother helped me get on here. Vouched for me. I catch him a few times and make him put stuff back. We joke, and play. He takes my daughter to the park to play if I get stuck working late."

"Very few seem to believe in how good of a kid he is," Conner added, hoping to coax the truth from the woman.

"More than a few," she said. "I know he skips school sometimes, but he always gets on the bus there and most days gets back in time to ride it home, well back to the resort."

"Is that because of your daughter too?" Conner surmised and Nicolet nodded her head.

"She's seven and didn't like the kids on the bus. There were bullies. At least until Derian started riding with her. In school, it's not so bad, but the driver doesn't care what is done to the kids."

"Why are you showing us Derian and not the men fighting with Patrick?" Serena asked again.

"People in the office have quotas, Alfonzo is big on pushing them," she began. "It's been a slow quarter I guess."

"You think scuba lessons are free with a timeshare?" Conner asked, and dread washed over her.

"Would they really toss Derian into jail for a couple of time-share contracts?" she questioned.

"Derian is young," Nicolet replied. "Charged as an adult, but our jails are near bursting. Ten years, maybe fifteen, a bit of money promised and he could be out early."

"That doesn't calculate," Conner stated, his eyes showing he was doing the math in his head like the matrix was downloading code.

"You took the tour, didn't you?" she asked, then her eyes widened. "No, you haven't yet. If you had I wouldn't have been asked to show you activities."

"We have a certain set of skills," Conner said. "A way of dodging salesmen."

"Or convincing them they are over charging if we can't move around them," Serena replied. "I'm notoriously cheap."

Conner gave her a slight nudge. "Besides, the rooms are nice—"

"Rooms? Those are for people coming through on a vacation," Nicolet explained. "Timeshare here is more than first dibs on the evening restaurant of your choosing."

"Why do I feel I'm about to get a sales pitch?" Conner asked.

"You're not," the woman assured. "But there are levels. Bigger rooms for those who will come a few times a year. Some stay for the three months their passport allows. Free access to activities and they enjoy the place where their beds are made and all their meals are free."

"I thought this wasn't a sales pitch?" Serena challenged.

"It's not." Nicolet stroked a few letters on her keyboard and pulled up the image of a house. "But there are villa-level packages. You pay a yearly fee, but the home is yours. It's not a room that might be different the next time you show up. Your family and friends can stay, just alert the management of the arrival and it will be cleaned. Have you seen people without wristbands?"

"Not that I noticed," Serena replied.

"Donald doesn't have one," Conner pointed out, rotating the plastic band on his wrist. "Never thought about it until now."

"Bethany does though," she replied. "But there's no way she's going to wear it for the wedding."

"Probably because her access will be granted to this part of the resort. Those who live there usually have a lanyard or key they flash. Some even own a golf cart to make getting around the place easier."

"How much are these houses?" Conner asked.

"Lowest, a simple two-bedroom is around two hundred and fifty thousand dollars," she said.

"That's not that bad," Serena said, tilting her head to the side and seeing fear in Conner's eyes that she was being sold on the place. "Cleaning, all you can eat food, made to order, year round."

"That's for the house," Nicolet stated, sending the spike of miserly bargain hunter off in Serena. "Then there's the yearly fee. Whether you come to the island or not."

"And with most of the people able to afford it aren't the ones to take vacations from their nine-to-fives," Conner said. "They can make a pretty penny on an empty house."

"What's the yearly fee?" Serena asked.

"Highest I've heard is three hundred thousand, U.S."

"That's one hell of a HOA." Conner let out a low whistle. "Even with the food costs."

"And liquor," Serena added, though she wasn't really sure it all washed out.

"You think Alfonzo or the resort would sell out Derian for a villa sale?" Conner asked.

"One?" Nicolet shook her head. "No, but two or three."

"It is hard to get out of those contracts," Serena pointed out. "That's years of paying money with little to no return unless you're free to travel. And those three don't seem like they get out of the city often."

"Four," Nicolet corrected. "The woman, the blonde, she bought a property too."

"Kaitlynn?" Serena questioned, the frozen image from her being comforted by Emma on a screen to the upper left.

"Yes."

"That's a lot of money changing hands," Conner thought. "But still, that snippet couldn't convict Derian. He was running away."

"That's not the one the police focused on." Nicolet's fingers clicked again and a new image, sunrise lighting up the sky in the background on a different set of cabanas.

One with a man waking from a night of sleep played. Derian walked along the bottom of the screen and soon the man was yelling. Taking off in the faux sand of a different set of cabanas and knocking Derian down. The teen gathered sand in his palm and tossed it in Patrick's face, making him stumble back far enough Derian could scramble toward a set of steps to the beach below. Patrick chased him with wild abandon.

"That's what is convicting Derian," Nicolet said as the video kept playing.

Serena prayed she would see Patrick, resigned, coming back up the stairs. Anything to prove that the kid got away, and the man was alive. At least long enough, Derian could have gotten on the bus. It did explain him standing over him at the beach. Trying to see if he recognized the man.

"What's that?" Conner said, pointing to an object abandoned on the cabana.

The shape was familiar and one Serena knew from the beach. Having blown to her feet, confirming Patrick's identity. He'd left his hat. The one he had on when he was killed. Or at least had near enough to him he caught the breeze having been removed from a caved in skull.

"If he left his hat, that means—"

Nicolet hit the fast-forward button, moving ahead twenty-five minutes, and an exhausted Patrick stormed up the stone stairs to the cabana. Pulling his hat on his head and leaning forward. Fingers steepled as if he were some villain in a B movie preparing a plan to get all who wronged him. When his head turned sharply to the side, his profile was unmistakable, jaw hard, rage boiling over, and not toward a now invisible Derian. He had made his way to the school bus by now. Patrick was looking at someone else. Someone who'd wronged him and was going to pay.

"You know it isn't Derian," Serena began softly. "Why not help him get out?"

"The contracts are signed, the checks cashed," she replied. "This job affords me more than a paycheck to feed my family."

"Timeshares can be canceled," Conner said.

"For many, they are resigned. It is not worth the hassle," Nicolet said. "And wouldn't you rather pay for a bit of paradise instead of a jail sentence?"

It made sense. Only one thing Alfonzo, Nicolet and the others weren't considering.

"Any contract can be broken. Especially one being reviewed by lawyers," Conner stated.

The video paused with Patrick stepping out of the frame. "Or people sleeping with them," Serena said.

EIGHTEEN
YOU'VE HAD NO SLEEP, SAW A DEAD BODY LESS THAN A DAY AGO

The time stamp let Conner know they had passed when he and Serena had gone for a run. Had the murder occurred while they were running? The window for when the murder occurred was slimming down to a near sliver.

"Where did he go?" Conner asked, assuming Nicolet would simply pull up a new view of a pool or bar, maybe. A path at the least. The property tended to meld naturally from one place to another in a seamless fashion to make one think a bush naturally surrounded a pool and there wasn't a wall on the other side.

Much like coming to this shack housing video equipment. The gate, though locked was like the old movie the Labyrinth where one would step forward not realizing there wasn't really a wall there before turning to find the latched gate and make their way to the building. The illusion was simple once you knew an opening was there, but nearly impossible to make out when one was wandering by. Resorts were like casinos, people allowed themselves a bit of disconnect and checking out of the realities of the world.

He took in his wife. The woman who had basically kept him balancing on the edge of complete disconnection. Bills were paid automatically, politics were fleeting at best, and more about the place they were visiting than the land they called home. Discovery was around every corner, keeping him engaged in a world brimming with life most miss. Growing up and even in college, if he wasn't in in a gym he would immerse himself in a first person video game even though a whole world with beautiful parks and trails was less than a stone's throw from his home. Missed opportunities for discovery in his youth now refused to him because even when they were at home, Serena would search out the neighborhood diners and hidden waterfalls in a metro area with the highest rank of parks per capita in the world.

True, at times, they saw the darkness, it was impossible not to when you wanted more than the tourist view of the world. But at the edges of sorrow were glimmers of light. Like waves cresting and capturing the sunbeams. Stepping out into the Caribbean and watching fish in bright rainbow colors swim past you. The bright colors reminded him of the IMAX movies when he was growing up.

Having bright colors filling more than the sky, but painting the streets and people around you during Holi in India. Or stepping out of a cozy cottage in Ireland to be enveloped in a sea of emerald green he didn't know outside of movies and photoshopped pictures. The permanent vacation, turned profitable was Serena's to control. He was along for a ride where he wasn't an Instagram boyfriend, taking a thousand shots to get the perfect image to share with followers. Conner was her partner, getting lost in moments and places. Between the two of them, missing a shot because they were engrossed in the actual event had become a danger, and why they had hired Josh beyond the need for additional editing help. To be the witness to the memories others might think tall tales because they could not even fathom a phenomenon so magnificent.

Patrick was murdered while they were on a run, enjoying sunlight, a soft beach and waves chasing them. If they would have turned up the first set of steps instead of moving past to see what Derian had been looking at and continuing their run, they could have avoided the whole mess. It would have allowed Patrick to be found by someone else while they simply wondered why he hadn't come down to breakfast with the others.

"There are blind spots," Nicolet's words caught him off guard and pulled him violently from the comforting thoughts. "Some due to poor planning, others come from damaged equipment or in this case none at all."

"Where is it?" Serena asked.

"This is close to the lobby pool." Nicolet pulled up the current activity to show only half of the pool was visible with the people taking the scuba certification class. "Since we can see into the lobby management doesn't worry about it. I did try to follow where the man went yesterday after the police left with their copy of the surveillance video. It hasn't set right with me, no matter how many villas your friends buy."

"What about the other side of the lobby?" Conner asked. "Does the camera show any part of the pool in the background?"

Nicolet's eyes widened and quickly she flipped to the lobby video. Rewinding the last twenty-four hours in record time. Early morning activities, management straightening and arranging flowers. Front desk clerks passing off keys and bringing covered cups of coffee in as they arrive at work. The children of staff gathering to get on the bus showing Derian holding a small girl, her hair pulled into two afro poofs, holding his hand and smiling up as he spoke some words to her.

At the very top corner of the screen, he could see the edge of the pool. Shimmers of sunlight flashing white on the water, gray in the black and white video instead of the stunning blue from the tiles beneath the water. Unlike the black blob being held back by the security guard on the videos they reviewed, he saw sets of legs. Clearly visible. Eight legs, four sets, three with shorts, tight to their legs and fourth in suit pants.

"Eric and Evan were in wetsuits when they were being interviewed by the cops," Conner said, staring at the legs. Wishing he could see more than a bit above the knee, and the lower legs of Patrick.

They weren't standing firm. No intimidating stance or a you're not crossing this line type of vibe. In fact for men who had him pinned to a wall and tossing him out of a stairwell the night before were now standing as if nothing was out of the ordinary. One of the sets of legs moved out of view while the other three went in the other direction.

"So Eric and Evan, do we assume the other one was Joey?" Serena asked.

"It wasn't Don or Abaeze," Conner reasoned from the light skin coloring. "Unless it was the instructor and that's why he left."

"Was Joey in a wet suit?" Serena asked.

"I don't remember. He didn't have a shirt on so maybe the top part was hanging down," Conner replied. "I suppose we could try looking at the breakfast area from our part of the resort. I really wasn't focused on that at the time."

"Joey, Eric and Evan," Serena said, letting out a sigh because if four went down and three came up they may never know if it was a combined effort or if one of them did the deed. "I'd say Kaitlynn too, but she was already spa ready."

"I'm sorry about Derian. He deserves better and if Mr. Espinal is here when he gets released I'm sure he will quickly offer him a job in recompense." Nicolet knitted her fingers together on her lap. "Wilmarie is heartbroken, her wails last night could be heard throughout our building. Even with the raise they gave her it won't be enough to cover for what Derian made on the side. She lost more than her child. In a few months, she could be destitute."

"You mean Detective Espinal has the power to give Derian a job?" Serena questioned.

"Detective?" Nicolet questioned, then shook her head. "Detective Mario Espinal is my manager's brother."

"Isn't that convenient," Conner said, his heart beating a bit quicker than it should as it raced in his chest.

Homeless, on the streets. Her son locked away. Having traveled outside of the usual tourist traps of the city, Conner had noticed the men and women in little more than rags. In contrast to his smalltown existence growing up, while they had the reality of a problem, a mix of social, political and environmental things made people tighten belts and move in with family members wasn't the same as what people faced here. While this problem existed everywhere, for him it was still as foreign now as it was to him initially. Much like when he was finding new things to eat or strange costumes to wear when they traveled it was a momentary shift for him.

Would Wilmarie be that woman? Crammed into a doorway struggling to sleep and not wake with every late-night noise around her? Stepping into the ocean as the only way to clean herself without fresh running water from the tap. A shudder tore through him at the delicate balance most of the world lived with, a paycheck or few dollars away from destitution.

"Thank you for your time. I'll let Alfonzo know you even shared the villa amenities with us."

Serena stood, and Conner followed suit. His eyes focused on the signs about the scuba class. "Is that every day?" he asked, pointing to the blocked-off pool area.

"No, yesterday's class got canceled because of the death," Nicolet said. "It was rescheduled for this morning. Not a big deal since we have over twenty-five pools, blocking out one, especially in the morning hardly goes noticed by most on the resort."

"Guess losing a co-worker doesn't mean you should have to give up scuba lessons," Conner said once they were away from the shack and making their way back toward the lobby.

Lunch would be served soon in the communal dining areas. There were a handful of them with buffets galore. He wasn't sure he could face Wilmarie at the one for their buildings, but Serena needed something to eat. They skipped breakfast and she hadn't slept. If nothing else, it would give them a place to sit and sort out what they had seen.

"You have that passport thing?" he asked. "Lunch is being served so let's find a place to eat."

"Probably a good idea to get something," she agreed, and dug the little map out of her purse.

Following the painted cement trail, they found their way to a large open-air dining area. Covered like a hut, but the size of a ballroom they made their way into the area and were seated, tucked away on the side of a wall. He watched as Serena let out a sigh, holding her plate with two hands, her nails making tinks as she drummed them underneath the porcelain disk while staring at the salad bowl in front of her.

Placing salad on his plate, he used the tongs to drop the basic mixed lettuce and carrot shreds base on her plate. Her head turned to glance up at him, thanking him with a nod, and he continued to pile on both their plates. Triple cucumbers on hers, extra cherry tomatoes on his. Shredded cheese, croutons, diced ham on both and some beets for him while his wife enjoyed a dollop of cottage cheese on the side of her plate. When they got to the dressing he, being a true Midwest boy, drenched the salad in ranch, Serena went for the Italian. The first movement of her own.

They'd go back through for the rest of the meal. She wasn't in a hurry to eat and this was a grazing type of meal. Their drinks were the only thing brought to them by servers, in between clearing plates from the table.

"Thank you," she said as she unrolled her silverware from the burgundy napkin before draping the cloth over her legs. "I can't believe I zoned out like that."

"Let's see, you've had no sleep, saw a dead body less than a day ago, had to deal with your family and be social on other people's terms." Conner knew triggers when it came to his wife.

Things that could pull her into a shell and hide away from the world. No matter how outgoing she appeared, deep inside she was the kid who didn't want to make a mistake to shame her family. Get her father in trouble or worse yet cause an international incident. He asked her once how many times had there actually been an international incident when she was growing up, not on her, but in general. Had her father been throwing up one thing after another where the world was a moment away from nuclear war because a child got bored and rolled their eyes at the man across from them?

Serena responded with an eye roll, making his point beautifully.

"Still," she said, stabbing at her salad to create the perfect bite of veggies mixed together. "Exhaustion I get, but the rest—"

"Adds to your exhaustion, plus you were breaking things down in your head."

"I was, a bit," she confessed and ate her forkful before covering her lips a bit with her hand, the fork balancing between the extended fingers. "Then I was thinking about the World Traveler Channel deal. I don't know why I didn't blurt it out when I saw it. Even to laugh at the absurdity of it all."

"Maybe because it wasn't really absurd?" he offered.

"Hello, my lovely daughter," Mr. Isola said as the hostess seated him and his wife. "Can we sit at this table here?"

The table across from them was open and also a two-top.

"That would be fine. Just don't push the tables together," the hostess said and returned to the front.

Mr. and Mrs. Isola hugged Serena in turn, then stared at Conner. At this point it was awkward to stand and accept a hug, he'd sat for too long and the normal feeling of being out of place washed over him. Standing, he shook hands with his father-in-law, then accepted a kiss on the cheek from his mother-in-law.

"I'm going to get our lunch plates," he said, hoping to escape the family bonding about to take place.

"I'll come with you," Mr. Isola stated, and the men moved back to the buffet area to take in the offerings. "My daughter trusts you to bring her lunch?"

"Not normally, but we've had a long morning and she had trouble sleeping last night."

"Aye, the young man from New York who was murdered?"

Mr. Isola questioned with a mournful look in his eyes. "Such a sad state of affairs."

"The local ambassador, he was willing to talk to you about the case?" Conner asked, a bit of hope blooming in his chest as he scooped rice onto both plates and Mr. Isola added the same to his own.

"She, Natalie, as much as possible. It is customary to have an autopsy performed by an American in these situations, but we do have the preliminary report. Blunt force trauma is the cause of death, of course."

The dark coating on the baked chicken mixed with the smell of spice looked good, so he placed a piece on Serena's plate and three on his own. Though he'd found the flavors a bit muted, with the aged population of guests wandering around the buffet, it made sense. This was a place one could retire to. The hotel-level buy-in would provide a nice getaway where one could be taken care of. Who knew, maybe the resort was part of a group where one could move from island to island, each spot offering a few months before the person's passport or visa expired.

Would that be the life Serena would search for decades from now? Buying in a few timeshares and living out their retirement, still traveling, but for longer stays? Or would retirement have them settling into their home, the one with mail piling up and the thermostat set in the mid-sixties, just warm enough so the pipes wouldn't burst in the winter?

"I've seen the booking picture of the young man who has been charged with the murder," Mr. Isola said, moving them toward the dessert table. An Isola trait passed down to his sweets-loving daughter. Conner wondered if the man only got the chicken and sides because he was following Conner's lead. There was a chance the man was only in search of the triple-layer berry-drenched slice of cake. "Who's to say if he is the type to kill."

"He isn't."

"Oh, you're who says this," Mr. Isola stated. "This explains why my daughter chased the sunrise to a prison and is currently paying for the young man's attorney."

"Kid's attorney. He is far from a man."

"Agreed."

"And we are both paying for the attorney. From our joint account," Conner stated, having not paid a dowry he wanted to make sure his father-in-law knew Serena wasn't footing the bill.

"I have seen a bit of the video, the young man did fight with your friend."

"Barely knew the guy," Conner leaned in a bit closer to the man whose head barely reached Conner's rib, unsure of who may be listening. "But Serena and I saw more video than what was given to the police."

"A cover-up?" Mr. Isola questioned, then tsked.

"One that could end this child's life before it even begins," Conner stated, and Mr. Isola let out a long sigh.

"We shall have lunch and then I will do what I can to help you. I've known Natalie for many years now. When she was younger, she was like Serena."

"Steadfast in her belief in justice?" Conner asked, navigating around other guests lost in their own search for food while he balanced two full plates and two dessert ones.

"No, she grew up in the service and understands, not only the ins and outs of being a diplomat, but the strong desire of a country to save face."

NINETEEN
JUSTICE IS SECONDARY TO PERCEIVED SUCCESS

"Natalie Meyer?" Serena questioned, remembering the friend who taught her how to slip from a security detail. "She's the ambassador to the Dominican Republic?"

Serena met Natalie on her father's first assignment as ambassador when she was six. Before that, in a way, she had grown up like any other kid in the states. Natalie, on the other hand, had been conceived in one country, born in another and by twelve had seen more of the world than most in a lifetime. Her mother had been the ambassador in Nepal when Serena's parents were in India. Proximity and formal functions meant they saw each other frequently.

Although she was a year younger than Serena, Natalie was mature, snuck drinks, and had boyfriends in most of the places her family had been stationed. Hero worship by the awestruck pre-teen didn't negate the utter disbelief that Natalie Meyer was representing the United States on foreign soil.

"Natalie Valdez now," her father corrected. They had moved to a four-top table at the edge of the dining area. Both her and her father still working on their cake as the staff cleaned up the now-closed dining area. It was the second slice for her father and the third for her. "While she agrees the facts of the case are not lining up as nicely as Detective Espinal would like one to believe at this point she's not ready to activate the FBI to take over the case."

"Would she be willing to listen?" Conner asked. "Review the evidence we found."

"I'm sure she would, but from what you two have described we now have three suspects, but only one with motive," her father stated, his head shaking from side to side. "Between that and the rash of mysterious deaths two years ago at the resorts of foreign nationals, we are in a delicate situation."

"Wouldn't proving the murder was not from the Dominican help their reputation?" Serena asked.

"Yes, and no," her mother replied, letting out a long sigh. "Because in their rush to close the case, it would now be seen as they bungled it horribly. Especially since you saw video of Patrick alive and well and after this Derian character leaves the resort."

"Egg on their face, big disgrace." Conner's melodic tone captured the momentum of *We Will Rock You* out of habit more than his initial desire to belt out Queen lyrics. "Sorry, Serena has shown me so many times over how justice is secondary to perceived success."

"World-wide," her mother replied, snagging a blackberry from her husband's plate and popping it into her mouth.

"And still we persist for the greater good," Serena replied. "In this case, Bethany's dream wedding has to be secondary to Patrick's murderer being placed in handcuffs. Derian cannot be punished for their actions."

"There is little more Natalie can do beyond backing the evidence you find," her father stated. "But back you, she will. If I get involved—"

"I know, then it becomes formal and, well, you have limits I don't have." Serena stacked their dessert plates and motioned for the busboy, who'd been waiting patiently to clear the final set of dishes. Not to rush the guests, but he needed to completely close down the area. "See why I don't want to be official with the State Department?"

"And here I thought it was the dress code that kept you from taking on the position," her mother teased as they walked from the area and back toward the pool.

Her parents' assigned bodyguards lingered behind the group as they walked. When her parents veered off toward their room, a chill snaked down her spine from no longer having the long shadow of protection she had despised so much growing up. There was no immediate threat to Conner or herself, but she couldn't shake her unease.

"Serena," the now syrupy quality of Kaitlynn's voice grated on Serena's very soul. The woman, who had been closed off the first night, was emboldened with each encounter. As if emerging from a constraining shell with wobbly legs and now she was practically a full-grown bird ready to fly with little knowledge of the barriers set in place for her.

"Kaitlynn." Serena smiled and stood by the lounge chair where she was stretched out. Golden bikini, not meant for swimming if the chain along her hips was any indication. Connecting the Lycra fabric of the front and back of the lower half of her bikini. All very chic, now and impractical for anyone with a decent amount of hips and ass.

"Sit, sit," Kaitlynn urged, and Serena sat on the side of the lounge chair next to hers. "Getting a little sun before the wedding."

"Where is everyone else?" Serena asked.

"Around here somewhere. After the scuba lesson, Joey and Emma wanted a little alone time, so I figured why not work on my tan. Especially after that lesson messed up my tan lines." Gliding her hand along her arm, there was a slight line where the wetsuit would have blocked the sun. Kaitlynn bent her knee up slightly, but made sure to keep her toes pointed. A total girl move, *come get me, see how sexy I am.*

The action engrained early on in life, Serena wondered if most ever noticed they were doing it. Kaitlynn maybe, if the lowered sunglasses and eyes staring across the pool were any indication. Evan and Eric were both at the bar getting frosty sweet drinks with paper umbrellas.

"Where are the happy couple?" Serena asked.

"Donald is showing her the villa they own on the property. Have you seen them?" Kaitlynn asked. "I'm thinking of getting one for myself. This place is amazing."

"You get enough vacation time to make it worth coming down?" Serena asked, and Conner stepped away to the bar.

"I'll make a way," she replied. "Crazy how I was always under such pressure for years, and now it is as if someone removed the weight from my back."

"A few days on the beach can do that for a person." Serena wasn't sure at this level, but what did she know about working a nine-to-five? Or in the case of the lawyers, she knew it was before the sun rose to after it set.

"You know even after I left Tyler, Michaels and Kern, Patrick plagued me." Kaitlynn brushed her loose blonde hair to the side. "Don't get me wrong, I didn't wish him ill or anything, but if he would have moved to California and joined a law firm I wouldn't have been sad to see him go."

"Were you in competition for clients or something?" Serena asked.

"All the time. I swear I set a lunch meeting with a client and he'd show up at the same restaurant, say his pleasantries when passing and two days later my client would request his retainer back and would be moving his business to Tyler, Michaels and Kern. As if they didn't run half the city."

"How would he know about your lunch?"

"I have no idea. I started having meetings in the office, or the client's office and the same thing would happen." She shook her head. "People didn't realize the lower per-hour rate means nothing if they pad their hours on the back end. It is why I left.

Patrick was my supervisor and when a few clients demanded to see proof I had put in so many hours on their behalf I was aghast."

"Had he padded your hours?" Serena prodded.

"And then some. It wasn't as if the three hundred an hour was going directly to me, people don't think about that when they see the per-hour fee." Kaitlynn shifted her shoulders, straightening them in disgust. "A slice comes directly off the top to pay for rent, secretaries, paralegals, and all the other office needs. All they see is I made five grand and they want an itemized accounting."

"One you couldn't provide because he was slipping a few extra hours."

"A few," she scoffed. "That thieving bastard I found out got a bonus for working the attorneys under him to the point they billed a certain amount of hours. That was why he was always bringing in so many clients so he could keep us busy. But even that wasn't enough. For every four hours I billed, he added a fifth. Round up he said. After a while, three hours rounded up to five. When I threatened to bring it to the partners—"

Kaitlynn's body went from stretched out in relaxation to tight as both her legs bent at the knee and she sat forward, arms resting on her kneecaps.

"I had made a mistake early in my employment," she confessed. "Patrick was an attractive man, powerful, which I have to say is a draw."

"You two dated?" Serena surmised.

"I'm not Emma, it only took a few dates, a bit of pressure to my upper arm, and a closed office door to know boundaries had to be set." Kaitlynn turned and planted her feet on the pool deck as she faced Serena. "He had pictures of me, I was fresh from law school. Sure of myself in many ways, but under no delusion when it came to a man like him and what he could do, so I made a choice."

"You stayed."

"I stayed, working for him, all the while hoping I could find some way to trap him and get his ass fired. When I had the evidence, he showed me pictures, texts, manipulated in a way to make it seem as if I had been the aggressor. Certain parts were removed from the conversation. One, I had stupidly deleted from my own phone."

"When you left, he wasn't content to just let you leave," Serena said, guiding the conversation.

"Patrick believes—believed if you were a part of his life, in any way, you were always his. Eric, Evan, and even Donald all worked under him, or were working under him. It wasn't sexual. I'd met people he tutored in college. Now his clients, as if no one else could represent them." The men were walking over with drinks and Kaitlynn returned to lounging. "Patrick saw everyone as subservient to his greatness. As if he were God and we were blessed to be in his presence."

"Daquiri for the lovely lady," Evan said, passing a frosted glass with bright red, slushy, ice causing condensation on the outside.

"Evan, do you work at Tyler, Michaels and Kern?" Serena asked.

"That would be me," Eric said with a half-hearted wave. "Although there is an opening now, Evan could come back."

"Just Evan?" Kaitlynn admonished. "I see how you are."

"You in the office again? I'd never get any work done," Eric said as he sat in the lounger next to Kaitlynn while Evan mournfully eyed the one Serena was on before taking a spot next to Evan.

"We must sound like uncaring vultures," Kaitlynn said.

"I've met lawyers before," Serena said with a smile.

"Lounge by the pool or nap in our room?" Conner asked as he passed her a smaller cup with a pale drink. The smell of coconuts and the pineapple spear along the rim made her mouth water for the Pina colada.

Hatred for Patrick ran deep between the three currently

lounging by the pool, but there was little more Serena could get from the woman. Plus she was curious, the other Katelyn had said she didn't know which man this Kaitlynn was actually dating. Evan and Eric shared more in common than a first initial glance. Both had worked with Kaitlynn at the same firm, now only one did. Evan brought her the drink, but Eric sat next to her and made a comment about her distracting him at work.

There was something about these three, and Serena knew nothing would be made clear if they stayed around.

"Nap," Serena said, words crossing her lips, but not coming from her heart. Sleep would be elusive and more than likely nightmare filled if she didn't have all the pieces in place for this puzzle. Like an untyped paper. Plaguing her when she knew what the topic was, but was missing the conclusion. Thesis was in place, research done, but instead of having her find an ending to tie everything up in a nice neat bow, she suddenly had come to a fork in the road.

This fork had three tines, each with a similar motivation, but which stabbed first? Patrick had one forceful death blow, crushing the front of his face through his brain. Stealing life, while others questioned its actual worth, they didn't have the right to do it. Kaitlynn talking about purchasing a villa and vacationing more often here was more than an offhand comment. She knew about the under-the-table deal going on between management and the police.

A pittance to them, a life to Derian. She was sure one of the men dying to flank the woman was to blame until Serena stood and saw Joey at the kitchen door. An envelope being passed to Wilmarie, her face hard as she threw it back at him and bills fell like fall leaves from the unsealed stationary.

———

"I wasn't kidding about the nap," Conner said, his voice a bit harsher than he expected, as Serena stepped out on the balcony. "Should I have spiked your drink with sleep medicine?"

"Huh?" she questioned, not glancing over her shoulder to see he was standing in the open sliding glass door. "Is she playing them both? Or is it something else?"

"Is who whating?" he asked, stepping out on the balcony to see why they were spending time out there. The thing couldn't be more than three by six with a set of chairs and a table from a kindergarten classroom.

Serena had set her drink on the concrete railing with her right foot perched between two of the steel spindles, her palms pressed flat on the surface. Her focus was on the pool they'd just left. Maybe he should have parked her ass in the lounger and let the sun do its job and suck the unending energy she tended to find when she was working out a problem.

"Kaitlynn, see how Evan moved to the lounger I was sitting on?"

"So," Conner replied. "Maybe he didn't want to be next to Eric."

"Maybe it's the gold bikini, but what I see down there is a queen bee with her workers." Serena sipped on her cocktail as if there were a Shakespearian play unfolding before her.

"What did you talk about with her?" Conner asked.

"Why she left the law firm, how Patrick plagued her still."

"Still?" he questioned.

"Yeah," she said, turning and heading back inside the room, satisfied with whatever she believed she needed to see. "He kept stealing clients, even after she was at another firm. Showing up at the perfect time to introduce himself while she was doing the whole wine and dine."

"Eric worked with Patrick, but Evan works with Kaitlynn, right?"

Between Kaitlynn, Katelyn the red, Eric, and Evan, Conner was beginning to wonder if lawyers were made in a factory with a limited model line. Adding to the confusion and misdirection of the whole situation allowed four people to question more about who they were really dealing with among the cookie-cutter legal friend set. How did Donald slip past human resources without a tag from the lawyer factory?

"Yes," Serena said.

"Evan would know her schedule," he concluded. "And he had worked for Patrick too."

"Which in Patrick's world meant he owed him according to Kaitlynn." Serena plopped on the bed after setting her half-drunk cocktail on the nightstand.

"Why is that?" he questioned.

"Something about a minion army," she said with a yawn and he prayed she would actually drift off to sleep.

It was unlikely, but then again he'd seen many unlikely things in his life. Triple, triples in a championship game. The McRib out of season. Elvis officiating a stormtrooper marriage to a Jedi. True, that was in Las Vegas where he saw things against the laws of nature, God and man, but still the impossible was rarely that.

"Anyone he'd helped owed him." Serena rolled on her side, a pillow clutched in her arms.

"We know he controlled Emma," he said. "If Kaitlynn had worked for him, then wouldn't she beholden by that logic?"

"Yep, which is why she's now talking about getting a villa down here, because she's suddenly free to live her life."

Conner stepped back out on the balcony and took in the view at the pool. Kaitlynn had rolled over and laid the lounger flat. But what caught his attention was Eric untying the back of her bikini and lathering sunblock on over her back. All the while Evan was lotioning the back of her legs and ass. Both with the care of a lover.

"You might have a point about Eric and Evan," he said, stepping inside the room to see Serena had passed out on the bed.

Silently, he slid the door to the balcony closed and went for his computer. It was time to review a few things. Patrick's murder could be put to the side for a moment. There was a teammate he needed to check on.

Heading to the website for his old team, he went first to rosters. Dropping down to a decade before and moving forward. Clicking on a few pictureless members of the team. The center he remembered hadn't been on the team long enough to garner a photo session. He'd been tossed an old practice jersey as they waited to give him a formal number.

Clicking through the images, he searched through a few more years. Only two men fit the description of the man he remembered. The first had been killed in a car wreck three years after leaving the team. Dmitri Marcov, on the other hand, had been traded two more times before being drummed out of the league. It was one thing to be tough on defense, it was another to be violent to the point of injuring players intentionally. There was little tolerance for that. Pulling up the picture of the man, the majority of articles followed a line of arrests for violent acts.

Suspected mob ties. All of it was normal thug behavior. Maybe his nightmare wasn't his brain processing his enemies and bringing them to the forefront of his mind. Although Dmitri could hold a grudge against Conner for basketball, it seemed as if he had more than one way to process his rage.

He'd have to dig deeper, this man was physical, not mental, well not cerebral, mental was another level that would need a doctor to diagnose. Even going back in his history to the schools he attended before going pro, nothing screamed hacker. Though the Russian mob was moving into that territory. Why bust legs, when a few lines of code could garner ten times the income with little to no repercussion? Law enforcement seemed to be miles behind, not a few steps.

"A little late in the marriage to be cyberstalking old boyfriends," Serena said with a yawn and he turned to see her standing behind him.

Her nap clearly over as she rubbed at her eyes then stretched.

Almost an hour had passed since he began searching out his enemy. Wait? Had she said boyfriend?

"What?" he questioned, turning in the office-style chair at the desk in the room.

"Dmitri," she replied, her yawn less pronounced as her hand spun as if unwinding a roll of yarn to get to the end of the skein. "God, what was his last name? Mark—Monty—no it was more Slavic. Markovich?"

"Marcov," Conner said as he leaned forward, his elbows resting on his knees. "Dmitri Marcov."

"That's it." Her eyes waking a bit more. "I haven't thought of him for years. Why are you looking him up?"

"I played basketball with him," he stated, still a bit confused as to how his wife would know the mad Russian.

"Really? Small world. God, he put me off athletes for years." Her voice dropped and slipped into a poorly executed Russian accent. "Ball is life."

"When did you date him?"

"I don't know, freshman, no sophomore year—yeah that was it, I wouldn't say I dated him," she said. "He was on some exchange program, didn't even last the semester now that I think of it."

"Got kicked out?" he questioned.

"No, some team recruited him." Her eyes narrowed, not in anger, but as if she needed focus to pull up the memory. "I remember he tried to get me to come with him. Like I'd drop out of school and chase after him as if he were a superstar."

"You didn't date him, but he tried to get you to move to Europe?" he questioned, the memories not lining up to a normal conclusion.

"He was like Patrick in many ways I guess. Except if he wanted something, he assumed he could have it." She cocked her head to the side and finally registered the image he had pulled up. "Is that a mug shot?"

"Yep," he replied. "Want me to see if there's an address so you can become pen pals?"

"Nope, I'm good, but hey, it's good to know I have a backup with the ability to extort funds." She shrugged. "Not shocking."

"Can we get back to you two dating?"

"We sat next to each other in a computer science course they said was required for graduation."

"Otherwise you'd have never taken it," he stated, and she nodded in full agreement.

"Turned out, I didn't need it, but hey, an A's and A, right?"

"Computer science, you remember which one?"

"No geek," she replied. "All I remember were macros—or was I trying that macrobiotic diet to boost energy, then? Ugh, it was boring, and he didn't need it at all. Most days he was done with the exercise five minutes in and spent the rest of the time surfing the internet and sending tapes to coaches."

"He can code, then?"

"Sure, I guess." She moved toward the balcony and opened the sliding glass door. "Guess everyone went for a nap."

"Or more."

"What do you mean?" she questioned as she closed the door and moved back inside the room.

"Have you ever had two men slather you in sunblock at the same time?"

"Is that why you're reaching out to an old teammate? Trying to find my type? Sorry, no matter what that man told you," she assured, palms facing him. "Having a coffee after class does not constitute a date let alone a full-on relationship."

"I think your instinct might be right about Kaitlynn. Either she's dating both men at the same time and playing them both for fools. Or, and this is more likely based on what I saw, she's dating both men and they have no issue sharing."

"Like, poly-type sharing? One woman, two rings? Brother-husbands?"

"You're getting a bit too excited by the idea," he said, leaning back in the chair.

"Society may look down upon multiple wives, but only in theory. Reality and in some countries, it's still common and an okay practice. Can't I be happy that women are finding equality?" She spun on her toes, twirling until she got to the bed and sat on the edge, crossing her legs at the knee and posing like a dignified woman of the fifties. "The reason behind multiple wives I get, a man can knock up a dozen women in a day."

"With the right amount of oysters, sure," he joked. "While women can only be impregnated by one man, for the most part, unless she's fast and loose with those eggs."

"Propagation of the species aside," he began.

"Exactly, the world is overpopulated as it is. Why not have a woman being cared for by more than one man?"

To that, he stood and stalked across the room. Grasping her wrists he bent her backward and pinned her to the bed.

"Why are you looking for a brother-husband?" she teased.

"After talking with you, I'm pretty sure the son-of-a-bitch is who broke into the Gaming Love."

"Really? Why? His undying love for a woman he shared a coffee with once in New Jersey?"

"And the fact his attack on me got him traded," he countered. "You asked if I had any enemies. The guy played less than a week with us."

"Dmitri does fixate on minor interactions doesn't he?" she said.

"Seems that way," Conner said, being drawn into his wife in her prone position. She wasn't fighting him off. Even with his hands trapping her to the bed. If anything, her hands were relaxed above her head and he moved from her wrists. Intertwining his fingers with hers. The way he preferred to be with her. Locked in as her equal, with a bright smile beaming up from her full lips, letting him know the somewhat contented woman he married was in the mood to play.

"You weren't cyber stalking my ex like some jealous man spent on taking out all who wronged me in life?"

"No," he laughed.

"Dang, because there was this one guy in middle school that at least deserved a swirly."

"What would I get if I found him?" he offered. "Brought him to you sobbing in apology for the wrong and harm he caused your pre-teen self."

"Have you been properly vaccinated?" she teased. "Because what I'm offering could transfer cooties."

TWENTY

THAT'S JUST USING YOUR BRAIN AND I DON'T APPRECIATE IT

"Promise I'll send you my shot record from second grade," Conner panted as he lay staring up at the ceiling. "I distinctly remember getting vaccinations on the playground."

"Was it a government program?" she laughed at his silly, yet serious description.

"Privately funded," he replied. "And administered by older kids, those who had survived the outbreak a few years earlier."

"Ah, well then I feel protected," she replied. "Herd immunity and all."

"Exactly."

A light mist of sweat glistened on his bare chest. Serena wasn't much better. Lying face down, wondering if her heart would ever return to a resting pace. Afternoons with no agenda could lead down many paths. Love making one of the better ones she'd have to say. The power nap moments before had been more energizing than a full eight hours. Like she expected, her mind had drifted like a drone flying over the resort.

Flipping between the cartoon drawing of the passport and the real in some Roger Rabbit type world. All of it leading back to the scuba lessons offered. Each time. Maybe it was her desire to go beyond basic snorkeling she'd done on more than one occasion. The activity simple enough in execution anyone could do it with success as long as they knew how to swim. While she enjoyed swimming in waters clear enough to see the schools of fishes and below, she wanted to go further. Not have the limitation that came from going down too far and having water covering the top of the tube. She wanted to do more than skim the surface, she wanted to go down and touch. Feel the fish as they spun around her. Explore the plants and get an underwater camera she could take with her to capture images reserved for only a special few. When she snorkeled, it was as if she was watching a crystal clear scene below her. Engrossing for sure, because there was no getting away from the beauty all around her, but it was in three D not four. Only scuba could offer her an all-encompassing experience such as that.

Either way, the man next to her had restarted her brain, reset her life, and even brought her a few good laughs at the memory of Dmitri. The man had lumbered around the campus like a giant among Lilliputians. She'd put him in his place more than once, mocking him with a line from *A Funny Thing Happened on the Way to the Forum.* '*I take large steps.*'

"Dmitri Marcov, who'd thunk it," she said, rolling to her back and going in search of her clothes.

"I'll send his info to Huey. He'll backtrace and make sure it was him then launch a cyber-attack that will put the fear of God in the man."

"I think he was atheist," she replied absently as she took a swallow of water from a bottle provided by the hotel. "Or was it he was the laziest—no that wasn't it. Marxist? No, that would be too cerebral."

"Is this coming to a point?" Conner asked.

"Are the air canisters for scuba diving concave or flat?" she mused, her finger spinning in the divot in the bottom of the bottle she was holding before bringing the plastic to her face and sticking it on the end of her nose.

"You might need a few more hours of sleep," he stated, and she turned to see him staring at her as if she'd lost her mind.

Maybe she had. Going all Pinocchio with her water bottle. But anything in a canister could have one of two bottoms. Flat or concave. It was a simple fact of life. When Conner gave her a can of compressed air to clean out her computer, it was concave, but she had seen movies with flat-bottomed canisters. Were those medical or scuba ones? Her brain tripped along memories trying to connect them. All of it brought her back to the ring around Patrick's face. The nose was a bit to the side, but not smashed. Her mind remembered the cookies she made when she was younger, cutting them out, pressing hard to break through the dough, even though it was soft and mailable.

The human body, for all its hard edges and strong bones, could be beaten into a pulpy substance. One molded and conformed to the environment. Humans were basically water-filled beings floating around the world with only a bit of calcium and other elements giving them shape. Maybe she was exhausted. Now she was remembering a meme saying humans were basically cucumbers with anxiety. Water...mailable...hard... the heavy ting from the man lining up canisters for the scuba class had caught her attention like a siren song or church bell clanging those to gather.

"I need to see the scuba gear." Snatching the room key, she ran from the room.

Lost in her own thoughts she didn't hear the words being called at her from her husband. This wasn't about jumping in the water and taking in the view. This was about finding a weapon, hard, heavy, and able to do damage. Unlike the fists of the young man being charged with the crime. Everything was coming together at once. Evan and Eric had access to the canisters. Was Joey in the class? Why hadn't they reviewed the video? Oh right, she passed out.

When she came out from the stairwell, she saw the rental counter for their area. Jogging around the pool, she dodged a few people and went in search of the employee in charge of water sports. Getting ready to close up for the day, a sandwich board was being folded flat as she raced and slapped her hand on the counter to a very confused young man.

"We're closing up for the day, no more checkouts until the morning," he said.

"I'm good," she said, waving her hand to have him hold as she caught her breath. Maybe she did need to go running with Conner more if this little jaunt had her gasping for air like a fish tossed on the boat deck. A stitch in her side had her clutching below her rib with her left hand as her right kept waving as if she were calling out for a big sale at a car lot. "Just need...to see... your scuba gear...for rental."

Unable to get her words out without gasping between, maybe the guy would take pity on her and offer up pure oxygen to save her dang life.

"Check out, everything is included with your stay, but you need to show certification and more importantly, you can only check out until five." The kid pointed to a clock showing it was five to five. "Tomorrow, okay?"

"No, I just need to look at it. The air tanks," she said, finally able to complete a sentence without her lung exploding.

"Okay," the kid huffed and plopped a tank on the counter. "We good?"

"This isn't the same one they train with," she said, reviewing the tank that was as long as her whole back. Still, she bent it over to see a flat bottom making her heart sink.

"No, we train with smaller ones, no reason to use one good for an hour when the students only use ten minutes max. Filling them isn't as cheap as people think."

"Do you have any of the smaller ones?" she questioned, and the kid arched an eyebrow.

"If you want to check out a volleyball for the night I could do that."

How did those two things go together? Was he just offering her random things to get her to go away?

"I just want to see the training tanks," she said, pushing up and leaning over the counter, her legs kicking when her belly lay flat on the surface.

Hands gripped her hips and lifted her up in the air, spun her out of the building, and placed her down on the ground.

"I apologize," Conner said to the kid, who lowered the checkout window quickly to stop the crazy woman from jumping over the counter to go on a rampage.

"Eight A.M. we're back open," he said, closing the employee door to the building.

"What were you doing?" Conner asked and she crossed her arms.

"I was looking for the training tanks," she said, as if he should know where her train of thought had led.

"Okay, well, as much as I enjoy seeing your backside dangling half out of a window," he said, passing her the sandals she left behind in her haste to get out of the room and guiding her toward the lobby. "Why don't we ask our favorite manager and see if we can get a private viewing?"

"See that's just using your brain and I don't appreciate it," she grumbled, more because she should have thought of that. Hopping on one foot as she pulled on one sandal, then switching it to the other because the idea of slowing momentum at this point to actually stop would be tantamount to giving up. This was her first big discovery, a thought she wouldn't be willing to let go of until she knew if it was real or all some sick twisted want muddling up her brain with facts. "But what if we find the murder weapon?"

"Then let's tell him you want to snuggle with it and bring it back to the room."

She cut her eyes at him.

"What?" he said with a shrug. "Okay, what if I distract him and you stick it under your shirt? If we run into your parents, we can tell them we took their advice and in three to twelve years we're having a gas bubble."

With a hard smack, the back of her hand slammed into his chest. "You're not funny."

"We know he was willing to sell out Derian for a few home sales."

"True, maybe we should just break into the employee storage area," she offered as if the idea was valid and not one that could land them in a Dominican jail right next to Derian.

"Or," he said, coming to a full stop at the edge of the pool off the lobby. "We walk over and check them out ourselves."

With his hands on her upper arms, he turned her body toward the man loading up a rolling cart with canisters. "Well, isn't that convenient?"

Skipping like a ten-year-old from pure glee at an unexpected opportunity, she approached the employee. "Want some help?"

"I have it, Missus," the man said, snagging two canisters and placing them in an OCD-level perfect line.

"Honestly, it wouldn't be any trouble," she said grabbing two herself. "I had been hoping to take a class but didn't get up in time this morning. Does it really take all day?"

"No," the man said as she picked up another canister, this time her hand slid underneath to find a concave bottom. "We had to double up today because—"

The man stilled, as if the death of a guest was some secret and not a well-known fact. "There were complications yesterday."

"Ah," she said, placing her full palm over the indent on the bottom of the canisters. "These aren't too heavy."

"They're empty, Missus," he replied. "Trust me in the morning, they weigh a bit more, but when you're in the water, you don't even notice."

"Is that why you have to watch the gauge? Because you can't tell that it's emptying?"

"Among other reasons. How long are you staying?" he asked. "Because on Monday we'll have another class."

"Good to know. How heavy are these things when they are full?" she asked, hefting the tank up to her shoulder. One end held tight with her right hand, the bottom with her left.

"Training tanks we keep a bit lighter close to eleven or twelve kilos."

"About twenty-five pounds," Conner converted the weight quickly for her.

"Yes, sorry, pounds. The ones we take out can be up to...forty pounds max. Steel verse aluminum and how much time we think we'll be out. The ones you can check out are a bit heavier."

"They have flat bottoms," she said as her finger tapped on the now-empty canister she had hefted.

"Some of these do too," he replied. "Not a big difference, just a design thing."

He reached for the canister, tugging a bit to get it from her hands because she'd become lost in her thoughts. When he placed it on the rolling cart, she noticed an OCD nightmare unfolding.

"You're missing one," she pointed to the obviously empty spot from what should be a perfect twelve tanks.

"It'll turn up," the man assured. "I had been getting my equipment out yesterday from the shack and when I came back, one was gone. It happens, guests don't want to wait for check out or just want to mess around."

"Are you missing a concave or flat bottomed one?"

"Um." The man scanned the grouping of tanks. "Concave I think, why?"

"No reason," she said and then turned on her heel toward Conner.

"If you're here on Monday I'm sure I have an opening in my class. You both should join."

"We'll check in with the desk," Conner said, waving off the guy as he moved Serena along the pathway. "What was that all about?"

"I'm not trying to take lessons," she said. Then stopped

walking to look up at him with a smile. "Unless you're willing to change your mind."

"Serena," he warned, or maybe he just wanted to know why she'd gone all twenty questions on tank construction.

"Okay, hear me out," she said and eyed a bench along the path. "Did you check out Patrick's face on the beach?"

"Not really, no."

"It is seared into my brain like a bad bowl of guac."

"Cancun? I told you something was off about the stuff."

"Right, but do you remember the bowl?" she urged, hoping he could capture the visual.

"Not really, why?"

"Basically it had a round part in the center, the indent where the blood—I mean guac was."

"So Patrick's face was like a bowl of guac."

"More salsa I guess," she reasoned, tilting her head to the side then shaking it to get the red from the visual. Circling her own face with her finger, she explained the visual. "Basically his nose was near perfect, but around it was an indent, blood had pooled there from the damage."

"Concave bottom," Conner stated, catching up to her train of thought before it took off from the station again like a bullet. "Twenty-five pounds being slammed into a face could do that."

"And one of the canisters is missing."

———

Serena, in the manic stage had a few levels, entertaining, more than any drunk at a party, exhausting, and near impossible to stop without a syringe full of a heavy sedative. His wife was nearing the end of a puzzle, which meant she wouldn't stop until every piece was perfectly laid and glued together to be hung in a frame.

While the dilated pupils to some would appear pharmaceutically altered, Conner knew in this moment she was laser focused on finding the killer. Each comment, movement and clue would be popping out at her as she narrowed down who, of her three suspects, really killed Patrick.

"I have to say that makes more sense than being beaten to death with a rock or fists."

"It does, doesn't it? You'd think the coroner would have been at least trying to find a rock to use and make the pattern," she said. "But there is no way the perfect circle could have been made by anything but a scuba tank. I need to tell Mr. Ruiz. That should be enough to get Derian out."

"Derian would have had access to the tanks also," Conner pointed out, and she buried her face in her hands.

"And they won't give him the tape showing he had left while Patrick was alive and well."

"Even if they did, Derian had skipped school and came back to the resort," Conner added, and he could see the frustration on his wife's face. "Sorry, I have to put up roadblocks or you'll never find a way around them."

"This that stupid crap you put in your games?"

"Yes, and sorry, my love, you're on level twenty, not level one," he said, hoping to help her along. "We are down to three right?"

"Motive, opportunity, yes."

"Dinner should be interesting tonight."

With the sun having set, Serena readied herself for the rehearsal dinner. Not being part of the wedding allowed them a bit more time to make their way to the Brazilian restaurant for dinner. A choice her parents may find annoyingly common considering their current duty station. Once again, they had the option of a shuttle or to walk. Conner was torn. Leave early to allow his wife to suss out who did what, her mind flashing back through the groomsmen and all their actions since they had arrived, or hop on a shuttle which would force her to not go down that train of thought thus causing a backup in her brain and a minor overload of the circuitry. Even now, as he watched her apply the slight makeup she wore on special occasions, he wondered if she would even acknowledge those around her that weren't part of her finding the truth.

The stick she dipped in the lip vial on its third dipping had yet to be applied to her lips. While amusing, at some point they would need to move forward and the knock on the door proved a perfect opportunity as he opened to see his mother-in-law.

"Conner, we thought we could all go together," she said as she stepped inside to see Serena waving the lip gloss wand as if she were casting a spell in the mirror. "Serena, you have to put it on your actual lips not the reflection."

"Huh?" Serena woke from her dazed thoughts and then focused on the objects in her hands. "Oh, right."

The wand glided over her lips, creating a sheen of burgundy before she recapped the gloss and tucked it away.

"You okay, honey?" her mother asked, taking Serena's face in her hands. "Too much sun? Not enough? You look a bit queasy. Is your belly okay?"

"I'm fine, Mom," Serena assured and removed the hands from her face, offering to hold them instead. "Honest, just lost in thoughts, that's all."

"Are you sure? Because if you're not up to going to dinner we can make your apologies for you."

Serena's eyes narrowed a bit and Conner decided he needed to step in.

"I have a feeling Serena is trying to do a pro/con list to get me to stay a few extra days," Conner said, rescuing her from the parental care. "Because see, here's the deal. She wants to get a scuba certification and I'm not comfortable with the whole thing."

His mother-in-law glanced between the two of them, her lips pursing a bit. "Scuba lessons?"

"My dearest," Mr. Isola called from the hallway where he was holding the room door open. "Shuttles are on a schedule, which means we must be too."

"Exactly. They are sticklers for the reservations around here," Conner said. "She can tell you all about it on the ride over."

The shuttle took off right as they arrived in the lobby, but they were assured another was less than five minutes away. Sadly, this allowed a deeper probing by Serena's mother into her strange state of affairs and unless Conner interceded with a better topic his wife would be bombarded with questions on her strange behavior. Not wanting scuba lessons was an acceptable and a more probable Serena activity. Scuba, sky diving, free climbing, hang gliding all the basic things those without a death wish would avoid like the plague and the things Conner had to redirect when brought up around him.

"Serena, honey, is there something you and Conner need to tell us?" Her mother's eyes were bright in expectation.

"Mr. Isola, I was informed I owe you money," Conner said, jarring the conversation and making Serena come out of whatever sleep-starved place she was at.

"Do you now? Well, pay up young man," Mr. Isola said, shoving his hands in his pockets, as they stood in a semi-circle. "I will happily take your money."

"Conner, I told you let it go," Serena admonished.

"No, I honestly didn't know about it until we came here and Bethany brought it up."

"She didn't really bring it up," Serena corrected. "A comment was made, mostly in jest, about Donald being willing to pay the bride price and Auntie Louise not being willing to accept because they were having an non-traditional wedding."

"Aye, aye, aye, I see, but it would not be my sister's right to accept the payment," Mr. Isola said. "My brother-in-law he would need to decide if Donald was making an acceptable offer and then counter if it was not enough to cover the raising of Bethany."

"The whole thing?" Conner questioned. "Because the woman wears designer sandals."

"My street market buys starting to look better and better to you already huh," Serena said with a nudge to his shoulder.

"That and the fact the U.S. government covered most of your formative years."

"Especially when she was in a growth spurt," his mother-in-law said. "I thought boys were supposed to be the bottomless pits. This one made me wonder if she had a hollow leg to hide all the donuts she ate."

"You're the one who brought me to Paris for a conference," Serena added. "They were pastries, fine, delicate, decadent pastries."

Serena's eyes glazed over a bit like a picture window at Christmas. A haze of memories just beyond the light.

The shuttle pulled up and soon they were all loaded in and the door closed when they heard a woman calling from outside.

"Wait," Kaitlynn called, with Emma hollering too. Ahead of them the men were running and Evan captured a bar on the outside of the bus and jumped on the running board to bang on the window of the folding door.

The driver stopped, unphased by the behavior of the guests, and opened the door to the bus. The bridal party spilled into the bus minus the best man, maid of honor, and Yvette. Evan was the last to get on the bus, holding his right shoulder and wincing.

"I told you not to do that," Kaitlynn admonished, her hand lovingly massaged the man's shoulder.

"Are you okay?" Conner asked, noting the injury that could be the death knell for his guilt.

"No, he's not," Kaitlynn growled. "He tore his rotator cuff three weeks ago, but didn't want to have surgery until after the wedding."

"I've been stuck doing all the heavy lifting for these two," Eric added. "But then again, I'm sure I'll be tasked with it after the surgery too."

"What are best friends for?" Kaitlynn said sweetly, while blinking her eyes.

"It is not that big of a tear," Evan said. "Enough to be an irritation and send sharp stabbing pain when I lift crap."

"How were you able to take the scuba lessons?" Serena asked. "Swimming must be unbearable."

"The instructor helped with the tank," Evan explained. "And he didn't make me swim, just use the equipment to go to the bottom of the pool. Hopefully, when I'm healed we can go out on a boat and explore."

"So you're coming back too?" Serena asked. "I know Kaitlynn said something about purchasing a villa here."

"We're all looking at places here," Emma said. "Don and Bethany will have a place, seems like a good way to escape the city from time to time and have friends around."

Emma's hand slipped around Joey's who moved them both to his knee. A look shared between the two of them deep and soulful. Patrick was a distant memory, gone as if the waves had taken him out to sea, never to be heard from again. While it had been barely a day since he died.

Serena and Conner were the last two off the shuttle, allowing others to exit, giving them time to lag behind.

"Do you think they are buying the places to cover up, or to make sure it doesn't come back on them? There is no statute of limitation for murder," Serena said.

"That's what's confusing me," Conner said. "Think about it, all of them are buying, why not just one of them? The guilty party is the only one who would be in danger."

"Unless others saw what happened."

"Either way, Evan is out," Conner said. "I've known guys who tore their rotator cuff, and even after surgery there is no way he'd have enough strength or power to smash straight forward and it sounds like that is what he did. Most he could do was bean the guy."

"Someone had to negotiate with the manager," Serena pointed out. "Was there anyone noticeably missing?"

"Abaeze," Conner said, "I'm not sure if he was even interviewed."

"No one came late?" she asked and he tried to remember when the men even showed up.

"I don't remember. I was talking with Huey about the hack."

"Video right?" she questioned, and he nodded. "Any chance the auto record was going?"

A few years before, Conner had been having people going back on contracts. Questioning deadlines he knew he had correct. Because of that, he started recording all video chats. At first, it was only important meetings, but he'd forgotten to turn off the feature, and at least once a month he needed to clear the cache of videos.

"You may not have been watching, but your computer might have seen what was going on behind you."

"Serena," Bethany called as she walked toward her with Yvette following and trying to fix a flower back into her bun.

Her crown tonight circling the knotted black hair on top of her head. A jeweled gate in a way with citrine coloring bursting from the gems with the pale blue flowers dotting her hair.

"Oh stop," Bethany said. "One flower missing does not kill the look."

"You say that now," Yvette said. "And then you see the pictures and you'll be all...why is there a hole there?"

"Fine, fine," she said as the bud was set back in place.

Long lashes batted at Serena as Bethany took her hands and smiled. Her gold eye shadow popped against the dark skin of Bethany with eyes outlined like an Egyptian Queen.

"Tell me why I have not seen you all day," Bethany cooed.

"You had so much to do and the rehearsal is for the wedding party."

"Oh pish," she said, waving her hand. "Tonight, you and me, please I need my favorite cousin with me to tell me everything will be perfect tomorrow."

"Nope, can't do it," Serena said with a smile. "But I will tell you from tomorrow on only happiness will come, even from the bad times."

Conner placed his hands on her shoulders. Leaning down to kiss the crown of her head. The sweet smell of coconut and warm sugar teased and tempted him as usual. The combination had become an aphrodisiac since he had been told of the scrub-down she'd received the day before.

"You two are so cute," Bethany gushed.

"Usman party," the host called out to the group, and people funneled inside the restaurant.

A photographer hovered on the edges, capturing moments of family, love, and friendship, but a moment of silence was taken. Remembering the man who couldn't be with them tomorrow. While others were bowing their heads, Conner lifted his enough to try to catch an inappropriate reaction. The click of the photographer, the only sound over the muted music, piped through the sound system.

"Let us proceed with the merriment," Uncle David said, and everyone raised their head.

Food was brought out, and meat was on display in all varieties as waiters walked around with steaks, chicken, pork chops, and roasts on giant skewers. Allowing people to point and have anything placed on their plate. The atmosphere was light as drinks were poured and tales were shared. In a way, it reminded Conner of the first night. When hopes were high and the world was theirs.

"Excuse me," Conner said, pushing back from the table.

"You okay?" Serena questioned.

"Absolutely, get me a cut of that steak when it comes back around." Stepping away from the table, Conner headed toward the bathroom but turned toward the hostess stand instead.

The photographer was packing up his equipment and Conner approached him.

"Hey, what kind of camera do you use?" he asked, making sure to approach like the interested geek. His size at times had a negative effect, especially when dealing with a man as short as the photographer.

"Canon," he replied holding it up, strap wrapped around his wrist. "80D."

"Us too," Conner said, stepping forward. "But I've been having issues with wider shots."

"What lens are you using?"

"I think the one that came with it," Conner lied.

"How wide are you going, because that's not an issue, even when I'm capturing a beach shot."

"We were up on the mountain," Conner said, then realized he needed to push further. "Were you able to get most of the room?"

"Yes," the photographer said and flipped the camera around showing him the screen and slipping through the shots.

"May I?" Conner asked. "I won't delete anything."

"I guess." The photographer passed it off and Conner spun the dial.

Images flipping, Conner used the zoom feature to see Kaitlynn and Eric sharing a moment. Evan's eyes turned down, but his hand holding hers. They had to be a thruple. Words were being spoken with that look. Setting the image back to the regular size, he flipped a few more. Abaeze's eyes were not down, they were staring directly at Joey. His eyes were straight forward and his face fixed.

All of it showing, this situation was growing, and the bigger it was, the easier it would be to make it all fall apart.

TWENTY-ONE

GET A CHICKEN FOOT FROM THE KITCHEN

Serena waved over a waiter and requested tea. Her belly was bursting and she needed the digestif to help her meal settle and found warm green tea worked the best for her. The caffeine would help sharpen her mind at the same time the warmth would help the questions swimming in her brain. Or it could turn horribly left. Both options were fun at parties.

"He really was looking at Joey?" Serena asked, wanting to storm to the main table to demand answers, but answers to what?

"It was eerie."

"Did you text Huey?" Serena asked since there was no chance they would be allowed to leave the festivities until too late. Which meant neither of them could watch the replay of the meeting held at the same time as Detective Espinal had been interviewing the other groomsmen.

"Yes, he's a bit grumpy about being recorded."

"Do I need to have a discussion with him, because I'll do it. I'll take his ass down and make him do his job." The words were rapid fire, like a machine gun, causing Conner to lean back in case a bullet actually hit him. "We pay him to work, we can stop doing that. Does he understand we have that power? He's not in charge even if we let him pretend to be."

"Okay, no more tea for you," Conner said, sliding the ceramic mug from in front of her. "Do you think anyone here keeps Ativan on hand?"

"Possibly, but I don't need it. Honest, I'm good."

Conner pressed Serena's nose, then pushed it to the side a bit.

"What are you doing?" she asked, her eyes crossing to focus on his finger.

"Seeing if I can get you back to normal speed." He pressed her nose a little further right.

"I will hurt you," she replied.

"Promise," he said with a wink, then brought his hand down to take hers. "My love, you're running on vapors. If we figure this out before or after the wedding, it will be okay."

"No, it won't. Bethany can't look at her wedding pictures and think, he's in jail, she's in jail. We need to know before she walks down the aisle. Before her perfect forever has people she'll need to photoshop out. Or worse."

"Will there be an aisle on the beach?"

"Of course there will be. I know her, it will be epic. Probably sprinkled with diamonds that somehow turn into Louboutin red bottoms as they meld perfectly with her bare feet."

"Wait? What would be worse than photoshopping?" he questioned. "And if your cousin can do that, we might need to check on her magic skills. Is this a traditional family Voo-doo?"

"Nigerian, not Creole," she pointed out. "But Haiti is only a few hours away. Do you think I could get a chicken foot from the kitchen here or would we need to get to the other side of the island to make sure it's powerful?"

Conner's eyes widened, and even she knew she needed to slow down.

Reaching for a goblet of red wine, she sipped. It was far from her favorite drink, warm, smooth, but horribly tart in her mind most times. The good part would come in about fifteen minutes if the alcohol actually hit her. Slowing her down. Depressing the hormones that were in hyperdrive right now. Spiking her need to solve a murder like she had spent years at Quantico dissecting criminal behavior instead checking out an elective in abnormal psych and picking up a criminology class one semester.

Taking a full swallow this time, she let the liquid slide down her throat. Praying for the alcohol to find her bloodstream. It was strange how hard liquor had one effect on her, while beer and wine had another. It wasn't the strength or proof. Whatever it was, warmth slipped from her chest, down her arms and into her fingertips.

Speeches were being given, but all she could do was watch the men and women sitting around them. Toasting happiness with little to no regard to the man who would be flying home with the luggage. Had his family been contacted? Why weren't they rushing to the island demanding the truth of it all? Or had they been told the same lie as everyone else and were happy to know the criminal was rotting away in a jail.?

A call made her phone buzz on the table in front of her. The number, recently saved. Even Conner wouldn't tell her no, it wasn't the time. Her eyes were transfixed on the electronic while others were staring at her for a very different reason. Grasping the phone she realized Auntie Louise had been talking and while her mind had been wandering the wilderness of crime scenes, guilty parties and way too many hours of grainy video, everyone else had been listening to…well probably a commentary on the wonders that were Bethany.

"I'm sorry, I have to take this," she said, sliding her finger across the answer button as heat flared in her cheeks and she rushed from the restaurant praying more for good news on the other end of the line, the thought trumping whatever thoughts on rudeness, etiquette, and decorum she'd blasphemed against. "Mr. Ruiz, please tell me you have good news."

"Mrs. Love, I have been in contact with the prosecutor all day and at first I believed we had a good chance at coming to a plea agreement."

"No," she bit, rage spiking through her whole being at the

thought the man was ignoring every part of their discussion in his office. "Derian did not do this. We told you there is no possible way this child did what he is accused of."

"I said at first," he rebutted. "But then I received the discovery information from their office. In their mind, showing me an open and shut case."

"And what pray tell was the damning evidence?" Serena asked, her free hand fisting in pure outrage.

"If I were to lock a gate with a chain from the circumstantial evidence linked together a newborn pup could push it gate open with a nudge of his nose."

Shaking out her fingers, Serena breathed out, hope blooming in her chest.

"Then I went to visit Derian," he continued. "Compared the crime scene photos and information from the autopsy. Even if the victim had been drugged and was passed out on the beach, there is no way Derian would have the strength to do what was done to the man."

"Can you get Derian released? On bond or bail or whatever it is down here?"

"No, not for a capital offense such as this."

"We've narrowed down real suspects," Serena said. "Or we had, the resort held back key videos."

"Not surprising," Mr. Ruiz said. "Any that could clear Derian completely?"

"Possibly," she said. "There's video of Derian leaving the resort and then video not long after of Patrick talking with the other groomsmen."

"Leaving the resort doesn't mean he didn't come back and go to the beach."

"But getting on a bus that was going to school would mean others saw him."

The other end of the line became silent. A bit of scratching broke through, but nothing she could discern to know what was going on.

"Mr. Ruiz?"

"Si, yes, I was making notes for Ms. Peña to follow up on. It is late, but we could possibly get Derian out in the morning."

"That would be wonderful," Serena gushed.

"The best way to do that would be to have the guilty party on a platter, so the prosecutor wouldn't have to answer to those higher up."

"Is he an honest man?" she asked.

"She," he corrected. "Feels similarly to myself. We see the corruption and do what we can to stop it. A very fine line is drawn between the needs of the country and town versus one individual."

"Thank you. My husband and I will do everything we can to bring you the guilty party tied up in a very nice bow."

"It would be helpful," he replied. "And Mrs. Love, we will do what we can on our end."

Conner's hand slipped along her shoulder as the line went dead and she turned. Sleep be damned, she would need to call in every favor she could to set this right. People would be leaving in less than two days and getting them back could happen, but it would be years. Lost years that would haunt her dreams. Maybe that is why she couldn't sleep. For fear of the nightmares swimming at the edges of her consciousness.

"Serena," her mother's voice broke through the spinning cogs, sending them flying like a clock smashed on the floor. "Serena Anaborhi."

Middle name, twice in so many hours. Disappointment abounded in the Isola clan for the child blessed with a name about being destined for goodness.

"Mother," she replied, turning, but only seeing Conner's chest in front of her. Lifting her eyes to him, the sigh unmistakable.

"Oh, I'm mother now, you know better than to leave a formal engagement," she stated.

"As if daddy never stepped from a room when tapped on the

shoulder," she countered. "At times there are more important things than ceremony."

"And that would be?" her mother questioned.

"In this case, a young man's life."

"The one we spoke about at lunch?" her mother's voice softened a bit. "What has happened?"

"Beyond them offering him a deal to say he did it, very little from the legal front. But our attorney is working on it, I gave him some directions based on what we've learned."

"Well, that is something."

"It feels like nothing to me," Serena protested, tears warming her cold cheeks as the breeze cut along the abandoned pathway. The hostess for the restaurant trying to not pay attention to the woman about to have a breakdown steps from the front door. Milling around, Serena found that this resort had so many nooks and crannies. Perfect for lovers to sneak off to, but also for murderers to hide away.

Every person around the table set for a celebration of life and love, a future unencumbered by the passing of an associate. Why did she care? Well, she and Conner. The man silently standing aside her. Allowing the processing, grief, and injustice to stew inside her until the ingredients melded. The flavor unmistakable.

"Huey sent me a screenshot," Conner said as she swiped the tears of frustration from her cheeks.

"And?"

"And everyone wants Bethany to have a perfect wedding," he said, flipping his phone toward her. On the screen behind the crystal blue eyes of Conner, midsentence, if his rounded mouth was any indication. The more important image was over his left shoulder.

Abaeze was standing with Mr. Espinal, their hands locked in a shake with Detective Espinal over Conner's left shoulder. What the man didn't know was the woman whose son was being tossed to the wolves was adding pastries on a back table, unaware of the Devil's deal taking place steps away from her that would forever destroy her son's life.

———

"He was part of it," Serena said, resigned to the devastation taking place with a simple deal of an attorney caring for his client over the truth evident in her tone.

"We don't know what is going on here," Conner said. "Between the wind and me running my mouth, even Josh couldn't pull the background audio."

"You think he was simply saying, thank you for your kind words?" Serena asked and like the image was Batman's beacon, Abaeze rounded the corner.

"Oh, I'm so glad I found you," Abaeze said with a wide grin, unaware of what at least two of the people standing there were thinking. "Bethany is having a minor meltdown wanting you."

"Me?" Serena questioned, her head turned to the side as she glanced over her shoulder as if Donald would be there. Or some other person of importance.

"Yes, of course," Abaeze said. "You and I both know the importance of cousins to only children."

"Right, um. I guess I'll head back." Serena headed back, but Conner couldn't move, Abaeze's comment hitting a bit too close to home at the moment.

"Abaeze," Conner said and the man turned back.

"Yes," he replied.

"I have siblings, so cousins weren't exactly my first best friend," Conner said, wondering how to broach a subject of evidence tampering.

"I too have siblings, but they came later and Donald and I had already become close. Less than a few months separate us. I can't remember a time without him."

"That is wonderful," Mrs. Isola said, placing her hand on the best man's shoulder, guiding him over to a bench. "I'm an only child, from only children, my family came from friends and co-workers. Well, more associates since Drew is the one who works."

"Do not undercut the hard work of the woman behind the man," Abaeze said. "I know Bethany believes she will be working for years to come, but with the path cleared for Donald, she will need to be the support for his growth."

"And their families," Mrs. Isola continued as she sat on the bench and Abaeze obliged. Manners overtaking the need to return to the party.

"For a moment only," he said, settling in next to her. "It seems my duties never end with Donald. I'm not sure who is the bigger bride at this moment."

"What does Donald do?" Mrs. Isola questioned and Conner stepped in, catching her up on the bigger picture.

"He's a lawyer, at the same firm as Abaeze. Isn't that correct?"

"Yes, most of us interned there and were hired after law school," Abaeze said. "But Donald is the most successful of all of us."

"Since Patrick is gone," Conner added. "Wasn't he doing better?"

"Patrick was not part of the group that came in together. We've had a few fall off and out of the firm, but Patrick had been there for five years prior."

"Five years? And still a good enough friend to be added to the wedding party."

Abaeze's jaw tightened and with a slight nod he tried to stand only to have Mrs. Isola clasp his hand in hers before placing them all on his knee. The motion simple, yet firm in the you're not going anywhere young man.

"I really need to be getting back, I'm sure there is a speech I am supposed to be delivering."

"You'd do anything to keep this wedding on track, wouldn't you?" Mrs. Isola questioned with her head tilted to the side, a mother's gift when it came to saying young man you won't be going anywhere until I am done with the conversation. "Let me tell you, Bethany has been demanding since the first time I placed my hand on Louise's swollen belly. This is a hard undertaking."

"Much like others say a labor of love in a way. Family, we take care of each other."

"And friends are now family," Conner said. "Buying property next to the one your family owns."

"Yes, how fortunate. Referrals are good for a few perks."

"Like covering up the person who killed Patrick," Conner stated, standing over Abaeze. While the man was tall, Conner had more than a few inches on the man. When seated, that difference was more prominent and the man tried to stand, but Conner's mother-in-law had the iron grip of a woman not willing to let go of a child dangling over a cliff.

"If you two care for Bethany at all, you will let this go," Abaeze stated. "Patrick's loss will be a blip in the office. A solemn moment of silence, a bit of oh dears, followed by an office being boxed up."

"And clients redistributed," Conner surmised. "How many had he taken from you?"

"A few, but that's why I don't care which of them did it," Abaeze said. "And what does it matter? They'll pin in on some kid who will end up in jail, anyway. So he gets there a few days sooner."

Fire sizzled up Conner's spine, his hand fisting at the disregard for Derian. Abaeze didn't even know who they pinned the murder on. Never looked in the kid's eyes. He probably took a dish from the kid's mother with a smile and thanks, never thinking of the fact he'd destroyed her life. Derian didn't have the luxury of being a kid, never had from what they learned over a couple days. But his heart was in the right place. He was taking care of his family, no matter how small it was, his mother was all he had in the world. The one person who loved him, no matter what others said.

"That kid is fourteen and now being brutalized in a jail for adults," Conner fumed. "Tossed away before he even had a chance to grow. We met him when we first came here. Nearly every person had tossed him away like garbage, from the time he was born. Now I understand you don't get that. But as a broke ass busted kid from a farming community, I understand hand-me downs and trying to get the smell of manure out so people could see me as more."

"You did it, they wouldn't have—"

"That kid was on a bus making sure a six-year-old girl he's not even related to got to school safely. That's what he was doing when Patrick was killed."

"That is not my problem."

"A wedding is a moment in a life," Conner said, flipping through images on his phone until he found the one he needed. "One, while precious, isn't worth another's whole existence. If Derian survives, what will he become? Exactly what you say he is and you've never so much as looked at the kid."

Flipping the screen once again to Abaeze, he showed the smiling face of the kid leaning into Serena at Carlos' bar. His cheeks puffed out from the taco he'd stuffed in his mouth seconds before Conner said, *'smile you two'*. There was no way a man could see a child smaller than Serena and not realize what they had done.

Burying his face in his hands, Abaeze's shame came out in heaving shoulders as he tried to gather himself enough to face the people around him.

"The men assured me they could make everything go away," he said, lifting his head. "Patrick only wanted to come because he was sure that Donald was wining and dining some clients while we were down here."

"Still, I don't get why Donald brought him in, and Emma. Invite sure, but making him part of the bridal party."

"Bethany doesn't have many female friends," Abaeze said. "Your wife wasn't answering and she had it in her mind she needed five attendants on each side."

"Social media versus the reality of the world." Conner shook his head. "That explains Emma, but not Patrick."

"Patrick was seconds from taking over Donald's biggest case. He said if he was too busy being part of the wedding he couldn't take on the extra load," Abaeze said. "This case will give Donald the points he needs to become partner. Patrick has—had been at the firm longer, doing dirty deeds and has been put up for partner a handful of times only to be passed over."

"But when Patrick arrived, he spoke about a case that Donald had abandoned."

"Manipulation, the man is not one you would want to play poker with." Abaeze finally stood. "What he didn't know was Donald had already signed all the settlement papers before we left. We'd tried to make it appear as if there were outstanding issues. Knowing he couldn't resist staying behind. If it hadn't been for Emma, Patrick would have never shown up."

"Emma and Kaitlynn," Conner stated. "She'd been sending Patrick pictures of Emma and Joey."

"Those two." Abaeze shook his head. "Until Patrick says he's done with you, you are not to leave him. The world is not at a loss for him no longer being a part of it, and while I sympathize for the young man, I don't know what I can do to help."

"Because you don't know which one actually killed Patrick?"

"And I don't want to," he replied. "I can't be culpable for what I don't know. I also need to look out for my clients."

"Evan, Erik and Joey are now your clients?"

"I need to get back to the party." Abaeze held his hands up in surrender as he walked away. "I wish I could help."

"And this is the family my niece is marrying into," Mrs. Isola said as she slapped her hands on her thighs then stood. "I am glad my daughter chose better. Bring me back, and Drew is going to need be tapped on his shoulder."

The determination on his mother-in-law's face was near frightening as she looped her arm through his.

"There are many things I will do for family, but I will not allow another to be destroyed for my own. You are right, it is a moment," she said as they walked along the path. "One that should be about the couple, not the hearts that will be clicked on a social media post."

"You ever wish we would have done the whole big wedding?" Conner asked. "Instead of running away to Vegas?"

"A part of me did," she confessed. "But then I remembered how tired I was after three days of celebration for my own wedding, well weddings really. The confusion on my family's face because of all the ceremony. Oh, and the fighting that led up to the ceremony. I was embracing my husband's culture at the cost of my own."

"I wouldn't think that seeing you now."

"I didn't," she said. "We had things similar to the way I grew up, Lutheran style weddings, but I knew how important it was for my in-laws. I had a few ceremonies. Traditional for him and me, it was a crazy week I'd been stressed out about for months. I used to joke with Drew I was making sure he really meant it when he said forever. That's why I made sure he did it a few times just in case the answer changed."

"The green dress must have made your family freak out."

"Most of my family came to the wedding where I wore a white gown and veil."

"Oh." Conner could feel the confusion tightening his eyebrows together.

"Children from mixed cultures walk a strange line," Mrs. Isola said. "The world will never let them forget they aren't a whole anything, but the more we've seen the less Serena believed it. Instead, she saw herself as blessed to know more about the world than most and not because of Drew's job."

Could that be the reason she didn't want children? Because it would tie them to one place where they would be told they were less than? He'd never had a big draw to kids in the long term. For him, it was a lack of love growing up. He never wanted a child to think they weren't important and although he loved Serena more each day could he have the same connection with a child? Lord knows his parents never had.

Unlike Serena's who showed her love and let her explore. Boundaries meant less with a diplomatic pass, or so his wife told him. Like right now, the police were involved, but that meant nothing because she cared. She wanted to solve the puzzle and right now they had three near-identical pieces and as much as he'd like to smash one into place and call it a day, she wouldn't let him. Because there was enough dividing the world.

TWENTY-TWO
YOU ARE HER SAFE HARBOR

"It's not going to be right and I have no idea how to make it work." Bethany was freaking out in the bathroom with Yvette and Katelyn the red trying to calm her down. The complementary bottles of lotion were being lined up along the sink like chess pieces.

"Bethany," Serena said as she stepped inside, past Chelsea who was blocking anyone from entering the facility as if she were some sort of bouncer for a high-end club. "Are we having an OCD breakdown or normal jitters?"

"You tell us," Katelyn pleaded as she rubbed between Bethany's shoulders, only to have her shrug the woman off.

"Serena," Bethany called, reaching for her and pulling her to the display of lunacy on the countertop. "You understand. The perfect image, my father has paid for all this and now it isn't lining up correctly. I've tried to be calm about it, reasonable even, but the tables aren't even."

"Okay, so what are we doing?" Serena asked, glancing at bottles a mix of upright and strewn as if tossed to the side and bounced in place.

"Five, creates even and odd at the same time. Bridal Knots says it's the perfect number."

"Okay." Serena gathered all the bottles in both hands and passed them off to Yvette. Bethany turned to Serena with eyes wide. "First, let's calm down a bit."

"Four and four is nothing but even, you get that. We'd be out of balance."

"I can see that," Serena lied. Numbers were more of a Conner thing, but that and fifty cents wasn't going to get her anything off the dollar menu of crazy right now. Would she have had this type of meltdown if she'd gone all big time with the wedding? Probably not. She would have canceled the wedding and eloped if a bridal party member died. Then again, she wouldn't have invited a sworn enemy to stand up for her.

"My mother says it can all be arranged for a true ceremony, and this could be an engagement party instead of a wedding, but there is no way Donald could get more time off. And not the way we need for a traditional wedding. Tyler, Michaels and Kern is not a place you abandon for months at a time or even take time off for a few weeks here and there. We're already going to cut our honeymoon short because of Patrick."

"I'm sorry to hear that," Serena said with sincerity, her heart breaking a bit for the woman melting down.

"We can't use Conner unless he was on his knees the whole time for pictures and what would that mean when we were at the altar?"

"You have an altar?"

"Yeah, some pergola thing is being erected for tomorrow." Bethany's hand splayed across her chest and she began dry heaving. "Dear Lord, tomorrow I'm getting married. Not even tomorrow. It's less than—oh my God, where's the countdown clock."

"Don't show her that," Serena said, unsure who was the timekeeper among the women, only knowing the person was in the room and highly unnecessary at the moment. "Breathe, Bethany. This is normal. Completely normal."

In the world of the insanely cognizant of social media and believing what was put out to the world was real, not highlights.

"Really? You broke down when you married Conner?"

"Sure I did," Serena kept with the lie, if for no other reason than she hoped the little girl who had pledged to be just like Serena when she got older would get a grip. "Bethany, who do you want in this wedding? Honestly, if it was Donald and you before a preacher, who do you want if you need to reach out for another hand?"

"Katelyn," she snuffed and reached her hand out for her maid of honor, the woman smiling as she accepted and held tight. "And Yvette and you."

"Then that is your wedding party. Maybe I could fit into one of the other woman's dresses," Serena said. "And that's odd yet even. You don't need five people. You don't even need three."

Maybe Serena was hoping to be completely dumped from the bridesmaid tag, but it was true.

"Katelyn and Abaeze would be happy to stand for you."

"But then it would seem as if we had no friends. No one who loved us."

Serena held Bethany's face in her hands. "Trust me when I say, I've been around the world and found the most peace and happiness in the smallest of places. Ones where no one goes, but magic can be found there. You don't need a hundred attendants. The only thing you need is a man who stares at you from across the room as if his beginning and end are wrapped up in the curve of your hip and his tomorrows are locked in the smile on your lips."

The perfect, yet wrong at all times, young woman absorbed Serena's words like a dry sponge tossed into the ocean. Arms quickly wrapped around Serena as she was pulled into a constricting hug.

"This wedding needs to be perfect for you," Serena said. "And only you. Those who love you will see the beauty of the day. The rest can go to Jamaica. I know a good cliff they can jump off."

"Any chance on your travels you found a good shrink?" Bethany laughed.

"I wish," Serena said. "But in New York there has to be a couple."

"Oh, why did I let it get this crazy?" Bethany asked.

"Because you're basic," Serena teased and got a slap on the shoulder for her troubles.

"Please, I'm about to be Bethany Usman, and she is anything but basic."

"Damn right," Serena said, adjusting Bethany's latest crown to make sure it was perfect.

"Oh, my goodness, my make-up," Bethany said as she took in the running colors on her cheeks.

"I've got you," Yvette said, tossing the bottles of lotion in the basin and opening her purse. "And not having to do all those women's makeup tomorrow means I'll be able to bring the gorgeous bride out of you."

"Serena, are you sure it will be okay?" Bethany asked, swallowing hard. "People won't think I'm foolish?"

"Not even slightly," Serena said, thinking besides, one of the groomsmen is going to be taking Derian's place in the jail cell so they won't have time to deal with another meltdown over balancing the bridal party. "We good here, ladies?"

"Yes, I've got her," Katelyn the red assured. "As always."

Stepping out of the bathroom, Serena rounded the corner to see Conner escorting her mother back to the party. Donald approached her with panic on his face.

"Please say she's not leaving me," he said, the worry furrowing his brow.

"Not even slightly, but you might need to talk with your attendants," Serena said. "I've been reminding her what is the most important part of the wedding for a bride."

"Please, not the dress," he said.

"No, the groom," Serena said. "And if he's not then none of the rest of the ceremony matters."

"Oh, she's not going to like that," Donald said with a light laugh.

"Of course she will, because she knows the most important part to the groom is the bride." Serena stepped away and found her own husband. "My love."

"Does the whole world revolve around Bethany?" Conner asked. "Because after speaking with Abaeze, I believe it does."

"It might," Serena laughed. "Why?"

"It was one of them," Conner said. "Abaeze doesn't know which and doesn't want to."

"Plausible deniability if the cops actually did their jobs."

"Pretty much." Conner led her by her elbow to their seats. "All three of them are covering. Buying property, paying off the locals."

"Can they all afford that?" Serena asked. "Realistically?"

"I doubt it," Conner said. "Which means…"

"Which means if someone is paying for another man's choice, their loyalty will only go so far."

"That's what I'm thinking," Conner said. "This party is going to be moving on to a bar soon."

"Will the guilty be overindulging or trying to keep the ducks in a sober row?"

"Let's retire to the bar and see," Conner said, offering Serena his arm.

Her mother and father, like those in their generation, had peeled off when the group made their way to the next stop of the evening, but it wasn't toward their room and the security behind them did not appear amused. Wherever they were going was off script.

"At least Abaeze isn't the guilty party."

"Not directly," Conner said. "But could he be an accessory after the fact?"

"You think they care about that here?" Serena asked. "Or has the family paid enough to be forgiven?"

"More they need a person to blame, but honestly, Derian may have the city wired in his own special way. He needs a new start somewhere," Conner said. "Even if it's a new tourist town.

Somewhere he doesn't have everyone seeing him as a no good kid."

"It made me think of our driver the other day. Moving out to the country to give his kids a chance to be kids."

"True, we could save him this time, but next time he might not be so lucky."

"I wouldn't have come to this stupid place," a howl made the Loves turn to see a flash of blonde as Kaitlynn turned on her heel. "Lord knows my life would be a hell of a lot better if I hadn't."

Conner tugged on Serena and they tucked behind a potted plant. The leaves giving ample cover, even for Conner, the stem reaching high in the air.

"Kaitlynn, baby, come on, think about it," Evan said. "We can go back to Tyler, Michaels and Kern. Both of us now, you know they'll take us."

"Why would I want to?" she questioned. "Was that your goal? Because it wasn't mine."

"What was yours?" Evan asked. "Torment the asshole?"

"You know what he did to me," she snapped. "If Eric wouldn't have saved me where would we be now? Ugh, Evan, even now, what are you really doing for me?"

Kaitlynn shoved him and he stumbled a bit into a bench. Serena's heart was thudding in her ears and she needed it to stop so she could hear the conversation.

"Why do I put up with you? I could have stayed back home if it wasn't for you."

"Trouble in paradise," Serena whispered, and Conner covered her mouth with his hand.

"Donald is one of my best friends, and even if I'm not in the wedding I would have come down here to support him." Evan pulled Kaitlynn into his arms, nuzzling into her neck. "If nothing else, we needed time out of the city."

"No, I needed time away from Patrick and his bullshit."

"Then why are you upset? Because you're not getting a bouquet and having to stand up front."

"I bet she cut us all out so she'd be the prettiest." Kaitlynn pulled away and tossed her long blonde hair to the side. "Because lord knows Katelyn with that horse face would never steal the queen bee's thunder."

"Or, now that Donald isn't being blackmailed, they can have the wedding they actually want," Evan said. "Come on, we're in a tropical paradise, so lets enjoy the unlimited drinks and have fun."

"Grow a backbone, Evan," she bit. "I don't know why Eric thinks you could get your job back. You wouldn't have the balls to approach Mr. Kern."

"I did plenty," he said, his voice lowering even with his apparent lapdog status.

"What, shoved Patrick?" she mocked. "Said a few choice words. Eric once again did what needed to be done."

"Did he?" Evan challenged, a bit of ire in his words. "Or did he take credit for what happened? I'm the one paying to get us out of the mess."

"Oh boo-hoo, your trust fund will never recover."

"You weren't there—you didn't have to see what I saw."

"I wish I had been," Kaitlynn said, her face twisting in ugly delight. "Watch the light disappear from his eyes. Knowing all the while who did it. Why couldn't you have gotten rid of the body? That's what I want to know."

"Because I told you that kid—"

"Kaitlynn," Bethany's voice came from up the path and soon the bride and groom to be were approaching the couple. "Kaitlynn, I do hope you understand."

"Of course," Kaitlynn's voice changing from accusing to appreciative, the perfect fake friend showing every bit of social media falsity. "This business with Patrick has been trying and in the last few days before your wedding. I couldn't imagine."

"The plus is that you are here to join us on our special day," Donald said with a clap to Evan's shoulder, the action making him wince. "This is what we truly want. Our loved ones to be with us."

"And they are," Kaitlynn said, her smile false.

"Now, which bar did we say we were going to meet up at?" Bethany asked. "Because if this is my last night as a single woman, I have some dancing and debauchery in my future

———

Conner and Serena pressed their backs flat to the wall. Others had joined the group going down to the bar where they should already be. Excuses could be made, but now they had to decide. Had there been a confession? Not really. Eric and Evan were usually attached at the hip, but four went down to the beach and three came back up. Evan's rotator cuff had him out of the running already, but did that mean Eric was the one who did the deed?

"Well, someone is full of herself," Serena said once they were free to step from the shadows.

"Evan is paying for the properties," Conner said. "You think all of them? Would he pay for Joey's?"

"I don't see why not," Serena said. "Whoever killed Patrick removed a large obstacle professionally."

"Evan said Donald was being blackmailed, but Abaeze didn't," Conner stated. "In fact, they were happy Patrick wasn't coming and was sure when they left, nothing was outstanding. Nothing could be used against him."

"Maybe Evan and Kaitlynn didn't know that," she mused. "Do you think Derian saw?"

"No," Conner said. "We've made it clear we're trying to help him."

"Did we?" she questioned. "Or to a street smart kid would we seem like another set of tourists fishing for information? Trying to cover up what happened."

Conner hadn't thought of that. The man was with their group.

It wasn't a foregone conclusion that Derian would see them as allies. Just because the Loves were looking out and agonizing about the fate of the young man, it didn't mean he believed them.

"There is no way to see him tonight," Serena said, pulling him from his thoughts. "But that doesn't mean we can't confront the trio and let them think when we spoke to him, he told us everything he saw."

"You that good of an actor?" Conner asked, unsure of his own ability to keep the lie straight. Even if it was for only a few minutes. If they did, it would be he said he said and not admissible. Voice recording was necessary, but he was going to have to double down. Luckily, at this point, he knew where to stand in most places to have the video to line up with the conversation.

Finding the bar wasn't hard, as music spilled out onto the pathway. Pulling random passer-byes with the promise of fun and a good beat. Stepping in the bar the bass from the music vibrated in his chest. A thudding beat overtaking his body as they moved through where the group of wedding goers had blocked off an area. Chelsea, Yvette and Katelyn the red were dancing with Bethany and Auntie Olivia. Sitting in the back of the area, Emma rubbed Joey's back as he nursed a drink. Three empty glasses already littering the table in front of him. Melted ice cubes showing the length of time since they'd been served and abandoned. The liquor no longer leaving a trace of brown at the bottom.

"Relief has shifted to guilt," Serena pointed out, then lunged forward, causing Conner to have to catch her.

"I'm so sorry," Eric said, his palms facing the couple in surrender. "I wasn't looking where I was going."

"You're rushing around," Conner said once Serena was righted. "Any particular reason?"

"Last minute wedding stuff," he said.

"Still helping then?" Conner questioned.

"Don's a good man, probably will be my boss when I get home. No reason to rock the boat." Eric gave a clap to Conner's bicep. "I better get going since Kaitlynn's in a mood and Evan can only do so much when it comes to her."

"Before you go," Serena said, catching the man's wrist. "It's none of my business, I get that, but I do have to question, the three of you are pretty close."

"In public, Evan gets all the glory," Eric said with a wink. "Just makes it easier for the three of us. Not everyone is so open-minded, and the last thing we need is some scandal."

"Patrick didn't know, did he?" Conner asked. "Because from all I've learned about the guy he seems like the type to hold it over someone."

"He goaded me, mocking me for losing Kaitlynn after—" Eric stopped and Kaitlynn's words about Eric saving her came front and center. "I really should—"

"That has to be expensive, having multiple homes, especially in New York," Serena said. "And with you three working so much it seems to be a waste because you'd never enjoy it."

"Evan is old money," Eric said. "That's why he took the hit and left the firm first. He could afford it. Besides, his family owns enough property. Kaitlynn's the one who has to do all the juggling. Rarely are we all together. Honestly, I need to get going. Evan says she's having a meltdown of sorts."

"If it's Eric, Evan will bail him out," Conner surmised once the man left.

"Or let him take the fall," she countered. "He's the one with the money, the open relationship with Kaitlynn…Joey's the one in panic mode."

"Something tells me he's worried about being blamed," Conner said. "Kaitlynn set the man up, expecting a confrontation only to have Joey cower."

"The party is over here, my friend," Abaeze said, pressing his hand between Conner's shoulder blades and moving him toward the group. "Your wife should be dancing and we should be drinking."

"He's right, I can't have my auntie being the life of the party," Serena said with a tap to Conner's hip.

Tasked again to discover the truth, or at least lead them further down the path. With a nod, he followed Abaeze to the group and they waved over a waitress.

"Tell me," Don's voice near yelling to be heard over the music. "The secret to a happy marriage."

"Love the woman," Conner said. "It's not really a big secret."

"Ah, loving Bethany is not the part that worries me," Don replied. "It is all the other things."

"What other things?" Conner wondered.

"Living, working, the day to day."

Was that why Serena had never slowed down? The natural progression of their life had them on the road, travelling all the time. There was never time to sit and reflect unless it was in a picturesque local where the moment surrounded them with beauty. Drawing them into a peace and allowing their brains to slow, reset and go again at a later time. Their routine, their normal wasn't one others could duplicate. Even with Serena's tips on traveling, their ability to be in moments made them precious and appreciative.

Conner shifted his gaze to the dance floor, his wife's laughter known to him. Even over the music, he could hear her, or maybe it was a memory replaying. Smile wide and eyes a bit narrow with her hands high in the air. The group of women lost in the music and not caring who was watching. Being free of judgment placed on them most of the time.

"Love her," Conner repeated. "In the insanity of moments, when she's being selfish, when she's being giving. Let her know in your eyes she can do no wrong because to the world they will only see her as incomplete. Missing one thing that no one will ever achieve. Women have it hard."

"Do they now?" Abaeze said with a laugh. "They are at home, not stressing beyond dinner most days."

"And yet, every decision they make comes into question.

Work, or stay home. Wear red or wear green. Short hair, braids, natural. All of it coming at a price between family, friends and the world if they post a simple picture. Everyone is judging them." Conner took a sip of the bourbon that had been placed in front of him. "But you are her safe harbor. The one who, even when you don't want to do it, approves of her choices."

"That is why your wife drags you around the world?" Donald asked.

"Not a bad way to live," he replied. "The view is constantly changing."

"But what about children, a family?" Donald questioned. "Bethany and I are both only children, and we do not want that for ourselves. When I see her face, I want twenty little girls running around the house just like her."

"Just like her?" Conner questioned. "Because that is a lot of tiaras."

Donald and Abaeze roared with laughter.

"All women do is manipulate you," Joey said, moving from the corner where he'd been sitting, his gait altered by the alcohol as he stumbled toward the men. Liquor spilling over the top of the glass tumbler he was holding between his thumb and middle finger. "Play as if they love you until they get what they want."

"Come on, let's get you back to the room," Emma prodded only to be shrugged off by Joey when she attempted to move him.

"Get off me," he howled. "You got what you wanted, you're free of him. Now you're crying as if you hadn't wished the man dead for the past few months."

"Joey," Emma replied, her eyes cutting to the floor. "Don't say that."

"Why? Because it's true, everyone here wants the truth of it all."

Conner reached for his phone. Hoping to find his voice recording app before it was too late.

"You wanna know the truth?" Joey's words slurred as he set his drink on the table only to have it spill, making Donald and

Abaeze jump up to avoid getting wet. "Fuck, I need another drink."

"Hey, Joey," Eric said as he and Evan flanked the man. "You need a little help."

"Oh, aren't you two the dynamic duo?" Joey shoved at both men and Conner noticed the security moving closer to the roped off section. "We should get you guys capes."

Joey tripped and Conner reached out to catch him. Getting a shove for his efforts.

"Anyone have a cape for these two heroes?" Joey howled as merrymakers moved aside to let the crazy man through. "Seriously, Evan needs one for his credit card and Eric—why do you need one, Eric? What have you done? Oh that's right you—"

Eric and Evan rushed Joey from the bar, their hands up, assuring the security they could handle their unruly friend as Conner trailed behind. Extending a hand to Abaeze and Donald to have them stay. Fumbling with his phone, Conner found the app he was looking for and started the recording. Running to catch up to the men, hoping to put the loud talker, full of guilt to bed before all the truths were spilled about what happened on the beach.

"Hey, you guys need any help?" Conner offered.

"No, were good," Eric called back.

"We spoke to Derian," Serena's voice cut through the abandoned pathway. Sweat on her brow from the dancing as she clutched her stomach from having to run to catch up to them.

Conner glanced around and knew they would need to move over toward an abandoned pool bar to get the men on camera.

"Who's Derian?" Evan asked as all three men turned toward the Loves. Joey's eyes bloodshot and lids heavy. The alcohol dulling more than his self-preservation button.

"The kid they arrested," Joey said, his head lolling from side to side. "What? You didn't even care who got blamed? As long as it wasn't us, right guys?"

"Well, we do care, and that kid is scared and alone in a prison cell," Conner said.

"Doesn't matter," Eric said. "The kid will take a plea and be done with it."

"No, he won't," Serena said with a hard scowl. "We won't let him. Already got him a lawyer."

"Why would you do that?" Evan asked, stepping a bit closer to Serena than Conner would like.

"Because he didn't do it," Serena countered. "And we all know who did."

TWENTY-THREE
YOU DO KNOW HOW TO PUT ON A SHOW

Serena's pulse thudded along the column of her neck. Her skin goose pimpled and stomach tightened. Though that could be from the smell of whiskey and meat wafting from Joey's direction. Evan, on the other hand, was stone cold sober and not her suspect, just her greatest threat at the moment. Inches from her face, standing over her in a way as if his size were truly a factor for her. In a way his height left her at an advantage defensively.

"What you think and what is the truth are miles apart," Evan said.

"That Joey can't afford to pay to cover up for you two?" she bluffed, hoping to hit a nerve on the man inebriated enough to lower his guard. "Can you? He doesn't have the trust fund you do, Evan."

"What would you know about my trust fund?" Evan questioned. His arm raised and Serena instantly grasped his wrist with both hands. Pushing up with ease and making the man drop to his knees with a howl of pain. Normally the move would do little, but with his injury and her ability to lock on gravity mixed with a searing pain brings about a result her defense teachers would applaud.

"You're gonna need that surgery sooner rather than later." She scowled at the man. "And we all know why."

"I didn't kill Patrick," Evan cried out and yanked his arm from her hands. Clutching the injured limb with his good arm to his chest like a broken wing.

"No, but you did a good job of tossing the murder weapon into the ocean," Conner said. "Those scuba tanks aren't light, especially when they are full."

The three men stared at Conner as if he'd watched the whole murder and was now moments from blackmailing them.

"It was you right?" Conner questioned. "Derian gave descriptions, but either way I figure it was you. Throwing away the evidence, taking your own bit of the blame in order to make it equal."

"Everything equal," Evan spat, still kneeling and clutching his arm. "But not, not even close."

"How much did the kid see?" Eric questioned, his jaw tight in rage and Serena could sense the truth moments from escaping.

"The shove down the stairs," Conner began, and Serena wondered if the bluff would work. "Patrick stumbled a bit on the last step. That's what caught his attention."

"I told you we should have chased after the kid," Joey said. "Offered him money. You should have followed up with him. Now he's spilling everything—"

"They aren't going to believe him," Eric assured. "The detective in charge of the case isn't interested in hearing the truth."

"Why? We did," Serena countered, and Eric's eyes burned with rage toward her.

"Why would we kill him?" Eric questioned. "You need motive."

"Like we don't all have motives," Joey cried. "Hell, you had to untie Kaitlynn when you found her in Patrick's closet."

"Shut up," Eric snapped.

"Why? Because he had pictures of you three together. Don't try to give me that whole she dates us both we all know better,"

Joey bemoaned. "And Patrick was so close to having Emma in the same sick situation. He stole all my damn clients and most of Evan's. What other motive do you need?"

"Yours, not mine. Fine, you take the blame," Eric replied. "I'm not."

"The video exists," Conner countered. "Of you four going down to the beach and three coming back."

"But there is nothing on the beach," Eric said. "We can say we left him there."

"And you left the canister too?" Conner said. "Because you're the one who grabbed it, Eric."

"So what if I did?" Eric crowed. "Doesn't mean Joey didn't get his pound of flesh from the man."

"But I couldn't," Joey said, tears streaming down his face. "Even when he pushed me all I could do was shove him back."

"And his head cracked against the wall," Eric accused. "Who's to say that didn't kill him?"

"He was still breathing," Joey whined. "Until—until—you smashed him in the face with that damn tank."

Eric rushed Joey, tackling him around the waist, sending the two men into the pool with a loud splash. The cold water jolting the drunk Joey who gasped for air only to be shoved back under the water by Eric. Expletives spewing from the man.

"Why won't you just die, your life is worthless anyway," Eric howled, his hands pressing down on Joey's head. Only hands flopped on the surface, desperately trying to combat the attack, even with Joey's dulled senses and bubbles of air floating to the top of the pool from the last of the air leaving his lungs.

Conner tossed Serena his phone and jumped in the water. First, trying to free Joey from Eric's grasp. The man thrashing at Conner with one hand. The muscles, hard and tense from the pressure of holding a man below him.

"You killed him," Eric screamed into the water below. "Not me."

Conner wrapped his arms around Eric, locking them at the

wrists, and flipped the man backward like some WWE wrestler. Splashes of water soaked the pool deck, wetting Serena's feet. Having tossed Conner's phone on a deck chair, she was ready to jump in if needed. Instead, she rushed to the side, reaching out for Joey.

"You did," Joey said, gasping hard for air, his hair flopped over his eyes. "I wish—I'd kill the SOB—but I didn't have—the strength to."

Joey trudged through the water, flattening himself along the edge of the pool, Serena helping pull him out of the wetness. Defeat on his face.

"Maybe I should take all the blame."

"Yes, you should," Eric snarled, being held back by Conner. "We've done enough to cover for you, and Emma will never love you, anyway."

"Take it all. Clear out two places at Tyler, Michaels and Kern," Evan spat, struggling to stand without using his arms. "I've paid enough to cover this crap up."

Serena clung to Joey's shirt, water being coughed up by the man she feared would let go and sink back into the illuminated blue of the water below. The pool less than four foot deep, but enough to drown a man, especially one not wanting to live anymore.

"Joey, will you confess?" she asked, sweeping his hair to the side, hoping the man with no courage could find a bit. "To your part."

"Did I kill him?" he sobbed, the whiskey and chlorine reddening his eyes. "Did I?"

"I don't know," Serena said, shaking her head.

"You do know how to put on a show," a woman's voice called from behind her and Serena turned to see her old friend Natalie standing, arms crossed with agents flanking her. The woman was older, but still sporting a blunt cut and smirk. "I take it these are unruly Americans your father believes may have killed one of our citizens on foreign soil."

"Unruly," Serena said, relief rushing through her veins. "On so many levels."

"Don't say a word," Eric warned, running his hands through his wet hair and then pushing up and out of the pool. "Not without an attorney."

"He killed Patrick," Serena stated. With a nod of Natalie's head an agent faced off with Eric. The man puffing out his chest until the agent offered a look that would make anyone relent and he cuffed Eric.

"You can't do this to me, I'm an American citizen I have rights."

"That you do," the agent said. "The first of which is the right to remain silent."

"And him?" Natalie asked, pointing to Joey, his body half on the pool deck. "What is his part?"

"That depends on the coroner, but it seems as if he knocked Patrick out," Serena said. "Have you reached out to the prison?"

"Your father called and asked for a favor. I was trying to find my way to his room when I heard the splashes and a man yelling you killed him, with a good New York accent I couldn't ignore." Natalie tapped her ear. "Gotta listen for my constituents you know."

"Didn't we avoid people we thought were American when we were younger?" Serena asked and sat back, forgetting the concrete was wet underneath her.

"We got old and I took on responsibilities," Natalie said. "How about we haul him in for good measure too?"

"I'm not a lawyer, and I don't know the law, but you might need a few more agents," Serena said as she glanced toward Evan, an agent taking her lead as much as Natalie's.

"What about the last pool boy?" Natalie asked as Conner crossed to the steps to get out.

"I'll keep him," Serena said.

"More importantly," Conner began, snatching a towel from

the shelves on the side of the pool to dry off his hands. "I'm the one who taped the confession if they give you any problems."

Picking up his phone he stopped the recording and then approached the ambassador to the Dominican Republic.

"You got an email I can send this to?"

"Are you innocent the Isola's husband?" Natalie asked, and Conner extended his hand to help Serena up.

"Innocent? Serena Isola?" Conner laughed. "Never met her, but I am married to a woman matching her description."

"Want to dry off and tell me all about her?" Natalie beamed.

"Natalie," Serena's father called, his hands outstretched and soon locked around hers. "Ambassador Valdez. I am so proud of who you have become."

"Ambassador Isola, always a pleasure."

"I see my niece's wedding has become a bit unruly," he said with apologetic eyes.

"We've contacted the local officials, but I see I'll need additional help from your agents."

"It happens," her father said, shooing away the imaginary issue. "Glad to be of assistance. Conner, you seem to be a bit wet."

"Yes, sir," Conner said with a nod.

"You say you have a full confession?" Natalie asked.

"Yes, Ambassador. It appears this man shoved the victim and knocked him out," Conner said, pointing toward Joey. "While this man used a scuba tank to kill him."

"That explains the indent," Natalie said, with the same glee in her eyes Serena had when it came together in her mind.

"The final man tossed the tank into the ocean," Conner concluded.

"And people wonder why we can't have nice things."

CHAPTER
TWENTY-FOUR

"*V*alentine's Day can be special no matter where you are in the world," Serena said, her make-up thicker than normal to cover the bags under her eyes, but at least the woman slept the night before. Crashing the moment Natalie made contact with Mr. Ruiz and they knew Derian would be freed.

Conner stood poised, assuming at some point during the walk along the beach his wife might reach for his hand and pull him into the shot. It was Valentine's Day after all. He'd even snuck away and found her a few chocolate covered strawberries for her breakfast.

"This special will be shown in a year, much to the dismay of our illustrious guest and head of Cofresi Beach Escape and Resort, Mrs. Cherise Mendoza who manages resorts across Latin America and the Caribbean."

The woman, smartly dressed stepped into view. "I'm happy Love on the Run came to us at this special time of year. While our temperatures are perfect year-round, what could be better than a beachside wedding with the ocean as your backdrop?"

"Thank you for taking us around for the final day of shooting," Serena said as Conner tucked away the camera. A few steps away, people were finding their seats at Bethany and Donald's wedding.

Instead of using the real beach, they were utilizing the faux one in the villa part of the property. On a cliff, Conner had been assured Serena would not be jumping off. At least not in her new dress. The larimar shade a perfect complement to her tawny skin. Braids were twisted and tucked back, creating a chignon and the pendent she'd found rested nicely below her breasts, the chain cutting between the soft mounds he would be handling later that night.

She reached for him, the bangles of silver bracelets making a metallic clatter as their fingers intertwined and they walked down the aisle and found a spot in the second row. Quickly followed by Mr. and Mrs. Isola who sat next to them. Music floated in the air and the smell of fresh flowers tied along the end of the chairs had Serena snuggling close. Or maybe she was still exhausted from her lack of sleep the last few days.

No matter the cause, his arm slipped around his wife's waist as family members from both sides filled the seats. A mixture of traditional and contemporary dress. Conner turned to take in his father-in-law. The tunic-style top and squared-off hat, while formal in Nigeria would appear casual where he grew up. His wife on the other hand wore a contemporary dress perfectly midwestern mother-of-the-bride style. Or in this case, aunt of the bride.

Auntie Olivia and her family, children included, went traditional. Unlike weddings when he was younger and just the father walked to giveaway Bethany, both sets of parents made their way down the aisle. Both traditional, and Auntie Louise, cross as usual, making him think when they were told to rise, the bride triggered a more full western style. The Bethian wedding style was on full display.

Instead, much like her cousin before her, Bethany took a bit of old and new traditions. Standing, they turned to see the stunning bride. Her strapless mermaid-style gown, hugging curves before fanning out. But her shoulders were not bare. Instead, the gift Serena had given her had been draped, reminding him of knights with ornaments placed on their shoulders to hold capes. The biggest surprise was the gele on her head. The traditional wrapping, hiding the long locks that had been on full display for the past few days. No crown was needed today. Instead the pale blue gele created a halo behind her head reminding him of the images of Mary when he was younger.

Her warm smile greeted the guests, all of whom had traveled far and wide to be here for the couple. Though some were missing, the important ones were not. Ahead of her, Auntie Olivia's daughters tossed flowers, and behind her, the maid of honor made sure her train was perfect before walking down the aisle ahead of the bride.

A few light-hearted jokes and twenty minutes passed before the newly married were allowed to kiss. The whole while Serena held on to Conner's hand. A connection he hoped would never break.

"Son-in-law," Mr. Isola said later, as the reception began. "Come with me."

Conner saw Serena had been distracted by Bethany and pictures were being taken. Mostly by cell phone cameras, but important, nonetheless. There was no shield to be created by Serena, the one and only child of the man to protect Conner, and he worried this would be the moment. The one where money was owed and grandchildren needed to be promised.

Money could be transferred, following the takedown of Dmitri by Huey and Josh combining a one-two punch that may have made it so the man wouldn't be able to turn a light switch on, let alone a computer made the revenue lost seem minute in comparison. No matter how tired and punchy Serena got, he couldn't allow himself to get on the bad side of those two men. Any empire he was building gaming-wise would take them two hours to destroy if he did.

Mr. Isola passed Conner a champagne flute, then tapped his own flute to the edge of the glass in cheers.

"Do you know why I allowed you to marry my daughter?" he asked.

"Because you don't know how to tell Serena no?" Conner joked, then got a bit serious. "It's an affliction most around her suffer from."

"Are you saying I spoil my daughter?" he questioned.

"There's a difference between spoiling, and allowing her freedom to blossom."

"Good save," he said. "Are you sure you two don't want to be diplomats?"

"Preferably on opposites sides of the world," Conner suggested.

"No, that would be no good," he replied. "You two are a team."

"I like to think so," Conner said.

"When I received the phone call from my daughter about getting married, I immediately phoned my deputy and told him I would need two days of emergency leave," he explained. "I would be rescuing my daughter and returning her home."

"What changed your mind?"

"The look in your eye," he replied. "There are traditions in my family—"

"The bride price," Conner said, holding his hands up in surrender. "I swear I didn't know. Can we do monthly installments?"

"It is the fact, seven years after being married, your first thought wasn't glad I dodged that bullet," Mr. Isola said. "That makes me beam with pride and certainty. You hear money is due and your thought is to pay. Not complain about the woman, who must drive you a bit crazy."

"There are good and bad crazy," Conner acknowledged.

"Ah, and this is why I never considered asking for a bride price," Mr. Isola stated. "Instead, I am content in knowing my daughter is loved, deeply, by a man. That is worth more to me than any amount of money. You complement her in so many ways."

"As she does me," he replied, his heart full of memories and love for his wife.

"Then we both have all we ever wished for in life."

"Mr. Love," Derian called, in his hand a dessert plate with a slice of cake on it. "You need to come, Missus is looking for you."

"Then I must go," Conner said, ruffling Derian's hair as he passed over the young man whose eyes were bright once again, hopeful for the future.

While Detective Espinal was put on leave, his cousin Mr. Espinal had been fired and brought up on charges. Derian had been released earlier that day, much to his mother Wilmarie's delight. Mrs. Mendoza promised to help the family move to another property and promote Wilmarie. There was little more that could be done until the woman learned English. But between Derian and being enrolled in classes, both would be sure to finish school.

For now, they were honored guests at the wedding, and it seemed, the smitten young man was being tasked as a gopher.

"My love," Conner said and Serena spun on her toes to face him, mouth full of cake with a bit of icing on the corner of her lips. Leaning down, he kissed, then licked before standing tall above her. "Buttercream."

"Get your own," Serena said with a smile once she'd swallowed her bite.

"But it's fun to lick it off you," he replied.

"Mr. Love, we are in public." She swatted at him, then passed him a plate. "I need one last shot."

She pointed to the wall at the edge of the reception area. Music was playing and the sun beginning to set on a beautiful Valentine's night.

"Is my work ever done?" he questioned, then slipped the strap of the bag on her shoulder off. Retrieving the camera and following her to the wall. Placing his cake to the side, work first, then sweets.

Serena sat, perfectly posed, her legs crossed and skirt hiked just enough to see her knee. Trying to focus on her face and not her body was always a challenge when it came to shots like this.

"Every day can be an adventure when you are with the one you love," Serena said, *her hands resting on either side of her before she pushed up and stood on the rock wall.*

Conner's heart leapt, watching his wife balance, taking a few steps along the wall.

"Serena," he warned.

"Getting their heart pumping is half the fun, but remember miles may expire, but love does not. Take the trip."

With her toe extended, she jumped. Forward and into his arms, where he would hold her, until their next big adventure. One he knew would come, like they all did, running full steam ahead. Taking on the world together, discovering new places and hopefully avoiding international incidents.

———

Don't miss out on your next favorite book!
Join the Melange Books mailing list at
www.melange-books.com/mail.html

Top 5 Spots in Puerto Plata, DR

1. Mount Isabel de Torres — Take the cable car
2. Zipline tour and Eco-tour — Two words: *Monkey Jungle*
3. Fort San Felipe — History
4. Casa de la Cultura — Town square
5. Ocean World Adventure Park — Animals and park rides.

Seafood Ceviche

Recipe provided by Dahlia Rose from her book
Soca Soul Food

1 lbs. Medium pre-cooked shrimp
    1 Cucumber (Fine diced)
    ½ Sweet onion (Fine diced)
    4 Roma tomatoes (Fine Diced)
    ¼ cup Chopped Parsley
    ¼ cup Chopped Cilantro
    1 Clove of garlic (chopped)
    3 Limes (juiced)
    2 tsp. Extra Virgin Olive Oil
    3 diced mint leaves
    Salt and pepper to taste.

Directions

- Remove all the tails from the shrimp and dice.
- Add all the ingredients except the lime juice then mix well.
- Add lime juice and salt and pepper to taste. Then chill.
- Serve chilled with tortilla chips or as a side for an entrée meal.

Chef's note: Diced jalapeno can be added to this for a bit of spice. You can also use grilled shrimp (diced) or grilled fish (flaked).

THANK YOU FOR READING

Did you enjoy this book?

We invite you to leave a review at your favorite book site, such as Goodreads, Amazon, Barnes & Noble, etc.

DID YOU KNOW THAT LEAVING A REVIEW...

- Helps other readers find books they may enjoy.
- Gives you a chance to let your voice be heard.
- Gives authors recognition for their hard work.
- Doesn't have to be long. A sentence or two about why you liked the book will do.

Michel Prince is a USA Today best-selling author who graduated with a bachelor degree in History and Political Science. Michel writes young adult and adult paranormal romance as well as contemporary romance. With characters yelling "It's my turn, damn it!!!" she tries to explain to them that alas, she can only type a hundred and twenty words a minute and they will have wait their turn. She knows eventually they find their way out of her head and to her fingertips and she looks forward to sharing them with you. When Michel can suppress the voices in her head she can be found at a scouting event or cheering for her son in a variety of sports. She would like to thank her family for always being in her corner, and especially her husband for supporting her every dream and never letting her give up. Michel has been awarded Elite Status with Rebel Ink Press in 2013, the service award for her local RWA chapter Midwest Fiction Writers in 2013 and 2014, won Sweetest Romance at IREA, is a PAN member of RWA, and the her novel The Amalgam is a finalist for the 2022 Minnesota Book Award. She lives in the Twin Cities with her husband, son, and dogs, Bolt and Sawyer.

www.michelprincebooks.com

facebook.com/MichelPrinceBooks

twitter.com/MichelPrince1

instagram.com/michelprincebooks

youtube.com/michelprincebooks

tiktok.com/@michelprincebook

ALSO BY MICHEL PRINCE

ADULT ROMANCE NOVELS WITH SATIN ROMANCE

The Growing Strong Series

The Guardian's Heart

The Queen's Heart

The Politician's Heart

The Teacher's Heart

Love on the Run Series

Always A Groomsman

Novels

The Rotation

NOVELS WITH FIRE & ICE YOUNG ADULT BOOKS

The Aberration Series

*The Amalgam * (finalist for the 2022 Minnesota Book Award)*

The Shield

The Seer

The Soul Reader

The Shifter (coming soon!)

www.ingramcontent.com/pod-product-compliance
Lightning Source LLC
Chambersburg PA
CBHW030500260626
47157CB00014B/678